THE MONK AND THE MAIDEN

The De Veres, Book 4

Leslie Vollard

ARE YOU SIGNED UP FOR DRAGONBLADE'S BLOG?

You'll get the latest news and information on exclusive giveaways, exclusive excerpts, coming releases, sales, free books, cover reveals and more.

Check out our complete list of authors, too!

No spam, no junk. That's a promise!

Sign Up Here

www.dragonbladepublishing.com

Dearest Reader;

Thank you for your support of a small press. At Dragonblade Publishing, we strive to bring you the highest quality Historical Romance from some of the best authors in the business. Without your support, there is no 'us', so we sincerely hope you adore these stories and find some new favorite authors along the way.

Happy Reading!

CEO, Dragonblade Publishing

**Additional Dragonblade books by
Author Leslie Vollard**

The De Veres Series
The Skull and the Lute (Book 1)
The Sword and the Damsel (Book 2)
The Broken and the Bold (Book 3)
The Monk and the Maiden (Book 4)

CHAPTER ONE

Winchelsea, 1183 AD

WILLIAM'S MORNING WAS going so well until Iselda de Vere showed up.

"Hildegard von Bingen clearly indicates that ginger cakes are the recommended remedy for stomach ailments," she said with the patient tone one uses with a young child. "After years of comparing the results of Galen's mint concoction with the ginger cakes for expecting mothers with morning sickness, I know that the ginger cakes work better."

It was only just past morning prayers, for heaven's sake. Usually, she at least let his breakfast settle before going on the attack. Little did he know when he agreed to lead the Hospitallers' effort to establish a hospital in Winchelsea that he would end up in arguments almost daily with the baron's youngest daughter. She was a sweet girl, and she seemed to fancy herself a healer and scholar of medicine. He knew she meant well, but her fanciful notions about medicine were causing nothing but trouble.

"I've also created distillations in my apothecary workshop of mint and ginger. A beverage made of ginger and honey mixed with hot water outperforms the mint as well," she said, her voice all sweetness and patience. Her crossed arms and tapping foot told a different story.

He was glad the stone walls of the hallway were thick so that their argument wouldn't disturb the patients, though he glanced around at the wood doors of the examination rooms, wondering if any of his brethren might overhear. He probably shouldn't have been alone with her like this, but he wasn't willing to have this conversation in front of the whole infirmary hall.

"For the last time, please don't interfere with my treatments. Hildegard's knowledge of medicine can hardly compete with the authority of Galen. She's a mystic, not a physician. And she's a woman. Why she would be foolish enough to put herself forward and write a treatise on healing, I don't know. What I do know is I don't have time for this. Lady Iselda, please stop interfering with my patients. This is my hospital, and I won't have it."

Despite the dim candlelight from the wall sconces, the deepening flush of her skin was plain as her lustrous, nut-brown eyes widened.

"Josela is my patient too. She's been seeing me for years. I assisted at the births of her first two children. And as for Hildegard versus Galen, I can show you the evidence, if you'd only agree to let me show you my records. As I've told you, I keep careful notes on every patient and every treatment and its success. I've tried both remedies, and the ginger consistently works better. I can understand your questioning the relative authority of experts, but I have hard evidence."

"Enough," he yelled a bit too loudly. Brother Joseph poked his balding head out of a room down the hall but quickly pulled it back in when he saw the two of them. Fortunately, Brother Joseph was a good friend. He wouldn't say anything about this to the other monks.

William wiped his hand over his face, and looked at the young woman before him who, he was irritated to note, was radiant in her anger.

He shouldn't be noticing things like that. Just like he shouldn't notice her lustrous, thick brown hair, barely visible beneath a linen veil held in place by a simple braided band. Or her soft, sweet lips, so pink and perfectly formed. Or the nip of her waist and curve of her slim hips in the demure and practical high-necked green wool dress she was wearing. She didn't dress like a noble most of the time, opting for simple attire that allowed her to blend in with the townsfolk, but there was a grace and elegance in her movement that belied her humble garb.

Looking at her made him feel things he knew he shouldn't. Much to his annoyance, she'd been showing up in his dreams lately, and not in the role of debate partner. He tossed and turned on his hard, stone bed beneath his thin, coarse blanket, the austerity of his monk's cell failing to mortify his rebellious flesh. It was embarrassing, really. But a man couldn't control his dreams, only his actions. He could only submit his thoughts to Christ and pray for strength. And in the meantime, he had to find a way to convince her to stop bothering him. She was distracting him from important work.

But what would the Lord Jesus do, confronted with such a woman? He would treat her with gentle compassion. He certainly wouldn't yell at her for tending to the sick and needy.

William crossed his arms, looking away, then back at her. "I'm sorry I raised my voice, my lady," he said in a quiet, measured tone. "Now if you'll excuse me, I have patients to attend to, and I believe you have a suitor up at the castle who should be occupying your attention." He turned and hurried down the newly plastered and painted walls. It was the opposite direction of where he actually needed to go, but he had to get away. Immediately.

"Isn't your examination room this way?" she asked sweetly behind him. He turned to face her, and she raised an amused eyebrow. He clenched his fists and failed to hide his affronted look as he walked slowly and deliberately past her to the correct door. "Here. Have some ginger cakes. Even if none of your patients have stomach troubles, they're a tasty treat." She pressed the basket into his hands, and the smell made his mouth water. "I wish you a pleasant day, Brother William. I'll see you at dinner," she called after him before turning and heading for the door.

Instead of entering the examination room, he ducked into the hospital's tiny scriptorium and sat on the stool in front of a small, angled desk. On a narrow shelf beside him sat his most treasured possession, a complete collection of Galen's Method of Medicine in the original Greek. He'd transcribed it himself from a copy at the monastery back home in Arundel. That was before he joined the Hospitallers, not that he had actually and fully joined the Hospitallers. *Always a postulant, never a novitiate.*

He rested his head in his hands with his elbows propped on the desk. Until the scent of ginger rising from the basket made him lift his head and reluctantly reach for one of the cakes. It was delicious. It was impossible not to take another one. He never had been able to resist sweets.

Maybe he was so on edge because his family was in town. Yes, that had to be it. A mere slip of a girl couldn't possibly be the cause of this much unease. But then he thought of the supper he would have to attend up at the castle in the evening. He'd have to face his family and Lady Iselda at the same time, and he groaned aloud. *Lovely.*

At least his parents had given up on convincing him to marry. Mostly. His Lordship still sent an annual donation to the Hospitallers to ensure they didn't let William take the vows. But now both he and his mother were focusing all their energy on their second child, his brother Michael, who was up at the castle this very moment being trotted out like a prize stallion in hopes of making an alliance with Iselda de Vere.

Poor little brother. He couldn't imagine two people less suited for each other than Michael and Iselda. Michael was never serious about anything, and Iselda was so unrelentingly earnest about everything it drove William mad. It would be interesting to see the two of them together up at the castle.

But before dinner time, there was a full day of work to do. It would be twelve whole hours before he was forced to endure Iselda again. He took a few deep breaths, put on his best *attentive physician* face, and headed into the examination room.

As he entered the back door, he lit several candles to brighten the dark corners of the room that weren't illuminated by the window. He took a quick inventory of the space, ensuring that all the supplies he needed were readily available. He checked a few of the small wooden boxes on the shelves to make sure Brother Cadmus had replenished them with herbs, as he did every morning before daybreak. The drawers in the apothecary chest held linen, scissors, needles and thread, and splints for treating wounds. They also held various poultices and unguents in earthen jars. The ewer on top of the chest was full of fresh water, and the bowl beneath was clean. Assured that everything was in order, he opened the front door.

A little boy and his mother were waiting for him on one of the wooden benches that lined the outer wall. Farmers, if he had to guess from their attire. The little boy was cradling his left arm, dried tracks from tears streaking down his cheeks.

William gestured to invite them in, and they followed.

"Mark, show the nice man your arm," the mother prompted. "Fool boy fell out of the hayloft and landed on his arm. I think he broke it. Thank you for looking at him…"

"Brother William."

The woman curtsied. "Thank you, Brother William." She took a seat on a wooden stool at the side of the room, and the boy took a step toward him, then stopped, eyes wide and tremulous.

William crouched down to his level to help put him at ease. "Well then, Mark, how old are you?"

"Seven," the boy mumbled without looking up.

"Seven! Practically a man. And were you fighting dragons up in that hayloft?"

The little boy turned red, and a tiny smile flitted across his face. "No. I was fighting lions."

"I don't know how many times I've told him not to play up there," his mother said, giving poor Mark a disapproving look.

William ignored her and focused on the boy. "Very brave of you fighting lions single handedly. How many did you defeat?"

The boy's smile broadened. "Four. I would have gotten more if one of them hadn't pounced and knocked me down from the hayloft."

"I see," William said, guiding the boy to place his arm on the wooden examination table and running his hand along the boy's arm ever so gently to find the location of the break. "And what did these lions look like?"

"They were giant and hairy, and they had big sharp teeth and claws like a kitty but huge. And they were jumping around and saying 'RAWR,'" the boy said, giving his most fearsome roar.

William gasped and pulled his face back in mock terror. "They made noises that loud, and you stayed and fought them? You must be braver than all the knights up at the castle!"

Having found the location of the break, he was relieved to note that all the bones were still in place, so there was no need for setting.

"Now, brave Sir Mark, I need to call on your bravery one more time. I need you to roll up your sleeve higher. I'm going to wrap your arm with some bandages so that you can't move it around and hurt it more. You'll need to be careful and take care of it for two months before we take off the bandages. Do you think you can do that?"

"Yes, Brother William," the boy said, fierce determination in his face. He gingerly rolled up his sleeve and placed his arm back on the table as directed.

"He will. You have my word," said his mother, narrowing her eyes at her son.

"Now, what do you think those lions are up to right now?" William asked as he gathered his linen bandages and a wood splint and began wrapping.

"I think they're RAWR-ing and chomping and trying to eat my brothers. They're very hungry, you know. My brothers would be very scared if they could see the lions, but they're invisible to everybody except me. So I have to fight them and keep everyone safe."

"Oh? How many brothers do you have?"

"Four. They're all older than me. They don't think the lions are real because they can't see them. Sometimes they tease me about it, but I know better. And they won't laugh when those lions eat them all up." The boy grinned and his eyes shone with fierce determination.

William smiled back at him, as he continued to wind the linen tightly around the boy's arm, binding the splint in place.

"But you won't let that happen, will you? I can see you're the bravest of your brothers."

"Of course!"

"Yes, you are indeed, and now we're all done."

With the boy bandaged up, William fashioned a sling out of linen.

His mother gave William a warm smile. "Thank you for seeing to our little Mark. You have a way with children, Brother William."

"Thank you, good woman. You see that our brave young knight here doesn't tangle with any more lions until his arm is healed, and all will be well. If anything happens to his bandage, don't hesitate to come back, and I'll fix it. And, brave Sir Mark," he said, turning to the boy, "wait right there while I get you a reward for your bravery."

William ducked out and snagged one of the ginger cakes from the basket. Upon his return, he held it out and said, "In honor of your valor in battle, I offer you this ginger cake. Now be good, stay away from those lions, and get better, you hear?"

"Thank you!" The boy was beaming as he and his mother left.

William sighed in the brief moment of quiet before inviting his next patient in. He couldn't help thinking, *wouldn't it be nice to have a child of my own?* But no, he'd made his decision nine years ago. This was where he belonged. He would have to content himself with caring for other people's children because he was never going to put a woman's health at risk by getting her with child again.

To quell the sudden wave of sadness that washed over him, he grabbed another ginger cake and ate it in three bites, licking his fingers when it was done. It did the trick, and he was ready to see his next patient.

Maybe these do have medicinal properties after all. Does that mean I have to thank Lady Iselda? He shook his head and laughed to himself. *What a woman.* With that, he walked to the door and called his next patient.

Chapter Two

ISELDA SHIVERED BENEATH her serviceable, brown wool cloak as a brisk February breeze blew in from the sea. Turning along Birdie Street, she hurried past a row of brothels, which were thankfully quiet at this hour. The row of neat and well-maintained half-timbered buildings looked like any other inns or taverns in the morning light, except for the bawdy signs that hung over the doors. Some of the pictures painted on those signs made Iselda want to giggle. Were such acts even anatomically possible?

Given her luck with men, she was unlikely to ever find out. Even on Birdie Street, Iselda was invisible. When her sister, Alais, visited, she always brought a guard with her. Her husband, Victor, insisted on it for her safety, and it was necessary, given the lascivious looks and catcalls she received from Birdie Street's denizens. But Iselda was practically a ghost, passing along the street as if she didn't exist.

Men never called after *her*. Not that she wanted them to. What woman would welcome such behavior? Her family tried to get her to bring a guard too, but she stood her ground and insisted it would interfere with her work. And as the years had passed without anyone expressing the least bit of interest in her, they'd given up trying to change her mind.

A frigid gust made her pull her cloak tighter around her and hurry as fast as she dared along the icy paving stones. It was a relief to reach The Bird's Nest, slipping through the heavy wooden door into the warmth of the common room.

A woman who looked remarkably like Alais, dressed in rough woolens, came bustling over as soon as Iselda entered. "My lady, I'm so glad to see you! Come in and warm yourself by the fire."

"Thank you, Jane," she said to the owner of this former brothel, which had been turned into a women's shelter. It was awe inspiring what she had managed to do with the place with some help from Alais and the Abbey. The only vestige of the shelter's former use was the layout—a large common room downstairs with a kitchen in the back and a warren of tiny rooms, each barely large enough for a pallet upstairs. The common room walls were now hung with tapestries depicting religious scenes, and the ladies all wore demure surcottes of undyed linen.

"Can I get you some mulled wine to warm you?"

"Yes, *please*. I'm practically an icicle after walking from the hospital." Iselda settled into a chair by the roaring fire in the common room hearth.

Three young women in various stages of pregnancy sat around her, sewing, and chattering together as Jane hurried away to get the wine. There was also an old woman with white hair who had fallen asleep and was snoring softly, a pile of knitting in her lap.

"Did you say you came from the hospital, my lady?" a young woman with honey blonde hair asked. Gwyneth, Iselda thought her name was. The ladies from Birdie Street came and went with such frequency, it was hard to keep track of them all. It was a shame so many went right back to their old profession after giving birth. Jane offered them alternatives if they wished to leave that life behind. She ran a thriving bakery and seamstress business staffed entirely by former prostitutes and women who had fled abuse or penury. Iselda wondered what Gwyneth would choose when the time came.

"Yes, I was at the hospital. Why do you ask?"

The young ladies tittered. "Did you see Brother William?"

Gwyneth waggled her eyebrows.

Iselda frowned. "Yes." She wondered where this was leading.

A young brunette whose name Iselda didn't know faked a cough. "Oh dear! I think I need the services of a physician. I'm feeling phlegmatic."

Gwyneth giggled. "We all are, my lady," she said, faking a cough of her own. "Can you tell him to come visit again? He was ever so helpful when he was last here."

"I think we all need thorough, *private* examinations," said the third woman, rocking with laughter, her jet-black braids swinging with her motion.

"Such a shame he's a monk," said the brunette with an exaggerated sigh.

"I know! With that thick, auburn hair and those soulful brown eyes..."

"And those long, skillful fingers..."

They all erupted into fits of giggles.

Iselda's face heated. She couldn't fault them for noticing his looks. Even she had to admit he was a handsome man, though she'd never say it aloud. It was too bad he was as prickly as a pincushion. Still, he was one of the few men who noticed her existence, even if it was only to argue.

Jane came back at that moment with an earthenware tumbler of steaming mulled wine, handing it to Iselda. Warmth from the vessel seeped into her fingers, thawing them as she breathed deep the honeyed and spiced scent. Cloves and a star anise floated on the burgundy surface, and she raised it to her lips, letting the delicious brew trickle down her throat and warm her from the inside out.

"I hope the girls weren't disturbing you with their gossip, my lady," Jane said, giving her companions by the fire a censorious look. "You'd think they had nothing better to do."

The young ladies all looked studiously down at their sewing.

"They weren't disturbing me at all," Iselda said quickly.

Jane narrowed her eyes. "You looked red as a beet when I

came over. They must have been saying something."

"We weren't saying anything bad, Mistress," Gwyneth said, all innocence. "We were just saying we wished Brother William would visit more often."

"For our health," said the brunette next to her.

Jane sighed and shook her head. "Brother William again, is it? Ever since he started visiting, they've been all in a dither over how handsome he is," she said to Iselda. "But they are barking up the wrong tree." Jane sent a pointed glance toward the ladies.

"I used to have a regular customer who was a monk," said the woman with the dark braids. "Believe me, monks are just like any other man when they take off their robes, however pious they might be when they are in them."

A momentary image of Brother William bare-chested as he practiced sword play with Victor flashed in Iselda's mind, and her cheeks heated even further. She caught an accidental eyeful just the day before up at the castle, and the memory kept popping up at odd moments, much to her consternation.

The ladies giggled, and Jane put her hands on her hips and glared. "I'll thank you not to go talking of naked men in front of Lady Iselda. My lady, why don't you come with me? This lot aren't fit company for your ladyship."

Jane guided her over to a sturdy trestle table in the center of the room and seated her on a bench close to a brazier. "Adelaide is upstairs with Bess, and I'm sure the others will be here soon."

Wrestling her thoughts back into order, Iselda focused on the prospect of seeing her friends, the midwives of Winchelsea. They gathered at The Bird's Nest once a month to share stories and trade tips. The gathering was Iselda's idea. She'd gotten to know them all independently over the years, but when The Bird's Nest opened, it seemed like the perfect place for them to come together.

As always, Iselda had her book of medical notes tucked into her bag along with a quill and ink. She meticulously recorded every birth they attended along with its circumstances so that they could all learn from trends over time. The midwives all thought her a bit mad at first, but in time, they'd come to accept her as a friend and welcome her at the bedsides of the women they served.

"How are the ladies with the cough and fever?"

"Wilhelmina and Ann are worse, I'm afraid," said Jane, sitting down across from Iselda. "We did everything Brother William said. We have them in a corner room away from the others, and we're airing it out regularly to get rid of any miasma. We're preparing the remedy just like Brother William told us, and they are drinking it three times a day. I don't know what else to do."

Jane's shoulders slumped, and she looked as if she bore the weight of the world on her slim shoulders.

"I'm sure you're doing everything you can," Iselda said, reaching across the table and patting her hand. "I'll check on them before I go."

"Thank you."

At that moment, Adelaide came down the stairs at the other side of the room, dressed in her usual serviceable green surcotte, all of her mouse-brown hair combed back into a snood. "Lady Iselda! I'm so glad you came," she said, hurrying over and taking a seat beside Jane. "I thought maybe with your new suitor up at the castle you wouldn't make it."

"What's this about a suitor?" Caterina asked as she bustled through the front door, her pregnant belly even bigger than the last time Iselda saw her. She was followed by Madeleine and her daughter Esther, who was learning midwifery at her mother's side. The two looked so alike with their round faces and generous figures, all except for Madeleine's gray hair.

Iselda wanted to crawl under the table. Why did they all take such an avid interest in marriage prospects? Surely, they had better things to do.

"Rumor has it that Brother William's family is visiting Winchelsea and that his little brother is courting her ladyship," Adelaide unhelpfully announced with a wide grin.

Reaching for her wine, Iselda took a deep drink. Couldn't they think of anything else to talk about?

"Is he as handsome as Brother William?" Esther asked, taking the seat beside Iselda, and nudging her gently with her elbow.

"You know I don't pay attention to such things," Iselda murmured into her cup, her ears burning.

"Bollocks," said Madeleine, squeezing in next to Esther.

"Madeleine, watch your tongue in front of Lady Iselda." Jane darted a stern look at Madeleine, who never watched her tongue under any circumstances. That was part of what made her so much fun to be around, though Iselda was grateful for Jane's intervention this time.

"If he's anything like his brother," Madeleine continued, undaunted, "he's a catch for certain. If I were twenty years younger—"

"You'd be married to father and seven months pregnant with me," Esther teased.

"Oh, go on with you," Madeleine said, elbowing her daughter.

"So *is* he as handsome as Brother William?" Caterina asked from the other side of the table.

Iselda took a deep breath and let it out. They weren't going to let this go, were they? "I suppose Michael is handsome, but he's nothing like his brother. All he talks about is tournaments. And he obviously has no interest in me. He's made that plain enough, though his parents are still angling for the match. Is Griselda joining?" Iselda asked, hoping to change the subject.

"Judith down at Glen Oak Farm went into labor this morning. Griselda is tending to her. She sends her regrets," said Caterina.

Iselda nodded. Rare was the meeting when they were all able to attend. As the population of Winchelsea had grown in recent years, the services of the midwives were nearly always in demand. "Well then, let's get to it, shall we?"

For the next hour, they traded stories of their most recent

births, and Iselda wrote down every detail in her book. There were six births since they last met—four girls and two boys. Two of the girls were twins. There were no maternal deaths to report, for which Iselda said a silent prayer of thanks. These women knew everything there was to know, but even with an experienced midwife, giving birth was an uncertain business.

Iselda herself had been present at two of the births, assisting and observing. Her familial duties made it impossible to commit to being present for the duration of labor, so she always paired up with another midwife, though there had been several occasions when the other midwife didn't arrive in time and Iselda handled the delivery. If only she was free to pursue her vocation as she wished! She knew she was as competent as the others, but her station in life meant she would never be able to become one of them.

All too soon, the meeting was over, and her friends had to hurry off to attend to business. After saying her goodbyes, she headed upstairs with Jane. She and Jane wrapped cloth around their noses and mouths so that they wouldn't breathe in the room's miasma.

Jane stood in the doorway, watching as she crouched down and took the ladies' pulses and listened to their chests. "What do you think, my lady?"

Iselda pushed up the sleeves of their shifts to examine their bandaged arms and pursed her lips. "He bled them."

"Yes, my lady."

Gritting her teeth, Iselda marked it down in her notebook. Bloodletting was a commonly prescribed cure that she absolutely opposed. It weakened the patient when they most needed their strength. It wasn't the first time Brother William had bled her patients, and she'd given him an earful about it the previous month. And here he was doing it again, despite her warning! She'd have a thing or two to say about that when she next saw him.

What was he giving these women as a remedy? She picked up

a half-empty cup and sniffed the concoction he'd asked them to prepare for the sick women, noting down the herbs. This, she approved of. It was very similar to what she would have used under similar circumstances.

Standing, she turned to Jane. "Their situation is serious, but you are doing all the right things to bring them through. Keep giving them the remedy as prescribed. Keep airing the room out once a day, and don't let the other women come near. We don't want this spreading."

"Yes, my lady."

They removed the cloths from their faces as they descended the stairs. "I'm afraid I must take my leave. I have several visits to make this morning before I return to the castle for lunch with Lord Michael."

Jane smirked. "Enjoy your lunch, my lady. And try to give him a chance. If he's related to Brother William, he can't be all bad."

"It isn't a question of whether I'll give him a chance. It's whether he'll give *me* a chance."

Jane tsk-ed. "Any man would be lucky to have you."

"Ha!" Iselda was going to die an old maid. She just knew it. And to be honest, she didn't mind that much, except for the loneliness. "My life is quite satisfying as it is. No one pays me any mind, and I'm mostly free to do as I choose. What do I need a husband for?"

Jane gave her a knowing smile. "Oh, men have their uses, my lady."

Out of nowhere, the mental picture of Brother William shirtless popped up again in her mind—the ridges and contours of his well-muscled chest, the sinuous strength of his arms. Why, oh why did she ever think that thought? She tried to ignore the general warmth that enveloped her because of this errant mental image.

Shaking herself, she pulled her cloak tight around her. "I should be going. Thank you for everything, and I'll see you again soon."

"Goodbye, my lady!"

Iselda hurried out the door, grateful for the cold blast of wind to cool her heated blood and determined to banish Brother William from her thoughts for the rest of the day.

CHAPTER THREE

BROTHER JOSEPH PEEKED into William's examination room right after the bell rang for Vespers, his robes hanging loose as always around his boney shoulders and skinny legs. "Aren't you having dinner at the castle tonight?"

"Thank you for the reminder," William said, peering around a round old man seated on a stool in the middle of the room. "I should leave now. Would you mind finishing up with Master Caldor here? He has a great deal to say about his gout and how it's all due to a curse from the baker next door to his shop."

"I see. Very interesting situation indeed." Brother Joseph nodded gravely.

William mouthed the words "thank you" to Brother Joseph and sidled through the door.

Grabbing his black cloak from a hook in the hall, he brushed the crumbs of the final ginger cake off the white Hospitaller cross on the front of his black monk's robe, then headed out into the clear, frigid night. The cobblestones of Castle Street were icy, and he had to watch his step. Few people were out on the street, but the inns and taverns were full to bursting, their common rooms brightly lit and the patrons boisterous in their carousing. He reached the castle gates and nodded to the guards. He wasn't a frequent visitor to the castle, but he'd come often enough in the early days when the hospital was under construction that they recognized him. Once inside, he shed his cloak and let a servant take it as she led him to the great hall.

He was the last to arrive, and everyone was already seated in the brightly lit space. At the head table, the ornate chairs were carved with starlings in flight in honor of House de Vere. Silk damask covered every cushion with a bright pattern of birds and flowers. The places were set with gleaming silver plates and goblets etched with French designs. Enormous candelabras stood at each end of the table, and a roaring fire burned in a hearth carved with mythical beasts.

Lady Isabella, Iselda's mother, rose and glided toward him in a wine-red velvet dress trimmed in ermine, the square neck exposing more of her imposing decolletage than he was comfortable seeing. She was a dark-haired beauty despite her years, and her features were echoed in different ways in each of her daughters. "Thank you for joining us tonight, Brother William. I'm so glad we were able to have the whole family present."

He bowed and answered, "Thank you for the invitation, my lady. It was kind of you to include me."

"You'll be sitting down here beside your mother."

William followed her direction, stopping to bow to Lord Daniel and Lady Carenza, the Earl and Countess of Winchelsea. The earl smiled at him and nodded, as did his wife whose resemblance to her younger sister, Iselda, was unmistakable.

"It's good to see you," Lord Daniel said. "I'm glad you could join us." The earl had been a generous supporter of the hospital and had been of immeasurable assistance during its construction. Having spent his youth disguised as a common shipwright, the earl was expert at anything related to woodworking. William was used to seeing him in the simple clothes he wore on the hospital construction site over the previous year, but this evening, he looked very much the earl, dressed in a deep burgundy brocade cotte that hung to his knees.

"You are always welcome at our table," said Lord Martin, the earl's father-in-law, and the local baron. Even he had eschewed his usual finely tailored sailor's clothes for a deep blue velvet tunic. William was starting to feel distinctly under-dressed for the occasion in his rough Hospitaller robes.

And there was his family, dressed in their usual stuffy finery. His father's auburn hair had more gray than when he last saw him. His mother's heart-shaped face had more wrinkles as well. It had been too long since he'd visited. His brother looked like his younger self, with wavy auburn hair, a strong jaw, and that arrogant aristocratic nonchalance of a young lord in his prime. William cringed inwardly at this reminder of who he used to be. Offering a quick nod to his father, he stopped briefly to clap Michael on the shoulder, then kissed his mother's cheek as he took his seat.

William took a passing glance at Iselda. She was wearing an inappropriately low-cut dress that squeezed her slim, boyish shape into something quite womanly. He'd tried very hard never to give thought to her breasts, but now it was impossible not to. They nestled in the silk of her dress like blushing apples on display at a grocer's stall. The emerald-green gown suited her, but it didn't look warm enough for a winter's night like this, not to mention what a gown that tight must be doing to her internal organs. Suddenly thirsty, he poured himself some wine and took a quaff before turning to his family.

"It's good to see you, Mother," he murmured as he settled in.

She shook her head at him. "Couldn't you at least have changed into some proper clothes?" she whispered.

"These are the only clothes I have. I took a vow of poverty," he whispered back.

"No, you didn't. Your father and I have paid good money to keep you from doing any such thing, you stubborn boy."

William smiled and kissed her on the cheek again. "I got it from you, Mama."

Her mouth quirked into a half smile, and she cupped his cheek affectionately.

"Brother William," Lady Isabella called from the other end of the table. "I know you've met Lord Daniel and his wife, and my husband, Lord Martin. And of course, you know our Iselda. But have you met our daughter, Alais and her husband, Sir Victor?"

William smiled at the man with blond hair and an eye patch seated directly across the table. "My lady, we are well acquainted," Victor said. "I met Brother William in Egypt. When I was wounded, I was in Brother William's care during my convalescence. I owe much to his knowledge of the healing arts. He's been practicing swordsmanship with me on and off since his arrival here."

"I've met him too," Lady Alais added. "Brother William has been kind enough to visit some of the sicker residents of The Bird's Nest. That's the women's hospice we run in partnership with the Abbey," she explained to William's parents who nodded in polite approval. "One of the residents had a lung ailment last month, and Brother William was most helpful."

Iselda, who was sitting opposite Michael, shot William a resentful look. That visit was the cause of their most heated argument in the last month. Iselda had been caring for the woman, who was not improving, so Iselda asked if he would be willing to examine her. It was obvious from the moment he entered the room that this woman needed a good bleeding. But Iselda didn't believe in bleeding. She claimed to have studied its effectiveness and found that it was harmful rather than helpful in the majority of cases, flying in the face of centuries of well-established medical practice. He overrode her objections and bled the woman, who recovered, proving him right. Iselda still insisted the woman recovered despite the bleeding rather than because of it.

His mother smiled tightly at the compliments about his work. She never approved of his vocation and made clear she thought he was shirking his filial duty. "Yes, William has always been concerned with those less fortunate," she said with obvious irritation, but then her expression shifted, and her smile broadened. She was up to something. William wondered idly what it might be. Thank heavens she was plotting about Michael and not him. "I understand you also care for the less fortunate, Lady Iselda? I've heard a great deal about your charity work."

Iselda froze and her eyes widened. "Yes, I… I…" She gave her mother a beseeching look, and her mother gave her an encouraging nod. It was surprising to see her tongue tied. She was never the least bit bashful around him. "Yes, I do charity work," she managed at last and then looked down at her plate. *Charity work, eh?* Was that what she called her medical dabbling in front of suitors?

His mother looked much too pleased, and he didn't like it. Whatever she was up to couldn't be good for Michael. It was odd, though. Michael had never given a fig about charity, or medicine for that matter, which was what Iselda was truly passionate about. Not that it really mattered, as long as his mother's plotting had nothing to do with him.

"Our Michael has a very different temperament. He's mad for tournaments. Did you know he took the prize in a jousting competition in Hastings last month?" she asked Iselda with an innocent lightness in her voice.

"Oh," Iselda responded, looking alarmed to find herself once again the focus of attention. "You must be very proud," she managed at last with a nervous smile. She was saved from having to say anything further by the arrival of the food.

It was a novelty to see her so tongue-tied. He wondered what caused it and whether he could inspire such a state himself. It would be nice to get some peace and quiet at work.

Five servants arrived carrying large silver platters. One had an elegantly arranged assortment of cured meats and cheeses, along with baskets of sliced bread. Another was dotted with perfectly seared scallops in sage butter. There was an enormous, caramelized onion tart, as well as a tureen of lamb meatballs. A tureen of mussels in saffron sauce was placed directly in front of him, and his mouth began to water at the delicious aroma wafting his way. Next, eleven servers came in with individual bowls of pottage. As earls, Lord Daniel and William's father were served first, followed by Lord Martin, then everyone else received their bowls in unison.

Lord Daniel stood, then folded his hands and bowed his head. His thick black beard brushed against his blue velvet doublet. Everyone else bowed their heads in their seats as Lord Daniel gave the blessing.

William echoed with his own murmured "amen," then helped himself to some mussels. This was far better fare than he usually got from his brethren. If he had to endure a meal with his parents and Iselda, at least he could enjoy the cuisine. The wine was good, too, and he found his glass empty far sooner than he should have. But it was only moments before a servant stepped forward to refill it.

As the din of serving and passing died down, Lady Carenza asked Iselda from across the table, "Where have you been all day? I feel like I've hardly seen you."

"It was a busy day," she answered her sister, clearly at ease in a way she wasn't with his family. "I visited the hospital first thing this morning where Brother William and I had a very interesting discussion about the relative merits of two remedies for stomach ailments." She glanced at him as if worried he would revisit the argument at the dinner table. "Then I stopped by The Bird's Nest to check on the ladies and see if any of them needed anything. I rode out to several farms to visit expecting women to check on their health and bring them food. Those poor women get no rest at all despite their delicate condition," she paused, clearly expecting some kind of response. William wasn't surprised when there was none; earls and their ladies rarely thought about the working conditions of the less fortunate. Unless of course, it affected them. He wondered why Iselda was different. But then again, why was he? He reached for his wine as she finished up her account of her day. "Then I came back for lunch with Lord Michael."

"Your chaperone talked more than you did," Michael grumbled, then winced. Father must have kicked him beneath the table, which he very much deserved. Lady Iselda wasn't easy to get along with, but there was no need to denigrate her in company.

She continued in spite of Michael's complaint, "And then I spent the rest of the afternoon studying the chapter on the medicinal properties of trees in Hildegard's *Physica*."

At that, William couldn't hold back. "You would be better served spending your time studying Galen or Hippocrates, you know. I assure you it's much more informative than this Hildegard. Although I'm not sure why I'm even suggesting this, as medicine isn't exactly a fit area of study for a young woman." He bit his tongue after he finished, realizing he'd been as rude as Michael, even if everyone around him was nodding in agreement. Why did she affect him this way?

Iselda squared her shoulders and glared at him. "I've read as many of the works of Galen and Hippocrates as I can get my hands on. Unfortunately, the nearest complete collection are in Canterbury. As for the fitness of the topic for women—"

Her mother clutched her arm in a fierce grip, and interrupted, "Of course it isn't appropriate for women to study medicine. My daughter is simply a voracious reader and has taken a great interest in charity for the sick and poor."

Ah, so the charity story is her mother's idea. Iselda turned her attention to her plate with a blush that traveled all the way down to her….

He looked away quickly, turning his full attention to the delicious mussels on his plate, spearing one's tender flesh and savoring it against his tongue. No, maybe the mussels weren't such a good idea either. He swallowed and cast about for something less sensual to eat. *There.*

Onion tart. There was nothing sensual about an onion tart.

His mother leaned close to him and whispered, "Michael can barely get a word out of her, but she seems to have plenty to say to you. Too bad you're so determined to take an oath of chastity.

You two would have made an excellent match."

William choked on his onion tart. She gave him an innocent smile.

"I'm not even going to dignify that with a response," he whispered back. No, on second thought, he would because if he didn't, she was bound to hatch some outlandish scheme to trap him into marriage. "Iselda is the most irritating, headstrong, interfering know-it-all I've ever met. If I was looking to marry, and thank heavens I'm not, she would be the absolutely last woman I would want as my wife," he whispered vehemently before glancing at Iselda to make sure she hadn't overheard. Fortunately, her sister Alais was occupying her attention.

His mother's smile widened. "Funny. Until this evening, she's been meekness itself. I was starting to worry she might be too meek for our family, but you've brought out another side of her. I like the new, feisty Lady Iselda."

He blew air between his lips. "You would, Mother."

Thankfully, they were interrupted by the arrival of the main course dishes. A roasted boar was the centerpiece. There were chicken and eel savory pies. At the other end of the table, there was some kind of fish in sauce. He couldn't quite tell what it was from a distance.

Lady Carenza asked her husband, "Would you like some pie?"

"Is it worth a try?" he answered.

Iselda smiled playfully across the table at the two of them. "Oh yes! Don't be shy."

Lady Alais's ears perked up. "With pie, you can't go awry."

Sir Victor leaned in to join the game. "May I have a piece of the boar's thigh?"

Iselda grinned broadly. "Sir Victor, don't cry, but Lord Michael is quite sly. He has taken the last thigh in the wink of an eye."

William couldn't resist joining the fun. "I cannot deny that I'd like to try that fish that I spy down yonder, by the by." Iselda's eyes sparkled in amusement at his contribution, and her smile was like a sunburst on a cloudy day.

"I don't get it. Why is everybody rhyming?" Michael asked, looking nonplussed.

Lady Isabella came to the rescue. "Oh, don't mind them. It's only a game they like to play. It started years ago with the earl and my Carenza," she said gesturing to her daughter. "They're both quite accomplished composers of troubadour songs. Did you know?"

"No, I did not," his father responded graciously. "Perhaps you might honor us with a performance during our visit," he said, turning to the earl and countess.

"Oh dear," Lady Carenza replied with a laugh. "I'm afraid we're a bit out of practice. We haven't had nearly as much time for that sort of thing since our children were born."

"Don't believe her," Victor interjected. "They could each hold their own with any troubadour alive."

The earl looked at his wife, smiling and tilting his head. "I've eaten my fill. Shall I send for my lute?" A look passed between the two of them that made William feel embarrassed to have seen it. *Theirs must be a very happy marriage indeed.*

As they waited for the lute, desserts were served. There was a tray of honey cakes, a terrine of cream custard, and a pyramid of sweet fritters sprinkled with sugar. Although William had already eaten more than his fill, he heaped samples of each sweet dish onto his plate.

Iselda glanced his way and raised her eyebrows at the formidable pile.

He shrugged. "I like sweets. It's not often I get to eat my fill."

She smiled, and the whole room brightened. "I like sweets too," she said, plopping a dollop of custard on top of a generous serving of fritters. "What's your favorite?" Taking a bite, she sucked the custard from her spoon, and he found himself staring at the perfect bow of her lips. *Lucky spoon.*

Oh no. I did not just think that. It must be the wine.

He jerked his gaze back to her eyes. "What's my favorite? I confess I love flavored sugar candies when I can get them, though such delicacies are hard to come by. But I have yet to meet a sweet I don't like. What about you?"

"I'm partial to custard, as you can see. I'd live on it if I could get away with it. It's so smooth and creamy on the tongue."

He emptied his goblet and tried very hard to ignore his body's reaction to the thought of cream on her tongue.

Fortunately, the servant returned with the earl's lute, giving William an excuse to turn away from the disconcerting charms of Iselda. The earl and his wife struck up a duet, playing the parts of two lovers who were separated and longed for each other from afar. Their verse was clever and poignant, and their performances were a delight to watch.

As Lord Daniel put down his lute and the evening drew to a close, William was sorry to have to head back out into the cold. Despite his fears, it had been a memorable and lovely evening. A servant fetched his cloak, and he was about to leave when a soft hand touched his arm. A tingling sensation spread all through him.

"Brother William, I hope you enjoyed yourself this evening," Iselda said, genuine warmth in her face. "These dinners with suitors have always made me feel terribly awkward. It was good to have a friend at the table. Thank you for coming. Truly."

Something inside him warmed at hearing her call him "a friend".

"It was a pleasure, my lady. Will I see you tomorrow at the hospital?"

"Probably. Someone's got to make sure you don't bleed all your patients to death." She said it with a teasing smile, and he laughed and shook his head.

"Good night, Lady Iselda. Until our next argument." He bowed to take his leave and found himself looking forward to their next meeting no matter what disagreements it might hold.

CHAPTER FOUR

A S SHE DID most mornings, Iselda woke right before dawn to the inevitable thumping and sighs from the bedroom next door. She loved Alais, and she was truly happy for her marital bliss with Victor. She only wished she didn't have to hear it so often.

She might be a virgin who had never so much as had been kissed, but between her sisters and her patients, she knew a great deal about what went on between a man and a woman, as well as the consequences. She'd heard more than one woman curse her husband's amorous attentions in graphic detail while in the throes of labor.

Frankly, the way Alais and Victor went at it, she couldn't help but wonder how her sister wasn't constantly pregnant. They'd been married seven years now and only had the two little ones. Perhaps they were taking precautions after her difficult pregnancy with Clara.

The midwives she worked with had been shy at first about letting her hear the advice they gave to desperate mothers that couldn't afford more children. But over the years they worked together, they'd given up on trying to protect her delicate sensibilities. Nothing was foolproof, but there were herbs one could take and ways a man could refrain from spilling his seed in his wife's womb. She herself had delivered this frank advice on more than one occasion, absurd as it was to be speaking about matters in which she had no practical experience. And perhaps she never would.

She was twenty-four years old and still unmarried, practically an old maid. Her parents had invited a string of potential candidates to visit over the years. Michael was only the latest. But not one had asked for her hand. Not one had even gone so far as to steal a kiss.

She supposed she could have tried harder to ingratiate herself, but something held her back. She didn't only want a husband and family for the sake of having them. She wanted what Alais and Carenza had. Her brother, Charles, too. And her parents. She wanted love. She wanted passion, devotion, tenderness, adoration—all the things she'd failed to inspire in a single potential mate.

She didn't have her sisters' showy beauty or their outgoing personalities. They had both rejected more offers of marriage than she could count before finding their true loves. But she was the quiet, mousy de Vere, the one everyone forgot was there.

There were advantages to being invisible. No one paid much notice to her supposed assistance to the healers and midwives of Winchelsea or to her studies of medical texts. She knew more about healing than anyone else in Winchelsea, with the possible exception of Brother William. It galled her to no end that, as a noblewoman, she always had to pretend she was only there to help and that she could never be a healer or a midwife in her own right.

At least no one had tried to stop her. Yet. Thanks to her invisibility.

But there were also disadvantages to being invisible, unworthy of notice, unremarkable.

Going over to her desk, she opened a drawer and pulled it all the way out. Then she reached to the very back of the empty cavity and retrieved a folded piece of parchment. She smoothed it out on the desk and looked it over with a sad sigh. Dipping her quill in ink, she added the name "Michael" to the bottom of the list. It was the twenty-seventh name on the left side of the parchment.

Across the top, she had drawn columns. She was a fastidious record keeper, after all. The titles of the columns were written at a slant so that she could fit them all in: "Kissed my hand," "Kissed my cheek," "Laughed with me," "Gave heartfelt compliment," "Kissed my lips," "Offered marriage." And then came the columns that led her to keep this hidden: "Caressed my body," "Touched my breasts," "Removed my clothing," "Aroused in my presence," "Made love to me," "Held me as I slept." She added an "X" to the first column next to Michael's name. He had dutifully kissed her hand when they were first introduced. He showed no signs of going any further.

She looked at the other names on the list. All of them had kissed her hand. Three kissed her cheek. Four had laughed with her. She didn't count the fake titters one made out of politeness. It had to be true laughter. Only one had given her a heartfelt compliment. His name was George. He said she was the most well-read woman he had ever met. None of the other columns had any marks at all. It had been seven years since she started this list, and nothing, not one act she couldn't perform in plain sight of her parents. She let out her breath slowly through gritted teeth, refolded the paper, and replaced it and the drawer.

After dressing in a simple, serviceable blue wool dress and pulling her hair into a loose braid, she headed downstairs in search of breakfast. She found Carenza in the great hall, nibbling on a sweet bun as she stared at a piece of parchment with furious concentration. Serving herself a sweet bun and an apple, she sat down next to her sister.

"What has you so thoughtful at breakfast this morning?"

"Hmm?"

"What's on that parchment that seems to be causing you such consternation?"

Carenza sat back and looked at her sister and narrowed her

eyes. "Disasters. I have a list. I'm trying to figure out if I've missed anything."

"Disasters?"

"Storms, floods, drought, fire, attack by sea, attack by land, plague, sinkholes, riots, windstorms…"

"What in heaven's name are you talking about?"

"We need to be prepared for any eventuality, however unlikely. The people will look to us to lead when disasters occur, and we need to have a plan, and preferably some preparations in place. I think our stores in the cellar are inadequate. We need more emergency provisions. We should also check on the emergency buckets we distributed around the town two years ago to ensure a quick response in case of fire. The Watch has a plan for going door by door to let people know in case of a predictable catastrophe like a storm or an attack. But I'm sure there are things I haven't thought of. And we need a whole different approach in the countryside."

Iselda stared at her sister. "Isn't this a little grim for the breakfast table?"

"At least this is more fun than grain stores. Yesterday, I spent all day going over records with Daniel to make sure we have plenty to get through the winter. It was agonizing. He enjoys that sort of thing, but it drives me mad. Planning for disasters is much more engaging."

Iselda couldn't help but smile. "I don't imagine most countesses do this sort of thing."

"Helisende does it," Carenza grumbled.

Ah, so that was what this was about. Relations with Helisende, Countess of Hastings, had improved significantly since Alais's marriage to Victor, Lady Helisende's nephew. But Carenza never quite forgave the woman for holding Iselda, Alais, and her mother prisoner several years back to gain a political advantage when Carenza's husband was fighting to become earl. Though, in Iselda's opinion, as captors went, Lady Helisende had been rather benevolent. Iselda's own distress was significantly lessened by free access to the countess's library.

Carenza, however, held a grudge and absolutely couldn't stand letting Lady Helisende be better at something. "I think I'll be spending my day directing an inventory of supplies and provisions." She popped the last of her sweet bun into her mouth.

"Do you need help? I have a few visits to make this morning, but I could help in the afternoon."

Carenza gave her a disapproving look. "Aren't you supposed to be letting Michael woo you?"

It was all she could do not to roll her eyes. "He's not wooing me. He's boring me to death with his endless tournament stories. I don't think I can stand another lecture on why ash is the best wood for lances."

A devilish look flashed in Carenza's eyes and then was gone in an instant. "Too bad his brother isn't in the market for a wife."

"What, William? You must be joking."

"Those expressive eyes, that chiseled jaw…. He has a pleasant, athletic build under those robes. Have you ever seen him practicing swordplay with Victor? Sometimes Daniel joins them. I confess I've peeked at them more than once, all sweaty and stripped to the waist."

"Carenza, you're married!"

"I'm not looking for me. You know I only have eyes for Daniel. I'm looking for you, my darling unmarried sister. I've never seen you get so worked up about a man."

"But all we do is argue. He's stubborn and backward, and he has no respect for research and evidence. He disregards everything I say because I'm a woman. I don't care about his nice eyes or his jaw or his delicious lips—"

"Delicious lips?" Carenza was smirking at her.

Iselda bit her own lip in consternation. She needed to be more careful with her words. She took a deep breath and retorted, "He's aggravating and impossible, and I'm very glad he's completely unavailable because I can't imagine a more exasperating person to be coupled with." Though perhaps he did have nice arms, and long, lovely fingers, and, yes, his lips looked delicious.

No. Some things simply shouldn't even be thought.

"I'm leaving," she announced, stuffing the rest of her sweet bun in her mouth, and fleeing the room.

"Wait," Carenza shouted after her. "Can you come to the cellar when the bell rings for Nones? I have an errand to run, and Mother asked for your help. She's already planning for the Feast of the Annunciation of the Blessed Virgin, and she needs help deciding which tapestries to hang in the hall."

She stopped and turned at the door. "Of course. Whatever she needs." She escaped before Carenza could ask for anything else.

Her morning visits were uneventful. She delivered four food baskets, gave ginger cakes to two expectant mothers, and changed the bandages for a woman who'd burned her arm cooking.

Right before the midday meal, she stopped by the hospital. The dormitory portion of the hospital was teeming with pilgrims awaiting a delayed ship to the Holy Land that had been scheduled to depart three days earlier, and she had to squeeze her way through a group of them to get to the door for those seeking medical care.

As she slipped inside, she caught Brother William's eye, and for a moment, his face lit up with a smile before it settled into its customary expression of annoyance. She wondered if she'd imagined it.

"And how do you plan to interfere today, my lady?"

"That's unfair. I'm not here to interfere. I respect your knowledge and expertise. It's why I send people to you." They'd had such a lovely détente the evening before. Why was he on the defensive with her again? She was trying to come in peace.

"And I help them. Except according to you, I'm bleeding them all to death." His voice was dripping with sarcasm, but he really did have nice eyes. And those lips...

"Has anyone bled to death today?" she asked sweetly, trying

to keep her composure.

"All of them, of course," he answered, deadpan. "It's very efficient. Once all their blood has been removed, they can never get sick again."

She felt a flush of annoyance sweep over her skin. "You're impossible."

"And yet you keep coming back to pester me. I notice you don't pester the other monks."

Oh dear. He had a point. Thinking of her conversation at breakfast with Carenza, she suddenly wanted to crawl in a hole. The best course of action, she decided, was to ignore everything he'd said and start over. She cleared her throat.

"I came here today to ask for your help. The two women you treated at The Bird's Nest have gotten worse. I'm concerned that there may still be a miasma in the building, or perhaps something in their diet is causing their humors to be imbalanced. I was hoping you might be able to pay another visit when you are able. I wouldn't want this to spread."

He closed his eyes and took a deep breath. His expression shifted to one of professional concern. "Of course, I'll go. I'll try to find time this afternoon to make a visit."

"But I have to ask, when you see them, please don't bleed them. It's only going to make them weaker."

His shoulders rose several inches as he tensed, frowning, and she braced herself for an angry rebuttal. She wasn't trying to pick an argument, but this was too important for her to let it lie.

"I won't if I can avoid it, my lady, but it may be necessary. I won't withhold proven treatments from patients in need."

The temptation to argue was almost irresistible, but she needed a second opinion. Loathe though she was to admit it, she had reached the limits of her own medical knowledge. So for the good of her patients, she took a deep breath and said, "Thank you. I'll leave you in peace."

He sighed and mumbled, "To my gruesome bloodletting."

She raised an eyebrow.

He raised one in return.

"I didn't say that."

"No, but you thought it."

True, but she was hardly going to admit it. "Good day, Brother William," she said and turned to go before she lost her temper completely. She tromped down the hall and out the door without looking back, and fortunately, he didn't follow.

The sea breeze whipped her face the moment she was outside, cooling the heat of her anger to a low simmer. How did he manage to get under her skin so easily? At least she'd managed to remain civil this time. It wasn't easy to walk away from a good argument, but it wouldn't have done any good to goad him when she needed a favor. And hopefully, he would honor his word and not bleed them if he could avoid it. That was the most she could hope for, really.

On the way back to the castle, she bought a meat pie. She didn't want to eat lunch with her family today. They were bound to try to force her into some awkward afternoon activity with Michael. Sure enough, as she was walking through the entry hall, she ran into Michael and his mother. She stopped and made a little curtsy, trying to look like she had somewhere urgent to go.

Michael's mother gave him a little shove.

"Er…uh…Lady Iselda?" Michael asked.

Pausing, Iselda turned to him with a patient smile.

"Mother says I should invite you out for a ride this afternoon."

Could anything possibly be more humiliating than a man inviting you on an outing because his mother says he has to? Her smile tightened.

"I'm afraid I have a bit of a headache this afternoon, my lord. I was heading to my bedroom for a rest." She didn't particularly like Michael, even if he was almost as handsome as William, but the look of relief on his face when she made her excuse gutted her. "Excuse me," she said, offering another curtsy and rushing upstairs before they could see the tears forming in her eyes.

She tore down the hall toward her bedroom and ran headlong into Alais.

"Iselda?" Alais's eyes were full of concern. "What's wrong?"

Iselda sniffed and knuckled away the tears that were spilling down her cheek. "It's nothing. I want to be alone."

Alais followed her into her bedroom. "It's obviously not nothing. You're unflappable. I've seen you in all kinds of crises, and nothing ever seems to dent your composure. What in heaven's name brought you to tears?"

Taking a deep breath, Iselda explained, "It was Michael."

"Michael?" Alais said, wrinkling her nose. "I didn't even think you liked him."

"I don't. But he asked me to go on a ride with him, and he said out loud that his mother told him to ask." And then she gave up on any attempt at composure and sobbed on Alais's shoulder. "I don't care about him or want his attention, but I wish for once someone would like me well enough to *want* to spend time with me. I know I'm not beautiful like you and Carenza. I know I'm awkward around men. But it's been so humiliating for so long."

"Oh, sweetling." Alais petted her hair and rocked her back and forth.

"You and Carenza found love. Neither of you ever lacked for suitors. What's so different about me? Why does every man who comes to meet me run away? Mama's brought twenty-seven men to visit since you got married. Twenty-seven. I kept count. And not one has proposed. Not one has even tried to kiss me. Alais, I don't want to spend my life alone."

"Oh, Iselda. You are such a special person. There is no one on God's green earth as kind and giving and considerate as you. And I don't care what you say, you are absolutely beautiful, inside and out. Carenza and I don't hold a candle to you. But—please don't take this wrong—you are a bit reserved with people you don't know, and with people you do know, your intelligence, determination, and capability are...a little terrifying. Someday, I hope that women will be able to study medicine and save lives and be appreciated for all that they can do. But at present, most men are too stupid and pigheaded to know how to appreciate someone like you. It will take a very special soul to love and appreciate you as you deserve. Don't give up, Iselda. I am certain you will find the love you seek."

Iselda rubbed her nose. "Thank you," she blubbered.

"Now, why don't you lay down and get some rest. I think I heard Mother say you offered to help her this afternoon. Is that right?"

"Yes," she sniffed.

Alais laid her down and took off her boots, then tucked her under the covers and kissed her forehead. "Take a rest. Think about what I said, and let Mother distract you this afternoon. And let me know if you want me to punch Michael in the face for being an ass. I'll do it. You know I will."

She couldn't help but laugh at that. "I love you, Alais."

"I love you too, little sister." Alais squeezed her hand and left her alone.

At first, she was tempted to get up for her volume of Hildegard, but instead she decided what she really wanted was a visit to the nursery. That always cheered her up.

When she arrived in the nursery, she found that all the children were out on a walk except Alais's little Clara and Carenza's equally tiny Roger, both two years old.

"I'm afraid it's nap time for these two," the nurse told Iselda.

"Let me help you. I know Clara always fusses."

She picked up Clara and rocked her while the nurse told Roger a story as he drifted off in his crib. Sweet little Clara took her coloring from her father, with her blonde hair and blue eyes, but the shape of her face was unmistakably Alais's. She had Alais's temperament too, all sweetness when adults were watching but adventurous and mischievous the moment their attention wandered.

Iselda hummed a lullaby and stroked Clara's hair to calm her wiggles, and she watched as Clara's eyelids grew heavy and closed. Holding this tiny person gave her so much peace. The little girl looked so angelic in her sleep. Iselda sat and rocked with her long after Clara drifted off, enjoying the peace and joy that came from holding her. At last, she reluctantly put Clara in her crib and headed back to her room to freshen up.

When the bell rang for Nones, she was ready to face the world again. She put her boots back on, fixed her hair, and headed down to the cellar. When she opened the door to the stairs down into the cellar, there wasn't any light below. Her mother must not have arrived yet. Iselda grabbed a candle, lit it, and descended into the dark to wait.

The cellar had always fascinated her. It was murky and mysterious. The rough stone arches that held up the stone floor of the castle cast shadows in all directions. Along the north wall was a row of enormous wine casks. The eastern wall was stacked with cask upon cask of ale. The western half of the cellar held shelves and shelves of foodstuffs put up for the winter—flour, oil, preserves, honey, hard cheeses, dried fruits and vegetables, dried herbs, fragrant sacks of spices, barrels of apples, braids of onions and garlic, and cured meats. The remaining space was occupied by a hodgepodge of furniture, supplies, weapons, and other sundries. When she was a child, she'd found the space terrifying, imagining ghosts behind every pillar, but now she found the peace and quiet soothing and the abundance reassuring.

She wandered through the shelves over to the dried herbs. While the collection had every imaginable culinary herb, there were some medicinal herbs that she planned to ask Carenza to add to the stores. She heard the distant noise of the doors opening and closing, then stepping down the creaking stairs. *That must be Mother.* She made her way back to the stairs and was surprised to see William. He carried the small satchel he always brought on medical visits.

"Lady Iselda, can you take me to the man with the injury?"

"I'm sorry?" She was certain they were the only people down there.

"A messenger said a servant collapsed in the cellar and that my services were needed urgently. I thought it must be something serious if they were bringing me in, since I know you are quite capable of handling minor issues."

Was that a compliment? The "minor issues" part rankled, but it was the first time she could remember him acknowledging her expertise in any way.

"I'm afraid there must be some mistake. No one else is down here. I'm supposed to meet Mother to help her with an inventory of supplies and make recommendations around medicinal herbs and other medical sundries to keep on hand for emergencies. I just walked through the whole space, and I'm certain we're alone."

Oh dear. They were alone! That wasn't good. It was unseemly for them to be by themselves, even if he was a basically a monk and she was an old maid. She could tell from the alarm on his face that he was thinking the same thing.

"Let's go upstairs and see if we can figure out what's going on," he said briskly.

He headed back up the stairs with his candle, and she followed close behind. He handed her the candle to open the door, but when he pushed up, the doors wouldn't move.

"What's wrong?"

"The door seems to be stuck."

"Try the right door," she suggested. "Sometimes the left side sticks."

He followed her recommendation and still nothing moved. He moved higher on the steps and wedged his shoulder against the door for better leverage. Still no movement.

"Maybe if we push together?" She set down the candles and climbed up next to him, careful not to touch him but close enough that she could feel the heat radiating from his body and smell his scent of herbs, soap, and a hint of something earthy that was all his own. It was suddenly very warm despite the chill of the cellar.

"On three," he said. "One, two, three."

THEY BOTH PUSHED with all their might, but nothing budged.
They were stuck.

CHAPTER FIVE

"IT'S NO USE. I think we're trapped here until someone comes along and lets us out," William said, letting out a frustrated sigh and sitting on the cellar steps. He was alone and locked in a cellar with Iselda de Vere. *Wonderful.*

She sat down beside him and smoothed her skirts. "Don't worry. Mother should be here any minute."

This wasn't good. They shouldn't be alone together. As long as it was only a few minutes, nothing too terrible could come of it, but if it went on longer... No, he wasn't going to think about that. Lady Isabella would come and let them out any minute now. There was no reason to panic.

Several minutes passed in silence as they both stared out into murky corners of the space. Iselda shivered beside him.

"Are you cold?"

"I'll be fine," she said, hugging herself.

He didn't quite believe her, but they wouldn't be stuck here much longer, he hoped. It didn't seem worthwhile to argue the point, so he went back to staring into the middle distance, trying to ignore his restlessness at sitting so close to her.

She shivered again. He turned to look at her, and he could see goosebumps on the small, exposed patches of skin at her wrists. "You're cold. Don't deny it."

"Fine. Yes, I'm a bit chilled," she said, her eyes narrowed in annoyance. "But it doesn't matter because we'll be back upstairs where I can warm up any moment now."

He nodded in grudging agreement, wondering why she could possibly be annoyed that he was concerned about her being cold. Did she have to argue with him about everything? It seemed to be her knee-jerk reaction any time they were together. She really was exasperating. It was one thing to debate about issues of medical authority, but was she truly willing to risk her health to spite him?

"Did you visit The Bird's Nest?" she asked, startling him.

"Hmm?"

"Were you able to visit The Bird's Nest before coming here?"

"Oh, yes. I stopped by right after my midday meal. I gave them more herbs to reduce their phlegmatic humors and bring down their fevers. I also recommended they give the rooms another thorough cleaning and air them out. And I'll have you know I didn't bleed them."

She smiled in a way that made him feel suddenly warm, despite the coolness of the cellar.

"You were right to suspect a miasma," he said, trying to ignore his reaction to her. "I suspect it's still lingering."

She pulled back her head to stare at him. "Did you just agree with my medical opinion?"

"Did I? That doesn't seem like something I would do," he said with a friendly chuckle. "Don't get used to it. It's unlikely to happen again."

"On the Ides of February, *anno domini* 1183," she proclaimed in a low, booming voice, "Brother William agreed with Lady Iselda's medical opinion. Henceforth, we shall hold an annual feast in honor of this strange and miraculous occurrence."

He snorted in laughter. "You sound nothing like the earl, you know."

"And yet you still knew exactly who I was imitating," she answered with an impish grin. There was a sudden flash of warmth in her eyes when he laughed. He couldn't help wondering what was behind it.

She shivered again.

"Lady Iselda—"

"Yes, fine. I'm cold. What do you propose I do about it besides wait for my sister?"

They were getting along so nicely for a moment there. Why did she turn prickly again?

"I was going to suggest we look around for something you can wrap around yourself until your sister gets here. Surely there must be something on one of these shelves."

She gave him a resentful look and stood up. "I suppose you're right. It's a reasonable suggestion."

"Ladies and gentlemen of Winchelsea, henceforth let us mark this day every year with fetes, music, and dancing in honor of Lady Iselda's declaration that Brother William made a reasonable suggestion," he boomed.

He could tell she was trying to keep a straight face, but her body was rocking in silent laughter. "It's all right to laugh out loud you know. I won't think less of you for it."

She burst into loud, unladylike laughter so explosive, she accidentally blew out her candle. He stepped down and tipped his candle to relight it.

For a moment, their eyes met. Something passed between them that he hadn't felt in a very long time. She was so close. His eyes dropped to her lips. A whiff of cinnamon and pear reached him, and he could practically taste her. He wanted to taste her. This couldn't be happening. It mustn't. He couldn't kiss Iselda de Vere. Or anyone. But especially not her. *Dear Lord in Heaven, help me!*

She broke the connection, looking down at her feet and blushing. "I think I know where I might find some bolts of cloth," she said, turning away and hurrying off toward the shelves.

He stayed put and watched her go, stunned and horrified. It had been nine years since the disaster with Luisa that had spurred his decision to run away to the Hospitallers. After all these years, he thought he'd perfected his system for equilibrium. His youthful lusts were in check. A combination of engrossing work, regular prayer, and consistent exercise seemed to be sufficient to allow him to avoid temptation most of the time. Every so often, when he got too restless, he allowed himself some solitary relief, then went to confession and did his penance. After all, celibacy was not man's natural state, and he was only human. For years, his system had worked. He'd been calm and in control.

And yet, moments ago, he very nearly kissed Iselda de Vere.

Even now with her out of sight, desire had him in its thrall. His body was tense, his breathing uneven. One specific part of his anatomy was stirring to life of its own volition, something that hadn't happened spontaneously since adolescence.

Worse yet, erotic images were flooding his mind unbidden, as he tried unsuccessfully to block them out. He didn't only want to kiss Iselda, he realized. He wanted to hear his name on her lips as he made her moan with pleasure. Even after all this time, he remembered what it felt like to lose himself in a woman, and for the first time in years he wanted it again with a desperation that shocked and shamed him. Worst of all, he wanted it with her, the terrifyingly intelligent and stubborn woman his brother was supposed to be courting.

He had to get out of this cellar. They couldn't be here together. He needed to leave, pour a cold bucket of water over his head, and stay the hell away from her, praying to heaven for an end to this madness.

He ran back up the stairs and started shoving at the doors again, pounding on them when they still wouldn't give. If they made enough noise, perhaps someone would hear them and come to their rescue.

"What are you doing?" Iselda called out, as she rushed toward him with a blue linen cloth draped around her shoulders, looking like a glowing Virgin Mary in the soft candlelight.

"I thought maybe if I made some noise someone might hear us and open the door."

"Be careful. You're going to—"

"Ow!"

"—hurt yourself." She sighed and climbed up the stairs toward him. There was nowhere he could go. He was trapped. She reached out and took the hand he was cradling. "What did you do?"

"Splinter. A big one, I think."

She took his hand and turned it in the candlelight until she saw the injury. A jagged sliver of wood several inches long pierced his skin on the outer edge of his right palm, where the meat of his fist had slammed against the door. A drop of blood was welling out of the long, shallow wound, but the torture of her soft, gentle touch was far worse.

"Yes, quite," she said in a calm, soothing voice he assumed she used with all of her patients. "Let's take care of this, shall we? And while we do, why don't you tell me about how you ended up joining the Hospitallers. I've always been curious. You don't talk much about the past."

"So now I'm your patient?" His voice was low and rough. Did she notice how it had changed?

"I thought you said you trusted me with 'minor issues.'"

"What does Hildegard have to say about splinters?" That was sure to dissipate any errant thoughts he might be having. A good argument would set things to right between them.

"As an injury? Nothing at all, though she does recommend wearing a ring with a splinter of linden wood as a protection against disease. But I hardly need a medical reference to treat a splinter. I only need to find a needle so that I can remove it. But I asked you to tell me about the Hospitallers."

He didn't want to talk about his past, not with her. He especially didn't want to touch on the reason he'd joined the Hospitallers. "What if I don't cooperate?"

"Would you like a peppermint sweet?" Iselda asked, halting his thoughts in their tracks.

"What?" Whatever he was expecting her to say, it wasn't

that.

"I made them. Father received a shipment of sugar from the East. It has fascinating properties. I'll give you one if you are very good and let me take care of your splinter."

Heavens, this woman was too capable for her own good! She knew nearly as much as him about medicine, *and* she knew how to make peppermint sweets? Not to mention that her bedside manner was exemplary. Why did she have to be so irritatingly competent? "Are you bribing me with treats like a child?"

"Do you want that peppermint or not?"

Archangel Raphael's wings, woman. "Yes. I want the peppermint," he ground out.

A slow, devious, triumphant smile spread across her face. "Then tell me all about the Hospitallers."

That smile did things to him, things he did not like one bit.

He cleared his throat. "I joined the Hospitallers when I was nineteen."

She turned and started wandering through the shelves. "Keep talking. I'm listening."

"I was a bit wild in my youth. I was fascinated by medicine from an early age, but aside from my studies, I was just as selfish, entitled, and hedonistic as any other first son of a noble. Maybe more so. I got myself into some trouble, and someone got hurt." *No, someone died,* he mentally corrected, ashamed that he was too much of a coward to say so aloud.

"Instead of staying and living with the consequences, I ran away to the Holy Land to join the Hospitallers. My parents worked out where I had gone and hastily bribed the Order not to let me take the vows. The Order valued my medical knowledge, though, and let me stay on as a postulant, providing care to pilgrims and crusaders, long after most other men would have been pushed out if they didn't progress."

She emerged from the shelves, pinching something between her fingers, presumably a needle, though it was impossible to tell in the available light. "Sit," she said in a light, friendly voice that nonetheless would brook no dissent.

"Where?" There were no chairs, after all.

"The floor will do." She plopped down on the packed dirt floor and crossed her legs beneath her skirts. It was entirely unladylike, and she looked absolutely at ease. She pointed an imperious finger at him and then down at the floor.

Complying instantly, he placed his candle on the floor beside her own.

"Give me your hand."

He reached out reluctantly and took a sharp inhale when she touched him.

"For heaven's sake," she said, giving him a level stare. "My six-year-old nephew is braver about his boo-boos."

His reaction had nothing to do with the splinter, but he couldn't admit that.

"Now," she said, as her fingers sent tendrils of temptation all through him. "Keep telling me about the Hospitallers."

She leaned over his hand to look closely in the candlelight. A strand of hair fell into her face, and she tucked it behind her ear. Following the trail of her finger, he found himself staring at her neck, right below the ear. It would be heaven to touch that little patch of skin with his lips. He wondered what it would taste like and whether it was as soft as it looked.

What was it she told him to do again? *Oh, yes. The Hospitallers.*

"After a month or so stationed in Jerusalem, they sent me to Krak des Chevaliers where I studied with master healers whose skills and knowledge far exceeded my own. I was there for a year and a half before they sent me to Spain along with a fighting force to support the King of Castille against the Saracens. That's where I met Victor. The campaign was foolish and disastrous, but I gained a great deal of practical experience treating wounds and disease in the field. I learned more about anatomy that way than I ever would have from a book."

As he spoke, pain and relief mingled as she slid the main bulk of the splinter out of his hand. It was over before he had a chance to realize what she was doing. He smiled at her technique, thinking of the many times he had done the very same thing to distract wounded soldiers. "Have I earned my peppermint yet?"

"No. Keep talking," she ordered without looking at him.

"After Spain, I returned to Krak de Chevaliers and continued my studies for another two years. By that point, my medical knowledge had grown too valuable for them to allow me to stay cloistered with my studies. I wasn't a full Brother because of my parents' bribes, but after all they had invested in me, I was more than a postulant. They sent me back to England to establish hospitals to house pilgrims and provide care for the sick. The one in Winchelsea is the fifth one I've started. I love my work. The only thing that would make it better would be if my father relented and let me take the vows."

As he spoke, he hardly noticed the prick of the needle removing the tiny splinters left behind. He watched the top of her head and the curve of her neck as she concentrated on her work, wishing he could run his fingers through her thick, dark tresses.

She looked up at him when he paused. "Do you think your father will ever relent?"

Once again, he was losing his bearings as he looked into her eyes. He blinked and turned away to stop himself from leaning in to claim her lips. She was so close, too close.

"I...I don't know," he said, trying to remember the question she'd asked. His father. She asked about his father. "I don't think so. He hasn't relented in all these years."

She looked up at him again. "You've been a very brave boy. You can have your peppermint now." She pulled a small cloth bag from a pouch tied to her belt and plucked out the small, hard sweet. "Say '*aaah*' Brother William," she said, with a teasing, sultry smile he'd never imagined her capable of.

"Aaah," he said in a voice that came out more like a low purr. She placed the sweet on the tip of his tongue, brushing his bottom lip lightly with her finger. *Oh, sweet Jesus in heaven, save me.*

"You know, I'm starting to think Mother isn't coming," she said, her brow adorably furrowed.

"Maybe she forgot?"

She shook her head. "Mother doesn't forget."

Oh no. "You don't think…"

"What?"

He was afraid to say it out loud for fear that it would make it true. "No, they wouldn't…"

"What?" The playfulness in her voice was replaced by worry.

"Your family wants to see you married?"

"Of course. Michael is the twenty-seventh man they've tried to set me up with."

"Twenty-seven? That's very specific." And a lot. Why were all these men unsuccessful?

"I keep meticulous records."

Of course, she does.

"How many proposals did you turn down?"

She averted her gaze and blushed. "None."

"None? Not one of them proposed? How is that possible?" He had assumed it was a matter of her being too choosy, but this… How did the rest of the world not feel the allure of this gorgeous, intelligent, *infuriating* woman? Men should be falling over themselves to beg for her hand. Not him, of course. He wasn't marriage material for so many reasons, and besides, they fought all the time. But other men. Men who didn't care what she thought about Hildegard. Men looking for a beautiful, intelligent, compassionate wife. Men he loathed for daring to court her, not that that mattered, since apparently, they weren't courting her, but even if they were, it shouldn't matter. Why should he care anyway?

Except that he did. A lot.

Her shoulders slumped, and she stared into her lap. "I'm too shy. I'm not pretty like my sisters. I'm too wrapped up in my books and my work. You're not the only man who doesn't want to hear about Hildegard."

He could agree with the last part, but the first part was utter nonsense. "Too *shy*? Have they met you?"

She shifted but still didn't raise her gaze. "I'm different with you," she told the floor.

Something deep in his chest thrilled at her words. It was satisfying to know he affected her too.

"I don't know why," she continued. "For some reason, I'm comfortable with you in a way that I'm not with most people. You understand me. You care about the same things, even if we disagree about them. When I try to talk about medicine, most people look at me as if I'm speaking Greek."

"Were you speaking Greek?" he teased.

"Only occasionally," she said with a laugh, raising her eyes to meet his. Saints above, that gorgeous brain of hers! He'd never met another woman with so much intelligence. It must have been so difficult for her to have been born a woman when she had the mind of a scholar.

"I approve," he said, leaning in closer against his better judgment.

"Because Galen and Hippocrates were Greek?"

Mary, Mother of God, that smile.

"As were all the greatest thinkers." He leaned closer still, drawn inexorably toward her inner light.

"The Romans might disagree." Her gaze dipped to his lips for a split second, and she licked her own unconsciously.

He was a hair's breadth from losing all composure and giving into temptation. Clenching his fist beside him, he forced himself to stop. "I think we've strayed from our original topic."

"Which was?" Her sweet lips parted as she looked at him from beneath long, lush lashes.

Hell and damnation, this was exactly what their families intended, if his suspicions were correct. "Why we're trapped down here together, and why your mother who never forgets anything hasn't released us."

She sat up straight and frowned. "You make it sound like it's on purpose."

He hated what he was about to say aloud, but he couldn't help but suspect. "It's very improper for an unmarried young lady and an unmarried young lord to be alone for so long without a chaperone, isn't it?"

"But I'm an old maid, and you're practically a monk."

An old maid? Her? Ridiculous. "You are not an old maid at the grand age of…what? Twenty-two?"

"Twenty-four," she said with a wince.

"Twenty-four." He stifled a chuckle. "If you are an old maid, I have one foot in the grave at twenty-eight. You, my dear, are an alluring young woman of a very marriageable age, and I am only practically a monk, not actually. My parents would love nothing more than to see their oldest son marry and ensure the succession."

"Are you suggesting our own families plotted our ruination to force us into marriage?"

He let his breath out slowly. "I'm afraid that's exactly what I'm suggesting." He hated it, but there was no denying the possibility. He had absolutely no doubt his parents were capable of such plotting. It surprised him to see the de Vere-Rossignol clan stooping to such depths, but perhaps they were getting desperate after twenty-seven suitors. Did she really write them all down? Someday he needed to see this list.

"How long does ruination take?" she asked. He hated that she rightly assumed he would know. "Are we already past the point of no return?"

"If I wanted to ruin you, I could have done so quite thoroughly by now." And oh, how he wanted to, though he would have laughed at such a notion even a short time earlier. Temptation flooded him at the mere thought—tasting her skin, touching her softness, sinking into her tender embrace. "But if I know my mother, she'll make sure we spend the night together so that there can be no question."

"We're going to be stuck here all night?" she gasped, clutching the cloth tight around her shoulders.

He looked around, his heart sinking. "We're going to be stuck together for life."

CHAPTER SIX

IT WAS IMPOSSIBLE to know how much time had passed down here in the windowless cellar, but Iselda was certain it was well into the afternoon, close to supper. Her stomach told her so. At first, she thought William's theory was outrageous. Her family would never do this to her. But as their captivity dragged on, and her stomach began rumbling with hunger, she was forced to give credence to what he said.

"Here, I found cheese, apples, walnuts, and honey," he said, laying down a platter he'd foraged on the floor beside her. He sat close enough to share the food but just far enough to avoid touching. "At least they locked us up somewhere with sustenance."

"And wine and ale, but no water. It's as if they wanted to addle our wits."

"That does seem to be the general idea."

She watched him assemble a piece of cheese, a slice of apple, and a walnut and then drizzle a bit of honey on top. He made an appreciative *mmm* sound as he devoured it in two bites and licked his finger and thumb. The sight made something clench deep inside her. An image flashed through her mind of licking the crumbs off his fingers, tasting sweet honey and tart apple as she sucked on his fingertips.

What was wrong with her? Against her better judgment, she

took a deep sip of wine.

"Have you had any further thoughts on how we might foil their evil plan?" he asked, interrupting her reverie.

"No. I still haven't thought of anything that isn't either profoundly humiliating or worse than the predicament we're in. I still think your claiming impotence is the most palatable option."

She was mostly teasing, but he still tensed at the suggestion.

"For you, maybe," he said, turning red. He was rather adorable when he was embarrassed.

"What does it matter when you want to take a vow of celibacy?"

"I don't know, but it does. Also, it's demonstrably untrue. My family knows why."

"But you won't tell me?" There was a story there, and someday, she was going to get it out of him.

"No." There was a finality in the way he said it that made clear he was not open to further discussion. "What about claiming you're barren? No one in Winchelsea knows more about medicine than the two of us."

"My goodness! Another compliment, William?" she teased, liking how his name rolled off her tongue.

"It's the truth, loathe though I am to admit it. Even Brother Joseph can't keep up with you."

It was the truth, but no one had ever said it aloud before. For all her years pretending to assist, she had always known her own expertise exceeded that of the people she supported. She was more widely read, had more experience distilling remedies, thanks to the apothecary workshop her brother had helped her set up, and she had never met anyone else who took notes like her and looked for themes across populations. She had no idea why she'd been obsessed with medicine and the human body from an early age, but her curiosity had been consistent and relentless for years.

Their eyes met, and there was a moment of connection and understanding between them that shook her to the core. He knew her. He saw her. Despite his protestations, he even respected her.

He shook himself and looked away as if nothing had happened.

"If we said some previous illness made you unable to procreate, who would doubt us?" he asked a neighboring shelf. "It would be impossible to prove wrong unless you married and had children, by which point none of this would matter."

"Except that I'd never be able to marry and have a family because no one would have me. Unlike you, I don't want to spend my life alone." She'd rather marry William than commit herself to a life of solitude, though she refused to admit that aloud. A thought occurred to her. "Oh!" She turned to him. "You could claim to prefer men."

His eyes widened and even in the gloom she could see his face flush. His nostrils even flared. "I don't understand how you even know about that, and I don't want to know, but it's also demonstrably untrue."

"Oh." She sighed and picked up a walnut, thinking. "How about claiming a secret wife?"

"Too easily put to the test. Making it credible would involve marrying a complete stranger, which would be worse than marrying you."

Why did her heart skip a beat hearing him say that? It was hardly a compliment, and yet his admission that she wasn't his worst option made an absurd wellspring of hope rise within her. *No, no, no, no!* She was supposed to be finding a way out of this marriage, not finding arguments for it.

"Consanguinity?" she suggested, knowing it was hopeless.

He shook his head. "Our families would have investigated that before Michael's visit."

"Coercion?"

"A difficult argument to make when the reason for the wedding is our having spent the night together."

She nodded and started assembling her own apple and cheese

tidbit. They'd considered various options for what felt like forever and had yet to come up with anything that was palatable to them both. "So we're getting married?" she asked, carefully keeping her voice light and casual.

He gritted his teeth. "If we can't find a way out of this, then yes, I suppose we are. I will do my duty, much though it rankles."

"I'm so sorry to burden you with my dreadful company," she said, unable to keep a note of bitterness out of her voice.

He looked stricken. "No, Iselda, that's not what I meant. Any man would be lucky to marry you."

That's what he thinks. And yet, none had offered. *But still.* She hadn't been even slightly intrigued by any of them, and had the list to prove it. "You mean, 'Any man except you'."

"I—"

"Don't bother trying to explain," she said, holding up her hand to stop him. Whatever his excuse was, she didn't want to hear it. "I've heard this story before."

He ran his hands through his curly, short-cropped hair. "It's not that I'm not…it's just that…I don't want to marry anyone." He seemed to be coming up with more reasons that while any other man would be lucky to marry her, he wasn't including himself in that luck. "And even if I did, I wouldn't choose someone I argued with nonstop. As we do." He waved his hands between them. "Iselda. You must admit this is a terrible idea."

"On that, we can agree," she said, taking another bite of apple and cheese to hide her disappointment, blood pounding in her ears. Of course, he didn't want to marry her. Why would he when they were constantly at odds?

But truly, it all came back to the same thing in the end. Men didn't like her.

When she was quiet and meek, she was boring. When she spoke her mind, she was irritating. She didn't have her sisters' spectacular beauty to compensate for her lackluster personality. Alais's encouragement from earlier in the day came back to her, but it rang hollow. There wasn't some magical, special someone out there who would offer her the love of which she dreamed. There was only compromise, and disappointment.

She took a deep breath and squared her shoulders, blinking back the unshed tears that pooled in her eyes. "Why do you think we argue so much?" she asked quietly.

He rubbed his hand over his face and let out an exasperated sigh. "You have ridiculous notions about healing and spend too much time reading the work of a quack."

She clenched her fist, took a deep breath, and released it. She should have felt angered, as usual, or at least annoyed, but instead she was surprised to feel disappointed. *He doesn't understand.* "You misunderstand my question. I know that we disagree about Hildegard, and I know you find some of my treatments to be questionable, just as I object to some of yours. That would explain one or two arguments. But as you pointed out, we have argued almost daily since you first came to Winchelsea six months ago. So. Why do you keep arguing with me, and why do I keep arguing with you?"

He looked at her intently, and she waited. There was more to this than pigheadedness, she was certain, and if they were to be married, she needed to know.

"I argue because I care deeply about my work," he began. "I don't want to see my patients come to harm. I don't want to see them risk their health with unproven treatments. If I stopped arguing, I would be failing them." He looked down at the floor before adding, "I could not guess why you keep arguing with me."

She waited until he looked at her again then met, and held, his gaze. "For very similar reasons. I argue with you because I am deeply committed to the health and well-being of the people of Winchelsea. My people. I don't want to see them come to harm, and I don't want them to receive inferior treatment when methodical observation has shown that other, newer cures are more effective. All of God's creation grows and changes with time. Our knowledge and understanding of medicine and healing must do the same. If I stopped arguing, I would be failing to give my people the care they deserve."

She paused to watch his reaction before continuing. He was absolutely still, focused on her with an intensity that almost made her turn away, but she held firm, knowing she could not back down at such a critical moment.

"I think we argue," she said in a quiet voice, almost a whisper, "because we are both passionate about our work and committed to the people we serve. We differ in our views on how to carry out that work, but we are alike in our sense of duty. We argue because we care. Would you agree?"

His hand rested on the blue cloth beside hers, and his pinky brushed against hers as he shifted positions. She gasped at the contact but didn't pull away, and neither did he. "Yes, we care," he admitted softly. "And perhaps that isn't the worst foundation for a marriage. But, Iselda, you deserve to be with someone who has chosen to be with you. And you certainly deserve better than me. I don't want this. Not with you or anyone else."

She hardly knew what to believe because as he was speaking, his pinky slid along hers in a gentle caress, and suddenly she could not attend to anything else. It was such a subtle touch that it might have been excused as accidental if he hadn't added another finger and then another, brushing ever so softly, barely moving but sending lightning through every inch of her body. She didn't dare call attention to it by looking for fear he would stop.

Like a tiny spark in a parched forest, his touch set her on fire. For years she had been waiting for someone to set her alight and make her burn. It took so little, only an inch of innocent flesh moving gently against another, and she was consumed. And yet his words, "I don't want this," echoed in her mind as he stoked her flames with his caress. Did he know what he was doing to her? What did he feel as he touched her? Was it anything like what she felt?

His gaze dropped to their hands, and his breathing grew ragged. He blinked in surprise, as if his hand had acted without his permission, but he didn't stop. His finger traced up her fingers to the back of her hand and then to the sensitive skin between her thumb and index finger. She bit her lip to keep herself from moaning aloud as he touched her there. Slowly he raised his eyes to hers, and she saw the fire inside her reflected in him, his lips parted, and his eyes darkened with desire. She'd seen her sisters and their husbands look at each other like this enough times to recognize what it meant, though this was the first time anyone had ever directed such a look at her.

"I shouldn't want this," he murmured as his index finger traced a circle on the back of her hand. She stared at him, caught, unable to do anything but surrender to his subtle seduction. He turned her hand over, running his thumb over the inside of her wrist, then tracing along the center of her palm, sending a shiver down her spine. He pulled her hand toward his face, pressing it against the rough stubble on his cheek and then brushing his lips against her palm.

A soft moan escaped her at his kiss, and he closed his eyes as if in pain. He nuzzled the inside of her wrist, then grazed it lightly with his teeth. She whimpered his name, pleading for something she didn't understand.

"Iselda, I can't. I mustn't," he groaned as he leaned toward her. Her lips suddenly felt dry, and she licked them as her head tilted toward his. She leaned in, her body inexorably drawn to his, unstoppable, her lips parting in preparation to meet his.

"God help me," he whispered, and then he kissed her. Despite his words, there was nothing tentative about his kiss. He tantalized her lips and then consumed them, as if sucking sweet nectar. One hand caressed her cheek as the other twined through her hair, undoing the simple braid in which it was tied until it hung loose down her back.

Her own response was timid at first, as she was uncertain of what to do and nervous about doing it wrong, but as she imitated him and he moaned in response, all hesitation evaporated. She had dreamed of this moment for so long, and now that it was here, she was ravenous for the affection she had been denied by other men. She savored the residue of honey and apple on his lips as her shy tongue darted out to explore after receiving an unforgettable lesson from him on how devilishly enticing a tongue could be.

As their kiss deepened, she caressed his neck and shoulder with one hand while the other ran through his hair, pulling him close. She wanted to touch more of him, hold him closer, feel his body against her own. If she was going to be forced to marry, at least she could enjoy committing the impropriety of which she would inevitably be accused. If he wanted her, she would happily give herself to him. If he wanted her…

That thought brought her up short. He desired her. Of that, she no longer had any doubt. But he did not welcome that desire. The life he wanted to live had no room for desire. The marriage that was being forced on them both would mean an end to all he held dear, and after sharing this beautiful, miraculous kiss, she didn't think she could bear to be the cause of such a loss. She realized she cared for him far too much to let him sacrifice himself in such a foolish way.

"William," she said, pulling away from the kiss even though it was agony to do so.

"Iselda," he answered in a husky voice that tugged her back every bit as insistently as his embrace. Once again, their lips met, and she was lost. He wasn't only kissing her, he was making love to her mouth, seeming to concentrate all his pent-up desire from years of abstinence in a passionate onslaught that took her breath away. She didn't stand a chance against the combined force of his need and her own.

He leaned in and loosened the ties on the sides of her gown with an expert hand. A distant corner of her mind still capable of logical thought wondered how and when he'd gained that expertise, given his austere life for the last nine years. His kisses blazed a trail of fire down her neck, and he nuzzled and nipped at a shoulder he'd just bared. He started tugging her dress lower to free her breasts, and she realized they were quickly approaching a tipping point beyond which neither of them would be able to stop. If she gave herself to him, he would *have* to marry her. If they stopped now, they could still throw themselves on the mercy of their families and pray that they would relent after forcing them together. She didn't want to be the one that took away that final, meager possibility of a reprieve.

"William, wait," she said, and he froze, panting hard with a wild look in his eye. "We have to stop."

He dragged himself back and groaned. "I know."

"I don't want to force you to marry me. If this goes any farther, I won't have a choice, and neither will you. If we stop now, we can still try to find a way out of this."

"If anyone had seen us, it would already be too late," he said rubbing his eyes with the heels of his hands. "Honor requires that I offer you my hand after taking advantage of you like that."

Did he just offer marriage? No one had ever proposed to her before. Her heart broke a little, knowing she couldn't accept. "First of all, you didn't take advantage of me. Second, my honor requires that I don't trap you in a marriage you don't want. I can't let you walk away from the life you've built with the Hospitallers just because we briefly got carried away, which, I'm certain, is exactly what our families were hoping for. Don't let them win, William."

"I'm so sorry. I'm ashamed—"

"Don't," she snapped. It was awful enough to pull away from his caresses. She didn't want to hear that he regretted this. Her body still thrummed with the memory of his touch, and she didn't want to taint that joy with guilt.

"But I should have known better, had more self-control. I had no right to force myself on you."

"I said don't." She could hear the venom in her own voice and tried to temper it. "You didn't force yourself on me. I was a willing participant. In case you don't remember, I kissed you back."

"How could I forget? The memory is likely to haunt me for the rest of my days. You set me on fire, sweeting. Even now, it's all I can do to refrain from taking you back in my arms and letting the flames consume us. But you deserve better than a tumble on the cellar floor with a man who doesn't want to marry you."

She winced at his words. It all sounded so sordid when he put it like that.

"You're an innocent," he continued. "I have an obligation to protect you, and instead I seduced you. I knew better and went ahead anyway. The blame for this lies with me."

She was finished with listening to this nonsense. "Fine. Wallow all you want. I'll leave you to it." She stood and walked away, wandering through the aisles of shelves until she found a satisfactory place to rest. She put together a makeshift bed using bags of grain and cloths and ate an apple to stave off hunger, since she'd left the platter of food with him. The temperature had dropped with nightfall, and she climbed beneath the cloths, trying to get warm, her fingers aching with cold. Blowing out the candle, she closed her eyes.

Sleep came, but it was fitful. Time and again, she awoke to find herself shivering violently. The cloths were insufficient to fend off the cold, and she wiggled and flexed her fingers and toes to ease the ache. A strange torpor crept over her that seemed different from mere exhaustion. Something was wrong.

She lurched to her feet in the dark, pulling her cloth blankets around her, and stumbled toward the distant flicker of William's candle, which was still lit. She found him sitting huddled, his back against a shelf, his arms wrapped around his knees, a cloth draped over him for warmth.

"Iselda," he said leaping to his feet upon seeing her.

"M'too cold," she slurred. "C-can't s-s-s-stop shivering."

He caught her in his arms and chafed her hands and shoulders, letting her lean into his warmth. "Curse them and their foolish scheme. If this costs you your health, I'll never forgive them." He stepped away from her for a moment to assess her condition with professional detachment. "Violent shivering, slurred speech, cold extremities. How do you feel?"

"S-so tired. Wanna sleep."

He shook his head.

"Whah? Yer sh-shaking yer head."

"Stay with me, Iselda. We've got to get you warm. Let's see… I can't start a fire down here. There's no ventilation. The smoke would kill us. Umm…"

"Yer warm," she mumbled, burrowing into his embrace. "Mmm…so warm." Nuzzling her face into his neck, she murmured, "Less go t'bed."

"Hell and damnation. That's the last thing we should do," he grumbled.

"D'you have any other ideas?"

He looked around desperately, hoping his eye would land on an answer he hadn't thought of, but there was nothing. He deflated and shook his head. "I suppose I don't have a choice. I can't let you freeze to death. Did you find a place to lie down?"

"S'over 'ere," she said shuffling in the direction of her grain sacks with his arms draped around her. He grabbed his candle and a flint and accompanied her back to her improvised bed. He settled her down onto the sacks, lay down beside her under the cloths, and blew out the candle.

He pulled her so that she was spooned against him. Every inch of her back connected with the warmth of his front. His warm breath feathered against the back of her head. His hand ran up and down her arm and her side. Slowly but surely, her trembling subsided, replaced by a delicious languor. At last, she dozed off with his strong, warm arms wrapped around her, his chest expanding and contracting against her with each breath. It was bliss, and sweet oblivion claimed her. Worries about the consequences would have to wait until morning.

CHAPTER SEVEN

WILLIAM RECEIVED A rude awakening. Someone yanked the covers off him, and he had no idea where he was. There was someone in his arms. A woman. How did that happen? Was he dreaming? One of his hands rested on a soft, shapely breast, and his fierce arousal pressed against her buttocks. He jerked away as if burned.

Next thing he knew, someone was hauling him upright, and, as he blinked in confusion, a fist connected with his face.

"No," screamed a woman's voice. "Victor, it's not what you think."

"I should kill you." His old friend's voice was cold and deadly. "I never would have thought you, of all people, could do something like this. What did you do to Iselda?" Victor roared.

Iselda.

Archangel Raphael's most holy gonads.

"Victor, you have to listen to me," Iselda pleaded, bolting upright. "We got locked in here yesterday. We banged and yelled for hours, but no one came to open the door. And then it got so cold. We couldn't light a fire. It was too dangerous, so he held me. It was the only way to stay warm. He didn't touch me except to keep me warm, I swear. My virtue is intact."

I didn't take your maidenhead, but I certainly did touch you. God help me.

William blinked away the stars at the edges of his vision and tried to ignore the fact that his left eye was swelling shut. He should have known he'd end up with a black eye if they were found by the wrong person. Knowing Victor, he supposed he should count himself lucky not to be impaled on a sword.

"What do you have to say for yourself, William?" Victor demanded in a rough, unfriendly voice, but his sword remained sheathed at his side.

"I am offering my hand in marriage to Lady Iselda, since it is the only honorable thing to do." When he ran away to the Hospitallers, he'd sworn to himself that he'd never take another woman to bed, but here he was, offering marriage. He had no choice, though, if he wanted to get out of this cellar with his head attached to his shoulders. Besides, he owed it to Iselda after the way he'd behaved. "What she said about our being trapped down here is true, as is what she said about the cold. This situation was not of our making, but I will not shirk the consequences. By the way, how did you find us?" All of that was true, even if he was leaving out certain damning details.

Victor looked him up and down. "Lady de Vere sent me down here. The whole household was searching for Iselda when it was discovered she was missing this morning. If what you say is true, then I am sorry for hitting you. You have always been an honorable man, and I appreciate that you will do right by Iselda without my having to convince you." He shook his head. "Locked in a cellar…what a way to find a wife."

"Where's Mother?" Iselda demanded, charging off toward the stairs. "I'm going to kill her."

He and Victor ran after her, and in short order they all found themselves in the great hall. All the women from his family and hers were gathered there, eating golden apple galettes and hardboiled eggs. As Iselda stormed into the room, her face bright red, she went straight to Lady de Vere.

Her mother took a deep breath, as if bracing herself, and wouldn't meet Iselda's eye. Meanwhile, *his* mother smiled at him like a spider that had caught a fat fly in her web.

"This is your fault, Mother," Iselda said loudly, her voice cracking with fury. "You're the one that asked me to meet you in the cellar. You always promised me that the choice to marry would be mine. I never ever would have suspected you'd stoop to subterfuge. How dare you do this to me!"

Her mother blushed slightly as she looked up, her face a mix of mild embarrassment and amusement. "I haven't broken my promise. When I agreed to this scheme, it was on the condition that you would still have a choice, provided your virtue was still intact." So it was true. Their families were scheming, but her family couldn't possibly know why he was so unsuitable for Iselda. "It is intact, isn't it?" her mother asked, glancing momentarily at him before returning her gaze to her sister.

"Of course, it is." Her hands clenched into fists at her sides. "How can you even ask?"

"In that case, it's up to you. He has no choice but to offer…"

"And I have," William interjected, glaring at his mother who was clearly the originator of this plan. How could she do this, knowing full well what his history was?

"But you," her mother continued, "are not obligated to accept, though I urge you to strongly consider it."

He couldn't contain his outrage any longer. Not only were they wrenching him away from the life he had chosen, but they had put Iselda in danger. "Do you have any idea how cold it was last night in that cellar? How could you risk her health like that?"

"I knew you wouldn't let her come to harm," her mother said dismissively.

"You didn't mind *me* coming to harm, though," he grumbled.

"Sorry about that," Victor mumbled behind him. "I had no idea they were plotting against you."

His mother looked up, still smiling. "We thought it best if the person who found you wasn't part of the scheme. Their outrage would be genuine, and you would be more likely to agree to offer marriage."

"This is cruel and heartless, even for you, Mother," he ground out.

"I'm tired of your avoiding your responsibility to this family," she answered. "It's time for you to give up this foolishness with the Hospitallers and do your duty. And I don't think you'll find your fate so terrible. It's obvious you have feelings for the girl. Might I assume from the black eye that they were, in fact, found in a compromising position?" she asked, turning to Victor.

Staring at the floor, Victor confessed, "They were asleep together, and he had his arms around her, though they were both fully clothed."

His mother's smile widened. This time, she had gone too far, and he intended to give her a piece of his mind.

Meeting her eye, Victor added in icy tones, "I don't appreciate being used like this, Lady Maud. William is my friend."

"I'm sure William will forgive you, my lord," she said, looking completely unabashed.

Iselda, still fuming, paced along the wall. "I understand your motivation regarding William, my lady, cold-hearted and manipulative though I find it," she said to his mother. "But I don't understand why my own mother would betray me this way."

Lady de Vere cleared her throat. "I know you won't believe me, but we did it for you, my dear. You want love. You want a family. You've said as much to all of us. But in seven years of trying to find you a match, the only man you've ever shown the least bit of interest in is William. We've been watching you for months now, wondering when one or the other of you would realize what is obvious to all of us. You're made for each other. You only needed a little encouragement to move past arguing over Hildegard."

"And you expect me to be grateful?" Iselda answered quietly. "How do you think it makes me feel to know that you think me so undesirable you had to force a man to propose to me? How could you ask me to be the one to tear him away from his life's work and force him into a life he didn't choose? If I was as madly in love with him as you all seem to think I am, how could I possibly start our union by hurting him this way? You should all be ashamed of yourselves." She turned to him, her face downcast.

"Brother William, I thank you for your offer of marriage. Since they have given me the option to decide, leaving your fate in my hands, I must follow my conscience and refuse."

Raphael's toes. She turned him down. He was free to return to the hospital and the life he'd chosen. Why wasn't he relieved? He had exactly what he wanted. He'd spent all night trying to reconcile himself to the necessity of marrying her. This match was a terrible idea. They both agreed.

But his heart lurched at her words, and all he wanted to do was fall at her feet and beg her to reconsider.

She moved to the table and picked up an apple pastry. "If you'll all excuse me, I'd like to be alone right now." She turned and left the room. What little sunshine there was went with her.

Suddenly all the exhaustion from his mostly sleepless night came crashing down on him, and he too longed to go back to his austere little room at the hospital to rest and be alone.

"I would also like to go," he said to his mother and hers, "but not before you promise me that this is the end of your interference. What you did to us was unconscionable, and I will not allow you to meddle in her life or mine ever again."

"I'm with Brother William," Victor added. "I never would have thought you would stoop so low." The mothers looked defiant. "If I hear so much as a rumor that you are interfering with their lives again, I'm going straight to Brother William, and I will do everything in my power to put an end to it. Were your husbands party to this?"

Both the mothers shook their heads.

"Good. I didn't think they would condone this. Be warned that I am going to find them and tell them right now. I'm confident they will join me in making sure this never happens again."

But it wasn't going to be enough, William knew. He demanded, "Your promises, ladies, if you please."

Lady Isabella nodded.

"Mother?"

His mother narrowed her eyes in challenge, and he held her gaze, letting her see the full force of his fury. Finally, she shrugged and mumbled, "Fine. I can't force her to change her mind, and her family won't make her, so it's pointless anyway."

With that, he turned and left.

Upon his return to the hospital, he made his excuses to Brother Joseph and headed straight to bed. Sleep took him almost as soon as he laid down.

Predictably, his dreams were filled with Iselda. She'd started haunting his sleep long before last night's incident in the cellar, but now his dreams were more detailed and specific. He knew the exact taste, shape, and texture of her lips. He knew that her sweet, pert breasts just filled his hand, though he had yet to see them. What color were her nipples? Were they pink, brown?

The way that she responded to him and moved in his embrace had changed too. When he'd dreamed of her before, she was always sweet, timid, allowing his attentions but not reciprocating. Now, she was passionate and hungry, her hands exploring, pulling him closer, her lips and tongue driving him to the brink of insanity with naive enthusiasm. She melded to him, desperate to feel his flesh against her own.

Their clothes melted away as the dream became more fevered. He sank into her, encompassed by her warmth and heat. It was exquisite, transcendent, but also deeply right. It felt like coming home, and he never wanted to leave. He moved within her, and she convulsed in pleasure.

"I love you, William," she murmured in his ear as she shuddered in release beneath him.

His eyes shot open, and he sat bolt upright. "No," he exclaimed to his empty room.

He looked down at his fierce arousal and realized he'd been moments away from spending himself in his sleep. He grabbed a cloth and with a few quick jerks expended himself into it with a guilty grunt. He'd been a fool to believe he could ever live with celibacy.

But there was still the memory of Luisa. He hadn't loved her. He'd used her and left her to live with the consequences, and she was hardly the first. Only she didn't survive those consequences, and neither did their child. He couldn't risk subjecting another woman to that fate, no matter how unlikely it was. Could he?

"Oh, Iselda," he whispered to the wall, panting and disheveled. "What have you done to me?"

CHAPTER EIGHT

I SELDA SAT DOWN at her desk and pulled out the drawer, reaching behind to find her list of suitors. As always, she had to document her experience for posterity, or so she imagined, not that she ever wanted anyone to find this particular document. To the bottom of the list, she added the name "William," and then she began adding the letter "X" beneath each column that applied. "Kissed my hand," "Kissed my cheek," "Laughed with me," "Gave heartfelt compliment," "Kissed my lips," and "Offered marriage" all received marks, as did "Caressed my body," "Touched my breasts," "Aroused in my presence," and "Held me as I slept." Only "Removed my clothing" and "Made love to me" remained unchecked.

A coughing fit took her, making her double over, distracting her. Instead of replacing her parchment in its secret place behind the drawer, she tucked it into the book with her patient records. Then she stripped down to her shift and climbed beneath the covers, still not fully recovered from last night's chill. She pulled the blankets up over her head and clasped her knees to her chest.

Her body ached all over. The confirmation of her mother's betrayal landed like a blow to her chest. Her mother loved her. She was certain of it, but then how could she do something like this? How could she be so wrong? Did she not realize the damage she was doing? Especially to William. She could find her way to forgiving what her mother had done to her, misguided though it was, but her manipulation of William was appalling.

The worst of it was that her mother was right about her. She did have feelings for him, and last night had been a revelation. She wished she could crawl back into his embrace and never leave. But both of their mothers had ruined it. They'd ruined everything. The tenuous, hesitant, desperate affection he shared with her last night might have grown into something if left alone, but their mothers had to dash it to pieces by trying to force it. And now she could never find out if she and William might have been able to find each other across the great divide that separated them. She would never know if he might have been able to love her for who she was, instead of the obligation she represented.

But there was something between them, wasn't there? Something had made him reach out to caress her, kissing her hungrily, and something in her had responded, tasting pleasure with lips and tongue that she had never allowed herself to even contemplate.

And then in the night, when she had been addled with cold and delirium, she still remembered his touch. His hand traveled up and down her side and her arm, warming her until she dozed, but that wasn't all. In his sleep, he'd pulled her against his arousal. That's the only thing it could have been, that stiff pillar of heat that pressed against her in the night. And when his hand had found her breast, it was all she could do to stay still for fear of waking him. She longed to tell him how much she loved his touch. She hungered for his body against her own. But it was not to be.

She drifted off into desperate dreams where he was always slightly out of reach, calling her name but never touching her fevered flesh.

"William, please, I need you," she murmured in her sleep, desperate for contact that would never come.

She didn't know what time it was when she awoke, but a tickle in her throat caused her to cough violently as her consciousness surfaced briefly. It was like she was breathing water instead of air. Chills and aches ran through her, making her restless and weary at the same time. Perhaps she had inhaled some of the miasma when she visited The Bird's Nest. The chill of the cellar certainly hadn't helped.

Rosamunda was fussing about her, irritating her fragile temper. "Oh, my lady, you're awake! Can I get you anything to eat or drink? You've been asleep for ever so long and with the covers up to your ears. I thought you might have taken ill. Perhaps an ague. My aunt has a cure for ague. You tie a live mouse to a rock and cover it in moss under the moonlight. If it dies, you've got ague for certain and need to eat nothing but honey for five days and then you'll recover as if nothing had ever happened. Should I go get a mouse?"

"No, Rosamunda," she managed to mutter. "I would like some clear chicken broth, and a tisane of ginger root. And tell Brother William I need to see him."

She drifted back to sleep, and William continued to elude her. She touched his lips with her own, and he was yanked away. She disrobed to entice him, but he was just out of sight. Her legs spread before him, desperate for him to come home to her, but he never did. Dear God, she wanted him here, touching her, caressing her, making her his own. But she was alone, alone, alone, and no one would ever make love to her because she was too repulsive to contemplate.

Someone poured broth down her throat, and she mumbled about Hildegard and whale brains, combined with goutweed and olive oil. Anointing. She was supposed to be anointed. It all sounded a little absurd to her, but who was she to doubt Hildegard?

"William, please," she murmured, not knowing if anyone heard.

Time passed. She didn't know how much. There were bad dreams but also some very good ones involving William stripped of his robes and worshiping her naked body in ways she'd never imagined when she was awake.

And then there he was. Rosamunda was by her side, giving her a gentle shake to wake her up. "William," she murmured, not sure if he could hear her. He looked at her, his eyes full of concern and anguish. "Don't you dare bleed me," she whispered, reaching out for his hand.

"I won't unless I must, my lady," he answered, the stiffness of his address mitigated by his thumb stroking her hand as he held it.

"Hildegard says to anoint with whale brains, goutweed, and olive oil for severe ague."

He stood beside her bed, and her whole body curled toward him.

"That's the most ridiculous thing I've ever heard," he said with a tender smile, leaning in to examine her, each chaste touch affecting her like a caress. Was she imagining things, or was he lingering, prolonging the contact between them? "Galen says to bleed the patient, but first I want to try a hot compress on your chest, cool water on a cloth on your head, and ginger and mint tisanes and bone broth to drink. We need to release the foul humors from your blood. You have too much phlegm and yellow bile. Since your head is fevered and your chest is phlegmatic, we have to cool your head and heat your chest."

"That sounds sensible," she agreed, gazing with longing into his eyes, wishing she dared caress him back.

"I need to listen to your chest to see if there is phlegm in your lungs. Will you permit me, my lady?"

She nodded, and he untied the bow at the top of her shift, giving him greater access to her chest. He slid the sleeves down over her shoulders, the thin linen now barely covering the tips of her breasts. He pulled the coverlet up to preserve her modesty, but not before a momentary slip made him avert his eyes and swallow hard. He saw, and she wasn't sorry.

"Pink," he whispered, barely audible as he rested his ear on her chest, right above her right breast. Her heart raced furiously, and she wondered if he would be able to hear her lungs over its thundering.

When he stood up straight, his forehead was creased with worry. "I'm afraid I hear liquid in your lungs. I know you don't want me to bleed you, but it's the best treatment I know for an infection like this."

She reached out and put a hand on his arm. "My book of patient records is on my desk over there. The summary of my findings on the effectiveness of bleeding is on the third page. If you'll only look…"

He pressed his lips together in a thin line. "Because you're sick, I'll humor you." He walked over to her desk and picked up the book, perusing it with his back to her. She could hear him flipping back and forth, presumably looking at detailed patient records that were cross-referenced with her summary. At one point, he raised his head as if in surprise. There was some more rustling, then the closing of the book.

When he returned to her side, he looked perturbed, fidgeting with his robe, and not meeting her eyes. "I should go," he said abruptly.

"Wait. What did you make of my evidence?"

He dragged his eyes to meet hers. "I can see why you drew the conclusion that bleeding is ineffective. Your record-keeping is impressive, quite as thorough as any I've ever seen. Far better than my own, truth be told. But have you considered that the outcomes in the cases where the patient was bled might be worse because the underlying infection was more severe?"

"I have considered that, but if you look at—" She was overtaken by a violent fit of coughing.

"You should rest, my lady. I'll come back tomorrow to check on you. If you are the same or better, I will refrain from bleeding you, but if you take a turn for the worse…"

"Thank you, Brother William. I understand."

"I must go." He turned and left abruptly, leaving Rosamunda to follow his instructions regarding a cool cloth for her forehead and a hot compress for her chest.

She closed her eyes and let Rosamunda fuss over her, unable to think of anything but the sensation of his head resting on her bare chest and what it did to her insides.

"Wilted lettuce," she blurted, interrupting another recitation about a specious cure Rosamunda had in mind.

"Wilted lettuce, my lady?"

"It has cooling properties. Perhaps it would ease the fever if I put it on my forehead with the wet cloth." And between her legs to calm the lustful throbbing she could not quell there. How Hildegard, a nun, knew of such things, she didn't know. But perhaps prayer was insufficient to quell one's natural urges.

"Yes, wilted lettuce please, if there is any to be found." Coughing took her once again.

"Rest, my lady. I'll see what I can find."

She lay back once again, closing her eyes and burning with twin fevers, one from her infection and one from her healer. The lettuce could not arrive too soon.

CHAPTER NINE

WILLIAM RUSHED OUT of the castle as if an armed mob was chasing him. Storming out the castle gate, he was blind to the world around him, ignoring his surroundings until he slammed right into Victor.

"Apologies. I was distracted," he mumbled, barely breaking stride and launching himself out into Castle Street.

"William," Victor called after him, jogging to catch up. "William," he called again, catching his shoulder, and bringing him to a halt. "You look like a man in need of a drink. Can I buy you a pint?"

Victor steered him with a firm and steady grip toward the nearest tavern and didn't let go until they were seated at a table with tankards of ale in hand. He didn't want to be here. All he wanted was to go for a walk in the woods and be away, somewhere he could breathe freely and not have to hold himself together. It was all too much.

"I'm glad I caught you," Victor said after taking a long pull of ale. "I wanted to apologize for that black eye I gave you. I had no idea what they were up to, I swear."

The black eye had faded somewhat and was now a mottled, greenish blueish purple. "I don't blame you, Victor. You had nothing to do with it, and I can't blame you for drawing conclusions. I know what it looked like." *And what it was.*

"I assume you were checking on Iselda? Alais told me she's got a fever. I still can't believe her mother participated in this plot after what happened to Alais. She knows too well what happens when a reputation is ruined."

William had heard the stories. Even years later, people liked to gossip about what may or may not have transpired between Alais and Victor's cousin, Robert.

"I can't believe they'd risk her health like this," he said, then took a swig of his drink. "This is a dangerous fever. If it gets worse, I hate to think what could happen."

"She's lucky to have you here to make sure she pulls through."

William stared into his drink, trying to push away painful memories. "I won't let anything happen to her. I promise."

Victor cocked his head to the side and gave him a penetrating look with his one deep blue eye. "You care about her."

William nodded, still staring at his drink. "A lot. Your point?"

Victor smiled. "And you were found in a…" He wagged his head from shoulder to shoulder. "…somewhat compromising position." He cleared his throat and took a drink. "Do you remember when you caught me with Rebekah?"

Yes, he did. How could he forget? He chuckled. "I still don't know how you convinced my nurse to bed you."

"I'm very persuasive." Victor grinned.

"Hmph," William said, smiling and shaking his head. "Does your wife know what a scoundrel you were?"

"Sadly, yes. She doesn't know about Rebekah specifically, but she knows in general terms. You know Jane from The Bird's Nest?"

Yes, he did. She was a force to be reckoned with. When one of her residents was ill, she pestered him relentlessly until he made a visit. Come to think of it, Jane looked a lot like Alais.

"Well," Victor continued, "she and I became acquainted when I first came to Winchelsea. At the time, she was doing something entirely different on Birdie Street. I'm sorry to say I took comfort with her in an attempt to rid myself of certain troublesome feelings about Alais, not that it worked. She and Alais are friends now, a fact that never ceases to amaze and terrify me. Even though Alais knows all about Jane, it still makes my gut churn when they spend time together." He took a drink. "Are you, perchance, struggling with some troublesome feelings?"

William stayed silent, not trusting himself to respond.

"I'm assuming it isn't your usual practice to cuddle your patients," his friend continued. "Or perhaps I should say…fondle?"

Raphael's cheeks. He did not want to be having this conversation, especially when he couldn't seem to stop thinking about what he'd glimpsed during his visit just now. *Pink. I can't believe I said "pink" out loud. If she knew what I meant…*Gritting his teeth, William grumbled, "Fine. Yes. I am having some troublesome feelings about Iselda."

Victor leaned in with an all-too-knowing grin. "Care to unburden yourself?"

No, he would not, but he wasn't foolish enough to think Victor was going to give him a choice. "I kissed her. Are you happy? I kissed her, and I want to do it again, even though it's wrong, wrong, wrong."

"Not so very wrong, I think, in holy wedlock."

"Ah, but she doesn't want to marry me. You heard her. And anyway, I shouldn't marry anyone."

"Oh? Why not? Other than those vows you haven't actually taken."

William emptied his cup, and Victor signaled the serving wench for another. "Our pasts aren't as different as you might think. Before I joined the Hospitallers, I was the lordly heir that made all the local girls swoon, and I took full advantage. They threw themselves at me, and I thought it was merely my due. I fucked around with impunity back in Arundel. I wronged more women than I care to count."

He took a swig from the new tankard that had just arrived.

Victor didn't say a word. He simply watched and listened.

"There was one girl, though, that I hurt worse than the rest. Luisa. There was something about her I couldn't resist, and I kept going back. I couldn't stay away, even after she confessed she was with child and married a farmer in haste. One day, I went to meet her and found her husband there instead. He gave me a black eye and told me Luisa was dead. It was because of the baby. Something went wrong, and the midwife had tried to help her, and then she'd died. He said I killed her. And he was right."

He'd hoped it would give him some relief to say these things aloud, but instead, it made him feel even worse.

"You didn't kill her," Victor said quietly.

"No? She never would have died if I hadn't gotten her pregnant. And then I neglected her care and let an incompetent midwife do her worst. I didn't hold a knife to her throat, but she wouldn't be dead if not for my carelessness and negligence."

It was all his fault. If he hadn't been so selfish, Luisa would be alive and well. Guilt churned in his stomach, and the urge to flee to the woods strengthened.

"You didn't kill her," Victor repeated.

William rested his face in his hands for a long moment before looking up again. "I ran away to the Hospitallers so that I could atone for my sins and be sure I'd never put another woman in danger. And I didn't. For nine years I behaved myself, and now, suddenly, Iselda makes me want to throw caution to the wind. I want to marry her. I want to start a family with her, even though that's exactly what I've been trying to avoid all this time."

As he said it, he realized it was true. He didn't want to go back to life as a Hospitaller, even though he knew it was the right thing to do. He wanted the life he'd imagined in the middle of the night, holding her against him in the cellar. There was no more peace to be found in running away. Sleeping by her side made him ache with wanting. He wanted to stay there forever and never let go.

"So by your logic, I shouldn't have married Alais, nor should I have bedded her, because of the chance she might die in childbirth." Victor stared him down.

"That's ridiculous. Of course, I'm not saying that."

"No?" Victor took a long, deep drink. "When Alais had Clara, she nearly bled to death. Fortunately, she recovered. But if I had lost her, would it have been my fault?"

"No." Seeing the look on Victor's face, he reached out and squeezed his friend's shoulder. He could only imagine what it would be like to see one's wife on death's door. This was all the more reason why he should ignore his dangerous infatuation with Iselda.

"Then why is Luisa's death yours?"

"You don't understand."

"I'm pretty sure I do." Victor sat there and watched him for a long moment, unblinking. "William, do yourself a favor and ask Iselda again. It's what you want, and I'm guessing it's what she wants too. She thought she was doing you a favor saying no, but she might change her mind if you prove to her that this is truly what you want."

"But I don't want—"

"Yes, you do. You already said so."

"I need to go take a walk."

Victor smiled at him and clapped his shoulder. "I know you'll do the right thing."

WILLIAM WALKED THROUGH the barren woods to the west of Winchelsea. At this time of year, the leaves were long gone, and the landscape was a study in brown. The gray brown of the tree trunks blended with the black brown of the leaf mulch beneath his feet, interspersed with tufts of dead grasses in light taupe and the red brown of leafless shrubbery. Wet slicks of mud sucked at the soles of his boots as he sought to lose himself, a hopeless endeavor when the castle where she slept was clearly visible through the bare tree branches.

She was trying so hard to be considerate and kind. He was sure she refused his proposal for his sake, not her own. If only he could believe she'd refused for her own reasons instead, everything would be much simpler.

But now he had her list, and he could no longer pretend.

He'd known about her list. She told him about her twenty-seven suitors. But it was something else entirely to see it, hold it, know that he was now number twenty-eight. He pulled it from where he'd tucked it beneath his robes. He swore he could feel it burning against him all through that chat with Victor.

It was beyond him why he'd taken it when he found it by accident amongst her medical notes. He'd reasoned to himself that it was too dangerous to leave it where it was, where anyone might happen upon it. Surely, she hadn't meant to leave it so exposed. Her illness must have made her careless.

Glancing around to make absolutely sure he was alone, he unfolded the parchment, his hands shaking as he looked at her neat columns. He could imagine seventeen-year-old Iselda starting this list full of hope, feeling a bit naughty after Alais's marriage. It was such a touching mix of sweetness and sensuality. Who would ever have thought Iselda de Vere dreamed of illicit touch, of inspiring a man's lust?

He was in trouble before seeing the list, but now he was done for. How could he ever recover? He lit the spark in that cellar, and she welcomed it. She was not shy at all in her response. And now he knew why. She had been waiting years for someone to dare.

The empty columns showing suitor after suitor offering only the barest courtesy painted a devastating portrait. She was nothing if not meticulous as she recorded these men's indifference. He ached for her as one man after another disappointed her. Not one had bothered to kindle her considerable passion. They never suspected what hid beneath her quiet, prim demeanor.

They hardly bothered to get to know her at all, it seemed. How could they have failed to laugh with her or give her a heartfelt compliment? It was insulting. He wanted to box their ears for being so stupid and heartless.

And then there was his own name. William. Number twenty-eight. Right after his disappointing brother. Looking across the columns, he realized how much it must have cost her to turn him down. All but two of the columns were checked. In his selfishness, he'd taken too much, gone too far, but he'd also given her nearly everything she wanted, from the innocent to the improper.

"Kissed my hand," "Kissed my cheek," "Laughed with me," and "Gave heartfelt compliment," made him smile. It was the least any man should do, and it was his pleasure to give her such simple joy.

"Kissed my lips." *Lord have mercy.* He should never have kissed her, but now that he had, he was desperate to do it again. Now that he knew she welcomed it, he didn't know how he could stop himself. But a kiss could not be undertaken lightly. A kiss led to other things. Dangerous things.

He had already "Offered marriage," and she'd said no. Her refusal gutted him, especially now that he wasn't only willing to marry her, but he wanted to. He needed to, despite all his fears and the lessons of his youth. If he offered again, would her answer change?

This brought him to the next three tick marks, the ones that troubled him the most: "Caressed my body," "Touched my breasts," and "Aroused in my presence." He'd hoped she hadn't noticed his body's unconscious response to holding her in his arms. He hadn't meant to take advantage of her in her sleep. It didn't matter that he was also asleep and not in control. He should have stayed awake and found a way to exercise restraint.

Before he saw this list, he could pretend she didn't know how far beyond propriety they had strayed, but here was proof she was well aware. And yet, she'd still declined his offer of marriage. Knowing how thoroughly he had compromised her, she still set him free.

"Held me as I slept," brought tears to his eyes. It was such a simple, innocent longing, a craving he'd never overcome in all his years with the Hospitallers. The previous night was the loneliest of his life. Having held her in his arms the night before, it was impossible to go back to the careful indifference he'd cultivated over the years. He hungered for the warmth and weight of her by his side. This, more than anything else, had done him in. There was no going back to his former life, not after this.

Looking down at the parchment once again, he saw that only "Removed my clothing" and "Made love to me" remained unchecked. He stiffened merely reading the words. There was no doubt what his body wanted. He also knew with absolute certainty that he could never allow anyone else to fulfill these two list items. It was unthinkable. And if he could not allow her to find happiness with another, it was clear what he had to do.

There was risk. But then, as Victor had reminded him, there was always risk. Despite the warning of his heart, he knew logically that lovemaking and pregnancy were not a death sentence. It was his fault Luisa had gotten with child, but her untimely death was not his doing. Victor was right. Whatever the sudden ailment that took her, it wasn't of his making. If he'd been there, perhaps he could have done something. Maybe he could have saved her.

Perhaps that was the key. He wasn't going to manage to stay away from Iselda. Not now. The desire he'd worked so hard to banish from his life was back stronger than ever. He wanted to taste every part of her, touch her secrets, feel her surrounding him, enveloping him. The dam of his control had broken irreparably, and he was awash in raw need.

He was going to ask for her hand again, and he hoped that she might give it. If, after their marriage, she got with child, he would be there to care for her, to make sure nothing could possibly go wrong. He would keep her safe and healthy at all costs. If he did his duty, then perhaps he could allow himself to give in to temptation at long last. No. Not temptation. Love. Because what he was feeling was more than desire. He knew this as well as he knew how to heal others. Yes, he wanted her, desperately, but he also craved her company and her conversation. He wanted to make her smile and laugh. He wanted to match wits with her and watch her intelligence sparkle.

It meant giving up his work with the hospitals, but there were other ways to practice medicine. He'd find a way to continue his life's work. It would be different without the support and guidance of the Order, but perhaps it was time for him to strike out on his own. He had learned what he could from them, and he had repaid their gift of knowledge with years of work on their behalf. And of course, he thought with a wry smile, his father had paid them quite a lot of money over the years. Yes, the Hospitallers would be just fine. It was time to stand on his own, to take a wife, and stop running from the mistakes of his youth.

He folded up the parchment, hid it in his robes once again, and strode back toward Winchelsea.

The hospital had a line out the door when he arrived, and the stranded pilgrims were still milling around, as their ship still hadn't yet sailed for the Holy Land. Squeezing his way through the press of people, he found Brother Joseph.

"Brother William, thank heavens you're here! I'll never get through this line without your help."

"Brother, I need to speak to you a moment."

"Can't it wait?"

"No." Brother Joseph made his apologies to the young woman whose burnt arm he was dressing, and they ducked into the hall together. "Let me guess. You've decided to leave the Order because you've finally realized you're in love with Lady Iselda."

William stared at him, stunned. "How did you know? I only figured it out about ten minutes ago."

"I've known this was coming for months, Brother. You two couldn't get enough of each other. I'm only amazed it's taken this long for you to figure it out."

"But we argued constantly."

Brother Joseph cocked his head to the side. "You and I have worked side by side for the last six months, and not once have you inquired about my views on ginger cakes. I'm with her, by the way. I'd much rather eat one of her ginger cakes than drink one of your mint concoctions when my stomach is off. Would you like to argue about it?"

"Of course not."

Brother Joseph smiled and shook his head. "Did you truly not realize you were inventing reasons to argue so that you could spend time with her?"

William stared in stunned silence. Joseph was right. He'd never bothered to argue over minor differences of practice with anyone else. Only beautiful, intelligent, infuriating Iselda inspired him to endless debate. On the rare days she didn't visit to cross swords, he felt bereft and restless. He couldn't wait to see her again, finding the least excuse to seek her out and quibble over some new minor point of practice. Good God. He'd been in love for months without realizing it.

More importantly, she'd been in love with him, at least he hoped so. Hadn't she admitted she was different around him, comfortable in a way she wasn't with others? Didn't she seek him out as much as he did her? Hope bloomed in his heart at this new evidence that perhaps she did return his love. Next time he asked, she would say yes. He was sure of it.

"I'm very happy for you," Brother Joseph said with a knowing smile. "Though I am sorry to be losing such a good friend and colleague. This life isn't for everyone. I thank you for your service and wish you well in your new life."

William wanted to hug the man, who had taught him so much, but he contented himself with pressing his hands to his shoulders. "Thank you, Brother Joseph. Your words mean more than I can tell."

"May I ask you one favor before you leave?" Brother Joseph asked.

"Anything."

"Can you wait to quit until tonight? I need your help with the crowd outside. There's a fever and ague going around, and everyone has it. It's been like this all day. Worst of all, the pilgrims staying in the dormitory have started to come down with it. I'm worried about the consequences if we don't find a way to curb this before it turns into an epidemic."

William thought of Iselda, feverish and coughing in her room. She'd probably caught the illness while serving the sick. No matter. He was her physician, and she would be fine, he had no doubt. She was strong. But these others? "Of course, and I'm happy to help at the hospital until the Order sends a replacement. I would never want to do anything detrimental to the Order's work."

William entered his examination room, marveling at how his life had changed in the space of a day. His mind spun with plans for a new future he'd barely begun to contemplate. But one thought dominated all the others. He could hardly wait to make his way to the castle and see Iselda again.

CHAPTER TEN

ISELDA WOKE UP feeling like she slept in a swamp. A hot swamp. Or maybe she *was* a hot swamp. Her mouth certainly tasted foul, and her lungs were full of muck. Not muck, phlegm. She was a hot phlegmatic swamp mess. Or maybe a hot mess of swamp phlegm? Was there a chapter in Hildegard about that?

Her sheets were drenched in sweat, and as she tried to sit up, she caught a whiff of her own ripe scent before coughing up a glob of phlegm into a handkerchief by her bed. *Ugh.* She was so disgusting. Her hair was sticking up in a matted mess on the left side of her head, while the right side was greasy and sticky. Why was it sticky? And why did it feel like there were wilted lettuce leaves between her legs?

She coughed again, making upsetting wet gurgles. "Rosamunda," she called. Or at least she intended to call. It came out as more of a croak. Fortunately, Rosamunda heard and came to her aid.

"Can you get me some mint tea? My mouth tastes like swamp phlegm."

"Of course, my lady."

"And when you get back, can you comb my hair? It feels all wrong."

"As you wish, my lady."

There was a knock at the door, and after several moments of

murmuring, Rosamunda let a man in. Iselda dove back under the covers hoping to hide…well…all of her. She wrapped the blankets around her head to form a deep hood in which she could conceal herself.

"Michael?" she asked in profound confusion, peeking from the depths of her makeshift hood. "What are you doing in my room? And why do you have flowers? You don't even like me." Wait. No. Something was off. "Michael, did you get a haircut?"

The man stepped farther into the room and laughed. That voice. That was not Michael's voice. And my goodness, this man was far more attractive than she remembered Michael being. The fever must still be scrambling her brains. Why was this attractive man standing by her bed, holding a bouquet of snowdrops when she was a hot phlegmatic swamp mess?

"Do I look that different?" asked a baritone voice that made her remember why she was sitting in lettuce. "I admit I borrowed the clothes from Michael, but I never expected you to confuse us."

"William?" she gurgled in horror. "You can't see me like this. I'm disgusting."

"I'm your physician. It's my job to see you like this. Would you mind coming out of your cocoon?"

"But…but… you're in *clothes*, and you have flowers. Is this a dream?" She narrowed her eyes. "Because I've been having a lot of dreams about you. Sometimes you're in clothes, but sometimes…" She clamped her mouth shut. She probably shouldn't have said any of that out loud, but she was at least two thirds sure this wasn't really happening. "I have a fever," she said idiotically, as if real and dream William didn't both know that. "I'm sitting in lettuce." Another thing she probably shouldn't have said out loud.

"Well, I don't know why you're sitting in lettuce, but I'm intrigued," he said slowly, trying to hold back laughter.

"It's the dreams. They're…." *Full of you with no clothes.* "I should stop talking." She had to anyway, due to another coughing fit.

When he heard her cough, his face transformed into an expression of professional concern. He reached out and gently pushed back her blankets. He didn't recoil, thank God. Pressing her forehead and neck to check fever, then checking ears and throat, he conducted a quick assessment, his chaste, professional touch setting her on fire even in her current state. Then he slipped the sleeves of her shift over her shoulders, pushing the garment down so that he could listen to her chest as he had the day before. She could swear he brushed his lips against her skin as he bent his head to listen.

"I still hear liquid in your lungs, and you are obviously still feverish. I'm afraid you're worse than yesterday. I really should bleed you."

"So why are you in clothes?" she blurted to change the subject. Maybe he'd forget about bleeding her if she could distract him.

"As opposed to naked?"

Oh, dear Lord.

"Why are you so attractive?" *Even worse, Iselda.* She really shouldn't speak at all.

He tilted his head to the side and smiled in a way that made her think she needed more lettuce.

"If you're asking why I'm in Michael's clothes instead of my robes, it's because I left the Order."

She was incapable of absorbing that information right this moment. It sounded like nonsense. "You left an order behind?"

"I left the Hospitallers."

"*Pshht.* No." She flapped her hand around in what she intended to be a dismissive fashion. He caught it and brought it to his lips, kissing the back of it so tenderly her whole lettuce-wrapped phlegm swamp went right up in flames.

Oh dear. She already couldn't think straight. And now he'd gone and made it so much worse. But there was something important here. If only she could hang onto what and why.

"But…". It was so very hard to complete a thought. "But I said no so you didn't have to." Producing that sentence was like trying to thread a needle while riding a horse. Her brain was done. She wanted her blanket hood back.

"And I realized I had to leave the Order of my own volition so that you could say yes." He was still holding her hand, and he pressed it to his heart. It pounded furiously beneath his fine wool cotte. "I don't think you're in any shape to be making life altering decisions today, but when you're better, I very much hope you'll agree to be my wife. I love you, and I want to spend my life with you."

She blinked several times, marveling at the clarity of her hallucination.

"I am definitely not awake, but this is a very nice dream." She wriggled back down under the covers until they covered her head, still hanging onto his hand. "I love you too, dream William," she said beneath the blankets. "Just don't tell the real William. He's not supposed to know."

He pressed another fervent kiss on the back of her hand.

"Sweeting, I have to bleed you. I know you don't want me to, but it must be done. If we don't drain the foul humors, I hate to think what might happen." His grip tightened on her hand.

She was silent for a long moment, wishing she had the energy to argue, but there was no fight left in her, not even a little. "If you must. I trust your judgment."

"Really? You never have before. You must be very sick indeed."

She closed her eyes. It was too much work to keep them open. She heard more people come into the room.

"William," she heard her mother say. "I didn't expect to see you here so early. How is she?"

"I won't deceive you. She is very sick. Her lungs are phlegmatic, and an excess of yellow bile is causing a severe fever. I was about to bleed her, but I will wait until you are done with your visit."

"Oh, my poor baby," her mother moaned. "We should never have agreed to that horrible scheme."

"No, you should not have," William grumbled. The fury in his voice was plain to hear. She squeezed his hand.

"Is she asleep?"

"No," she croaked from beneath her blankets to save William from having to guess. "But I don't want to talk. Still mad." She scrunched down deeper in the blankets but still hung onto William's hand. It was escaping her right this moment why she was mad, but she was certain of her outrage.

"What happened to your robes?" she heard Carenza ask.

"I left the Hospitallers."

"What?"

"I'm in love with you sister, and I'm hoping she'll agree to be my wife. She refused my proposal because she didn't want to force me to marry. I didn't think she'd accept unless I proved I was asking of my own free will."

"I accept, dream William," Iselda coughed, still buried deep.

"And I am not holding you to anything you say while you're this sick and feverish," he said, caressing the back of her hand with his thumb. But she could hear the smile in his voice. "I'll ask you properly once you've recovered."

"Oh my," her mother exclaimed. "My baby is getting married. I finally get to throw the wedding celebration I've always dreamed of!"

Iselda rolled her eyes under her blanket.

"Wait until I tell Lady Maud. She'll be beside herself. Don't worry about a thing, you two. We'll take care of everything."

"Before you run off to tell my mother," William said in a gruff voice, "Please wait until your daughter's fever is gone and she can answer while in her right mind. She's very sick and more than a little delirious at the moment. You should have heard what she said about lettuce a few minutes ago."

Iselda swore she could hear her mother's buoyant mood deflating. "Can I at least tell your mother you *might* be getting married? A wedding like this takes time to plan. I promise we won't make any arrangements that can't be easily undone until Iselda is better and confirms her answer."

William squeezed her hand a little too hard. Poor Dream William. Her mother was a trial sometimes. "Why do I suspect you're going to go ahead no matter what I say?"

"Come on, mother," she heard Carenza say. "Let's leave them alone. Rosamunda is already here to chaperone. She's still sick and needs care, and I'm sure he's needed back at the hospital with this ague going around."

"Thank you, Lady Carenza. Now, if you'll excuse me, I'd like to get on with bleeding her."

She tried to pull her hand away as she listened to the footsteps of her mother and sister leaving the room. He held on tight, not letting her pull away.

"Sweeting, you agreed if you got worse, you would accept my treatment. Ask medical experts anywhere in the known world how to cure a fever, and they will all agree this is what has to be done. Not only Galen. The Romans and even the Arabs agree on this."

He was right, curse him. She wanted to argue but knew she was in no state to do so. Slowly she stuck out her arm.

"I trust you," she croaked from beneath the blankets.

He rustled around in his bag and then she nearly yelped as he sliced a shallow cut near the crease of her elbow. It made her suck her breath through her teeth.

"I'm so sorry, sweeting. I don't want to hurt you, not ever. I wouldn't do this if I saw an alternative. You're being very brave. I wish I had a peppermint candy to give you."

Mmmm. Peppermint. Maybe that would get rid of her swamp breath? "Bag is on my desk next to my book."

She was starting to feel faint as she listened to the drip, drip, drip of her own blood into the small metal bowl he used for this purpose.

"Can I pull back your blanket to give you your peppermint?"

"Mmhmm," she murmured.

He pulled the covers back to find her head. She blinked her eyes open, fighting drowsiness as her blood continued to drip. "Say '*aaaah.*'" He placed it on her tongue, then caressed her cheek. Why did he have to be so sinfully gorgeous when she was such a mess?

"Thank you," she whispered, drifting off as the candy melted on her tongue. "I love you, Dream William." And with that, she passed out, only to meet up with him again in her dreams. Naked.

CHAPTER ELEVEN

HER FEVER WAS gone. She was sure of it, not that she wasn't still weak and coughing a bit. But the sickly heat was gone, and she was desperate for a bath. Oh, a bath. *Heaven!*

"Rosamunda?"

"Yes, my lady?" she said from a seat in the corner in a sleepy voice. Rosamunda had been watching over her all day during her illness, ready to take care of her slightest wish.

"Have you been here all night?"

"No, my lady. I came up about an hour ago to tend to your fire. My apologies for dozing. I wasn't sure when you would wake."

Iselda pushed up to sitting. "You really should take care of yourself. I'm worried you aren't getting enough rest. I wouldn't want you to get sick."

"Don't worry about me, my lady, I have this amulet here to protect me," she said, holding up a lumpen piece of stone on a string around her neck. "I haven't gotten sick once since I bought it."

"And when did you buy it?" Iselda asked, struggling to keep a straight face.

"Two weeks ago. And I haven't gotten sick once!"

Amazing.

"Well, I recommend you get plenty of rest anyway to ensure

your amulet continues to work," she said with the most serious face she could summon. "Since you're here, though, I'd like your help. I'm desperately in need of a bath, and it would be lovely to have my sheets changed. I'm certain I'll feel worlds better if I can get clean."

Rosamunda clapped her hands with a broad grin. "You must be feeling better, my lady. Lord William will be so pleased," she said, waggling her eyebrows in an insinuating fashion.

"All the more reason for that bath," she murmured to herself. William had promised to propose properly, whatever that meant, as soon as she was recovered enough. The one thing she knew for certain was that she couldn't bear for that to happen while she smelled like a dragon. Who lived in a swamp.

While Rosamunda was out of the room making the necessary arrangements for the bath, Iselda decided to test herself on her feet. She'd been in bed for almost a week now, and she was desperately bored. Even seeing her family—who she was still very mad at—would be an improvement on staring at her walls for hours on end.

Setting down one foot and then the other, she eased herself to the floor. *A bit wobbly, but mostly stable.* Staying close to the bed, she tried walking a bit. Even the short distance around the bed winded her. She must have been very sick indeed, although she still suspected the bleeding weakened her when she most needed strength. Someday, she was determined to win that argument, even if she was fighting against all the experts in the known world.

"My lady," Rosamunda exclaimed, coming back into the room, and rushing to her side. "What are you doing out of bed on your own? What if you'd had a spill?"

"I still remember how to walk, you know." It wouldn't do to be grumpy with Rosamunda after everything she'd done, but she'd been pent up too long.

"At the very least, let me put a robe on you so that you don't catch a chill."

She decided it would do no good to argue that she'd already caught a chill and appeared to be over it by now. Instead, she surrendered to Rosamunda's fussing, allowing herself to be wrapped in a long, soft, woolen robe and shod in woolen slippers.

"Now you take my arm and let me help you down the stairs. Your bath should be ready by the time we get down to the bathing room."

Together, they made their slow, wobbly way down, ignoring the curious glances of the other servants as they made their descent. As promised, the tub was full of steaming water, fragrant from the dried flowers and herbs that had been added. It looked like the best thing she'd ever seen.

"Help me in?" she asked, as she untied her robe and stripped off her shift. The sides of the wooden, barrel-shaped tub were high, and she didn't trust herself to climb in alone.

With Rosamunda's help, she stepped onto the stool beside the bath and cautiously lowered one leg and then the other into the hot water. It felt even better than she'd imagined. Lowering her whole body, she let out a low moan of pleasure.

"There you are, my lady. Do you need any assistance?"

"No, thank you."

"Then I'll leave you alone and go change the sheets. I'll be back in a short while with some clean clothes."

"Thank you, Rosamunda. Can you bring the blue wool dress with the scooped neckline?"

"Of course."

Alone in this glorious warmth, she sank down into the water, letting it soak through her hair, and all the aches of the last week leached away.

William was going to propose today, she was sure of it. Seven years of waiting, and today was the day. The thought of spending the rest of her life with him at her side filled her with a warm glow. And something else. Her fever might be gone, but she still remembered the dreams, and the cellar, of course—the way his hands felt on her body, the way his lips brushed against hers. She couldn't help wondering when she might taste his lips again. Would he kiss her today? There would be no more than a chaste peck in front of family, but perhaps if they could find a moment alone…

No. She wasn't going to think about that. This was the most important decision of her life, and she needed to be sure she was making it with a clear head. Even though the decision was a foregone conclusion, she needed to be certain she was making it for the right reasons. She knew, and wasn't going to think further about, all the reasons it felt right. Was there anything that concerned her about this union?

She blew out her breath in a puff and submerged her whole head for a long moment before reemerging and scrubbing herself with a rough linen cloth and soap.

If she was honest with herself, and set aside her ravenous lust and tender adoration for William, there was plenty to worry about. First off, there was his decision to leave the Hospitallers. It was a grand romantic gesture, no doubt, but how could she be certain he wouldn't regret it? And if he regretted it, wouldn't he end up resenting her? What would he do when he was no longer opening hospitals? She imagined he would practice medicine, but perhaps as a married man, he would feel obliged to take on more lordly responsibilities. Would his family expect them to move to Arundel? Could he truly be happy walking away from his life's work, even if it was his choice to do so?

Then there was the question of what he might expect from her. The arrangement she had here in Winchelsea with the midwives and healers couldn't continue. Her family was willing to look the other way when she was an eccentric old maid, but as the wife of a prominent lord, her days of invisibility would be over. Also, while William had acknowledged her competence and knowledge, he'd never taken back what he said about women practicing medicine. He might expect her to quit, and she knew neither her family nor his would approve of her continuing once she had a husband and household to tend. Could *she* be happy without her life's work?

If he was willing to sacrifice his work to be with her, then surely, she could sacrifice her own work for him. It wasn't as if she was ever going to be allowed to do more than assist, no matter how much she studied. It wasn't proper, and she knew it. Nonetheless, she couldn't help feeling a pang at the prospect of leaving her patients behind, even if there were compensations.

She poured scented oil on her hair and massaged it through the long, snarled strands, patiently pulling apart the tangles. If only her life was as easy to untangle as her hair.

One more thing troubled her, and it had to do with William's past. It was clear he was a very different man before he joined the Hospitallers. He hinted at past bad behavior, but what exactly did he do? Someone got hurt, he said, and that was why he ran away to join the Order. But she was certain there was more to that story. Was he hiding something? It certainly didn't feel like he was being completely honest. Then again, she had no claim on him when he told her. She had no reason to pry. But if they were to be married, she wanted to know.

None of these things changed her mind about wanting to marry William. She was going to say yes eventually. Aside from being beautiful to look at and sinful to touch, he was intelligent, driven, thoughtful… He bickered with her because he cared, and, she suspected, because he liked her company. She'd seen him with patients, colleagues, and friends enough times to know that with other people he was kind, humble, and empathetic. And, of course, profoundly competent, a quality she found deeply alluring. Much though it pained her to admit it after her family's tricks, she had to agree they were right. She and William were made for each other.

Nonetheless, she was going to ask some questions before she gave a definite yes. There was no reason to rush things. Well maybe one reason, having something to do with the infuriating heat that had taken up residence between her legs. Wilted lettuce only went so far. She wouldn't prolong things too much, just long enough to be absolutely sure.

Sinking back into the water one last time, she found herself smiling and humming one of Carenza's love songs. Love. What a terrifying, dizzying, sweet, and wonderful thing. After all these years of thinking she'd never find it, here it was, so unexpected and so right. And this was the day she would say yes. *Thank you, Lord, for helping me find love.*

She finished rinsing out her hair right as Rosamunda returned with her dress. For the first time in days, she was clean and confident and ready. The world was filled with possibility. She only needed to dress, go upstairs for breakfast, and let the day unfold.

Soon, she was seated at the breakfast table with her family, letting them fuss and flutter as she serenely consumed her eggs and toast. Daniel joined them and then Victor. Before long, William walked in, making her heart pound out of her chest. Thank goodness he always showed up around breakfast time.

"Lady Iselda, you're up," he said, gazing at her adoringly. "Are you feeling better?"

She granted him her warmest smile, melting beneath the ardor of his gaze. "I am."

He fell to his knees beside her. "I said I'd wait until you were well enough to ask, and here you are, up and about at last. Iselda de Vere, will you marry me?"

"Probably," she answered, offering what she hoped was a smile of mystery and promise. "Almost certainly," she said, relenting at the alarm that filled his eyes. "I would like to speak with you first." As every head turned avidly toward her, she added, "In a more private setting."

Daniel burst out laughing. "De Veres always have questions." Carenza elbowed him in the side, but she gave him an adoring look.

"I'd be happy to chaperone," Alais offered, jumping up from her seat, looking as if she'd just won a contest.

The mothers looked at each other and shrugged. "As long as

you come back with good news, I don't care who chaperones. After all, you already spent the night together," Lady Maud said, giving them both a pointed look.

Iselda gave William a fond look and nudged him to stand. Alais practically leapt around the table, grabbing both of their elbows and dragging them to the family sitting room.

"I never get to do this," Alais enthused, rushing them along. "This is my big chance. Alais the chaperone! Someday I'll get to do this for Clara, but I'll have to wait ever so long. I'm so excited that I get to hear what you say before anyone else. Everyone who wants the story will have to come to *me*," she exclaimed, pushing them toward a sofa. "Or you, of course," she said as an afterthought. "Forget I'm here. I'll go stare at a wall. You can kiss all you want as long as it doesn't go any further." She planted herself on a small chair in the corner and picked up some sewing, facing the wall, as promised. "I'm ready," she sang, announcing her invisibility, as Iselda and William collapsed against each other in silent laughter.

The sudden contact sent her heart racing, his too from the look in his eyes. He pulled her into a sudden, ravenous kiss that she would swear should have set her skirt on fire.

"Oh, you're kissing! I'm so excited," Alais enthused from the far corner, causing them to pull away from each other and look up.

"Alais," Iselda warned, ready to throttle her slightly older sister. She and Alais were only eleven months apart, after all.

"Sorry. I'm not here. I'm sewing and looking at the wall, I promise."

Iselda gave William an apologetic look and rested her forehead against his. He kissed her lightly, but sucked her lower lip between his, leaving her unable to form words for several moments after he broke contact.

"You have questions?" he prompted.

Yes, she did. What were they again?

She cleared her throat to buy time for her poor, addled brain, and that made her cough. When he started looking alarmed, she blurted out, "You left the Hospitallers," to distract him from her lingering symptoms and general wobbliness. He really did worry about her too much. "I know how deeply you care about your work. Are you sure you're ready to walk away?"

He caressed her cheek. "Yes, I'm sure. There are other ways to practice medicine. I've done my part for the Order. I'm ready to strike out on my own."

That made sense. She could accept that. He wasn't walking away from his calling, only adjusting how he approached it. She nodded.

"And what would your expectations be of me? I know my work is unconventional. I would, of course, put our family first. But would you allow me to keep doing my work at least some of the time?"

He her hands in his and looked into her eyes. "I'm not sure how I feel about you traipsing through the countryside attending births at all hours, but I'm sure we can agree on some sort of arrangement so that you don't have to give it up entirely."

His answer left her with a twinge of concern, but she reminded herself this was likely to be the most generous response she would get from any man. Most wouldn't allow her to continue at all. She nodded again.

Running her thumbs over the backs of his hands, she asked, "And what about family? I know you planned to live a life without one. I want children, and if we're married, I think we're likely to…likely to…" Why was this so hard to say? Was it because Alais was listening?

"We're likely to have them," he said with a laugh. "Yes, I agree. I'm not likely to manage to stay away from you." His lips were on hers again, hot and demanding, tasting her, devouring her as she clutched his cotte in sweet desperation.

"But do you want them?" she asked, breaking away. Of all her questions, this was the one she worried about the most. If he didn't want a family, she wasn't sure she could go through with this.

He was silent for a long moment and took a deep breath. "Yes, I do. I've always enjoyed children." She thought she sensed hesitation as he spoke, but he didn't elaborate. *Don't overthink it, Iselda.* He agreed he wanted children. That was enough.

"Would we stay in Winchelsea or move to Arundel?"

He tilted his head to ponder her question. "Do you know, I hadn't really thought about it? My parents will want us to go to Arundel, but I see no reason to return there if we prefer to stay here. I miss Arundel. I haven't been there for years, but I'm not sure I'm ready to move back. Perhaps we can visit and decide. Would that work for you?"

"Yes, that sounds lovely," she said with relief. She didn't have strong objections to moving away, but she wanted to make sure it was to somewhere they could both be happy.

"I have one last question, but I know it may be one you'd prefer not to answer." She sat holding his hands in her own, biting her lip, not quite ready to continue.

"What is it, sweeting?" he asked quietly.

Iselda glanced over at Alais and caught her sneaking a glance at them.

"I'm not listening," Alais chirped, facing the wall once again.

Iselda looked up at him, trying to find the right words so that she didn't cause offense. "Several times you've mentioned your youth and things you've done that you regret. I'd like to have at least a general sense of what happened."

He let out a long slow breath and nodded slowly. "I suppose I shouldn't be surprised that you're asking, and it's a fair question. It's only that I don't like the answer I'll have to give you. I hope you can forgive me for the sins of my youth." She squeezed his hands and gave him an encouraging nod. It was impossible to believe this man had done anything truly despicable, but she wanted to know. She didn't want to be surprised after they were wed.

"I was…umm…popular when I was young," he said, having

difficulty maintaining eye contact but glancing up at her frequently. "As my father's heir, I was given a great deal of license, in some cases more than I should have been. In particular, I was not very respectful toward women. They offered affection, and I took it, even though it was wrong for me to do so. My family shielded me from consequences, solving embarrassing problems before I was even aware of them. But there was one woman I dallied with that I knew I had impregnated. Something went wrong during her pregnancy, and she died. The baby too. It's what drove me to join the Hospitallers. I felt like I needed to make amends."

Her heart went out to him. He'd been carrying so much guilt and pain over this for so long.

"Oh, William," she whispered, brushing her lips against his. "I think you have long since made amends. What you did is no different from what most lords do in their youth. You only regretted it more deeply than most because you're such a caring person. You don't need my forgiveness, but if it makes you feel better, you have it."

She kissed his forehead and his cheeks before finding his lips and showing him with slow, gentle kisses how she felt about him, regardless of his revelations. "You've answered all my questions to my satisfaction, and I'm ready to answer yours. I would love to be your wife and have a family with you and torment you with Hildegard while you torment me with Galen. I still can't believe you left the Hospitallers so that you could be with me. I would never have asked it of you, but now that it's done, I can't say I'm sorry. I've been waiting years to find the right person. I'm so glad it's you."

"*Eeeeee*! You're getting married," Alais squealed from her corner. Iselda was tempted to chastise her again but let it go. After all, she wanted to squeal too, and she might have if William hadn't pulled her onto his lap and kissed her senseless.

Alais chose that moment to clear her throat. "Now, now, you two lovebirds, I'm afraid I have to exercise my sacred authority as a chaperone and stop you before anything too scandalous happens."

"Your sacred authority as a chaperone. Really," Iselda said in her most sarcastic annoyed-at-Alais voice. "Did God Himself appoint you?"

Alais rolled her eyes. "I can't be too lenient, or they'll never let me chaperone again. Besides, I'm dying to go tell everyone. Aren't you?"

CHAPTER TWELVE

THE DORMITORY HAD become a patient ward, and the Hospitallers still hadn't sent a replacement for William. For a week now, he'd spent every waking hour tending to the growing number of people that had fallen ill. Nearly every one of the pilgrims waiting for their ship to the Holy Land had come down with it. The few who hadn't moved from the hospital dormitory to inns to avoid the miasma he suspected were responsible for the spread. The only break he took was his daily visit to Iselda, who was almost fully recovered, thank God.

The mothers were in a frenzy of wedding preparations, now that he had formally proposed, and he left them alone to have their fun because he was otherwise occupied. The people of Winchelsea needed his help.

He and Brother Joseph walked from one pallet to the next, checking for fevers and bleeding the patients as necessary. One of the ladies from The Bird's Nest that he had helped was recovered enough to act as his assistant. She helped with cleaning and cooking and feeding the sixty-two invalids currently residing in the hospital dormitory, some on cots, some on pallets on the floor. They had lost seven patients so far. All had been elderly and in poor health to start with. Fortunately, most seemed to begin to recover after three or four days of severe symptoms.

He washed his blade and rinsed out his bowl and proceeded

to the next person on his bleeding schedule. Right after he made the cut, a gentle hand touched his shoulder, and he smelled a soft scent of pear and cinnamon. It was Iselda.

"What are you doing here? You should be up at the castle recovering, sweeting."

She looked pale and her face was a bit drawn, but otherwise she seemed as healthy as he'd seen her since she first got sick. And she was beautiful, even in the simple, serviceable brown wool dress she was wearing with all her hair tucked under a wimple. He longed to kiss her, hold her in his arms now that she was well enough. But he shoved that thought aside. There was too much work to do, and she really shouldn't be here. Not yet.

"I'm here to help. I'm well enough to be of some use, at least for a little while. Tell me what you need me to do, and I'll do it."

"No, you—"

"I promise to go back to the castle if I feel the least bit tired or ill," she interrupted. "I care about the people of Winchelsea, as do you," she said in a softer voice. "It's my duty to be here. Let me care for my people."

He could see the fierce determination in her eyes, and he couldn't pretend that he didn't need the help. Letting out his breath, he warned, "No Hildegard remedies. We need to give them consistent care with proven treatments. And you go home the minute you start flagging."

He saw her bite down a comeback, but she swallowed and said instead, "I agree to your conditions."

"Leonora from The Bird's Nest has recovered, and she's prepared a cough remedy. She has a huge pot of it boiling on the stove. Can you check the patients in that half of the dormitory," he said, pointing, "and see to it that they get the remedy? If they have other minor needs, I trust you to take care of them. If there's anyone taking a turn for the worse, please let me know or tell Brother Joseph."

"Of course," she said, all business.

"And sweeting," he added, catching her hand, "Thank you.

It's good to have you here." He kissed her on the cheek and immediately wished he hadn't because he wanted so much more. But this was not the time.

He continued his rounds of the patients with fevers, carrying out one bloodletting after another. At long last, he reached the end, only to find a line of patients with other concerns waiting in line outside the examination room. Brother Joseph had finished his rounds of the patients he was attending and had started on taking the people in line, but there was no chance he could see them all without assistance. He went to find Iselda.

"Can you help Brother Joseph with the line of people outside the examination room? He won't get through it before nightfall without help, and I need to make another round of the ague patients."

"Of course," she answered and headed away to carry out her assignment. No questions, no arguments, only work. God bless Iselda.

He went back to complete his rounds, and when he returned to check on her a while later, he found her being threatened by an old man with a headache complaint.

"Now see here, missy, you leave me alone and get me a real healer," the man roared in her face. "You have no business meddling in men's work."

Iselda responded with steely patience. "I'm sorry that you feel that way. As you can see the hospital is overwhelmed at the moment. If you don't want me to see to your needs, you are welcome to come back tomorrow."

"I have a headache now, young lady, and I don't intend to go anywhere until I see a real physician."

Iselda took a deep breath. "They will tell you the same thing I did. Drink some willow bark tea and rest. It will pass."

"Now see here," the man yelled in her face.

"Excuse me, is there a problem sir?" William asked, stepping between them, ready to give the man a much bigger headache if he didn't mind his tongue with Iselda.

"This little chickadee is meddling where she's not wanted. I'm having one of my headaches again, and I want to see a real physician about it, not some bit of fluff in a skirt."

William was ready to throttle the man, and it must have shown in his face because Iselda put a calming hand on his arm and shook her head at him ever so slightly.

"Lord William," she said. It was odd to be called that again after so long, but he supposed "Brother" didn't fit anymore. "I'm only a silly girl, and of course I don't know anything about real medicine." William's jaw dropped. Could this possibly be the same woman who fought him tooth and nail for months over the practice of bloodletting? She mouthed the words "trust me" to him. "Would you mind confirming for this gentleman what you would recommend for a headache?"

"Willow bark tea and rest," he answered staring at her like he'd never seen her before.

"Thank you, my lord," said the man, bowing respectfully to William, shooting a dirty look at Iselda, and then wandering away muttering about meddling females.

William took her elbow and steered her out of earshot. "What just happened there? Are you feverish again? For months, you argue with me over arcane medical texts and treatments, demonstrating a knowledge of medicine that exceeds most male physicians I know, and now you're only a silly girl?"

Iselda shrugged. "He was a patient, and he was suffering. Nothing I said was going to change his views of women, and it wasn't worth arguing. The quickest way to get him the relief he needed and send him on his way was to give him what he wanted. Some people need to hear a man say a thing before they trust it."

"But you never backed down on anything with me. You argued with me for months." How could she be so determined and tenacious with him and then not mind belittling herself in front of that obnoxious old man?

"Arguing with that man would have been a complete waste

of time. But you? You cared, and you listened, even when you disagreed." She smiled and gave his arm a little squeeze. "And I liked you."

He was trying to think of somewhere private where he could sneak a kiss when a man came staggering up carrying a limp woman with a badly burned arm.

"Help me, please, my wife…" The man looked on the verge of collapse.

William ran to him and took the woman from his arms, carrying her into the examination room and laying her on a table. "What happened, good man?"

The man was shaking visibly, and Iselda took his hand in hers to comfort him. "Tell us what happened, sir. Lord William will do his best to help her."

The man wiped his brow and stared at his wife. "She was fine. Everything was fine. My Marta is strong as an ox, always was." As the man talked, William cut away the woman's sleeve so that he could clean the burn. "Never seen her faint in my life. But she did today. One minute she was stirring a cauldron on the hearth and the next, she slumped against it." The man took off his cloth cap and started twisting it. "I came running and pulled her away, but not before she got burned badly. But… but…she didn't wake up. I don't know why she doesn't wake up."

Iselda guided the man to a stool to sit and went to fetch him a mug of water.

"You said she fainted?" William asked. "Was she feeling ill? Headache, cough, fever?" Perhaps the ague had struck this poor woman down. Something must have made her faint.

"Not at all. My Marta was never sick a day of her life."

Iselda handed the man a cup of water, and he drank it down.

William felt for fever and listened to her chest. She sounded completely healthy. Then Iselda gasped.

"She was with child?" she asked the man.

"Yes."

"Who's her midwife?"

"Caterina."

"Go find her now. *Run.*"

The man went running out the door, and Iselda pushed the woman's skirts up over her knees. Blood streaked the woman's legs all the way down to her ankles. William muttered a curse. How had he missed that? He should have seen. And here he was checking the woman for ague.

As Iselda tended to the woman with calm focus, he felt as if his lungs had lost half of their capacity. He could no longer draw a full breath and was forced to back away. His heart was racing, and his knees were shaking.

"William?"

He had to get out, get some air. How had he never noticed that there was no air in here?

"William, are you all right? You don't look well."

He swayed and staggered to the door and went outside. Putting his hands on his knees and his head down, he took deep, gulping breaths. To his deep relief, Iselda didn't follow him. As he slowly recovered himself, he made his way back to the ague patients and doggedly conducted another round of checks, using the work to block out what he could not face.

What would Iselda think of him after a lapse like this? No, better not to think about it. It was stuffy in that room. That was all. He needed a bit of air. It had been a long day. He needed rest, but he couldn't possibly stop. He would heal every patient he saw within an inch of their lives until whatever was happening in that room was done. But what if that woman...? No. Ague. Herbs. Bleeding. Rest. Next patient.

He had no idea how much time had passed when a soft hand touched his shoulder. Dread filled him as he turned to look at her. He could hardly meet her eyes.

"Are you all right?" she asked kindly, touching her hand to his forehead. "I was worried you might be coming down with the ague, but I don't feel a fever."

He grasped her arm. "The woman. She..." He couldn't bring

himself to form words.

"She had a difficult time, but I think she'll pull through. She lost the child. I was worried the bleeding wouldn't stop, but at last she passed the remaining tissue in her womb. She's no longer hemorrhaging. Once she was out of danger, I finished cleaning her arm, and applied the salve you were using. She'll be staying in the hospital overnight. I didn't think it was wise to move her."

Air returned to his lungs and blood flowed through his veins once again as it should. "The midwife. Did she come?"

She heaved a deep sigh of exhaustion. "No. She was with another woman who was having a difficult birth. I handled it."

"You knew what to…?"

"I've attended one hundred and fifty-three births, sixteen of which I managed myself because the midwife wasn't able to come in time. I've helped fourteen women through miscarriages, and she's the fourth I've treated by myself. I've read every text I can find on the topic of pregnancy and childbirth in Latin or Greek. I assure you, I know what to do."

He stared at her in awe. This was the one area of medicine where he was completely out of his depth, and it was the one that caused him the deepest anxiety. Men weren't supposed to be in the birthing chamber. And it was out of the question for men to study such topics. Nonetheless, he had surreptitiously read everything he could on the subject so that the next time a woman was in need like Luisa, he would be prepared.

But look what a mess he was. What good was he to anyone if he was so panicked, he couldn't breathe? Iselda knew what to do. She was calm and collected, and she saved that woman's life when he fell apart. She was a miracle.

He grabbed her hand and dragged her to the miniscule scriptorium, closing the door firmly behind them. Not bothering to light a candle, he pulled her to him and claimed her mouth with a desperation unlike any he'd ever known. She was life. She was healing. She was goodness, and he could not live another second without kissing her, without feeling her body pressed against his own. He needed to drown out his own fears in her sweet embrace.

He tugged at her wimple until it gave way and allowed him to sink his hand into her silky-smooth hair. As his tongue dipped into her mouth, she opened to him, tasting him, sucking as if she craved him every bit as much as he did her. It was too much. It was driving him over the edge.

His hands had a mind of their own. As one kneaded her breast through the layers of her demure, high-necked dress, the other pulled up her skirt. Even without seeing he could feel the perfection of her long lithe leg through her woolen stocking. He paused at her garter, tracing the line where stocking gave way to bare flesh. She shivered at his touch and arched toward him, inviting him to continue, so he did. Reaching higher, his fingers teased her dampened curls, and she pressed herself into his hand. As he parted her folds, she moaned into their kiss and trembled as he began to stroke the tender nub he found there.

She was so hot and slick and eager, he could hardly contain himself. His own arousal strained against the confines of his breeches as he petted her to a peak, sinking one finger and then another inside of her. Oh God, he had to have her. He needed her right now. He had to be inside of her, feel her surrounding him, enfolding him in passion.

As wave after wave of release rocked her body, and she trembled and quaked against him, he thought he might die on the spot if he didn't take her here and now.

"I want you, William. I don't want to wait," she whispered in his ear as she melted against him in the final throes. She traced her fingers down and grasped him through his breeches.

As a bolt of lightning went through him at her touch, the reality of what she was inviting him to do sank in. It was impossible. He couldn't take her up against a wall in a tiny cell that didn't even have a lock. Anyone could walk in on them at any time. Brother Joseph was seeing patients right down the hall. Somehow, he had to find the strength to step away.

He could hear the roughness and strain in his own voice as he gently moved her hand away and said, "I want you too, sweeting. But this is neither the time nor the place. We've both waited years. We can wait two more weeks."

"William," she pleaded, running her hands up his chest and kissing his jawline.

He took her hands firmly in his own and stepped away. "I'll take you back to the castle." He found a flint and lit a candle. What he saw nearly made him lose all self-control all over again.

Her lips were red and swollen from his kisses. Her eyes were dazed and sultry after her climax. Long strands of hair hung down around her face, framing it and making her look deliciously ravished. Her eyes dipped to his arousal, and she bit her lip. He had to close his eyes and take deep, calming breaths, trying to recall everything Galen had to say about putrefying wounds. Surely that would calm his blood.

When he opened his eyes again, she was tucking the last strands of hair back beneath her wimple and looked nearly as presentable as she had before, though the look in her eye was still far from the tame and demure.

Two more weeks. Only two more weeks.

He listened at the door until he thought it was safe and opened it as silently as possible. When he saw the hallway was empty, he beckoned to Iselda. Together, they slipped out into the deep blue of twilight and made their way silently back up to the castle.

At the entrance to the castle, she turned to leave, and he held her hand to pull her back. "Until we're wed," he murmured in her ear, "please don't go anywhere without a chaperone. If I find myself alone with you again..." He stared at the ground and shook his head.

She squeezed his hand. "Two weeks."

He looked up, and she nodded, serious, prim Iselda once again.

Instead of returning to the hospital, he headed straight to the inn where he'd taken a room after notifying the order of his decision to leave. He knew Brother Joseph needed his help, but he wasn't fit for company at the moment.

He did what was necessary to find the release he denied himself with Iselda, but as he lay on his bed afterward, he found his mind returning to the woman who had the miscarriage. All his good intentions of ensuring what happened to Luisa didn't happen again flew out the door when faced with a woman in crisis. And this was a complete stranger. How was he going to survive Iselda having children?

It was too late now. He was committed to his course. In two weeks' time, they would marry, and he had agreed to have children. She was innocent, but not so innocent he could take precautions against children without her noticing.

Two weeks until he was forced to surmount his greatest fears so that he could give in to his deepest desires. Two weeks. *Ave Maria gratia plena...*

CHAPTER THIRTEEN

I SELDA'S DREAMS WERE worse, and the lettuce was not helping. Every day, she went down to the hospital and toiled for hours giving aid to William and Brother Joseph and comfort to the sick whose numbers kept growing. And every day, she brought Rosamunda to ensure her own good behavior.

William was right. They couldn't be alone. The way her body reacted when he touched her... She didn't even know such sensations were possible. She'd ached with nebulous longing before their heated encounter in his office. Now, it was all she could do not to haul him off to some dark corner every time she saw him. Her desire was so specific and intense now that she knew what he could make her feel. It was like an illness, a fever. She couldn't concentrate. Her body was warm and restless. She hungered noon and night. There was only one cure, and he'd refused her.

She wanted to be grateful for his fortitude in the face of temptation. He was right to do what he did. But then why did she wish so desperately he was a little bit less honorable and decent?

Despite the frantic pace of their work, the days dragged. It felt wrong to marry in the midst of so much suffering. She prayed every day that the illness would subside before their wedding day.

With one week left, at last the numbers began to decline. Sixteen people had died. More than eighty currently slept in the hospital, too sick to be released. Nearly everyone in Winchelsea came down with it. For most, it was a few days of inconvenience, but for the unlucky few, it was a death sentence.

"Death can come at any time, and life should not be wasted," Carenza always said. Charles too, when he was around. Iselda needed that wisdom now more than ever.

"Iselda, are you listening? I asked you a question."

With a start, she looked up at her mother across the breakfast spread. "I'm sorry. I wasn't paying attention. Can you remind me what you asked?"

Her mother shook her head and sighed. "You're spending too much time with all those sick people. If you don't watch out, you're going to breathe that miasma and get sick again yourself."

Iselda clenched her fists and then released them below the table, then took a bite of bread with cheese. After swallowing, she asked again, "Your question, Mama?"

"Have you decided on the flowers for your bouquet?"

Flowers? When half the town is too ill to get out of bed?

"I thought I already told you that daffodils will do. Nothing else is blooming yet."

Her mother made a face.

"What is wrong with daffodils?"

"Oh, nothing. Nothing," her mother said, fiddling with a linen napkin. "They're just so...ordinary."

"And I'm ordinary, Mother, so we'll match."

"No, you're not. You're...you're..." Her mother trailed off.

"I'm what?"

Her mother stared at her plain linen napkin for far longer than such an item warranted. "Daffodils are fine, dear," she said at last in a quiet voice.

Iselda picked up her toast and marched out of the room, taking her cloak from Rosamunda who was waiting right outside the great hall door. With a nod of her head, she strode out the door and down Castle Street, not checking whether Rosamunda followed. By the time she arrived at the hospital, she'd finished her cheese and bread, and to her moderate dismay, Rosamunda was right behind her.

She caught sight of William and gritted her teeth as she tried to ignore the immediate heat that stirred between her thighs. *If only Rosamunda wasn't quite so attentive...*

Tearing her gaze away, she surveyed the beds. At least a dozen were empty. Either things were finally taking a turn for the better or...

"Lord William, how can I be of assistance this morning?"

She had started every day with this question since she first came to the hospital to help.

William smiled. It made her insides clench, and she squeezed her knees together.

"We're turning a corner. At long last, the number of sick is declining. May God's grace continue to rain down on us."

A wave of relief rushed through her. Perhaps the end of her people's suffering was in sight. The urge to embrace him was almost irresistible. She contented herself with squeezing his hand.

She spent her morning dispensing medicinal infusions and hot broth. More and more of the patients appeared to be improving. Things truly seemed to be turning around, praise the Lord.

Just before noon, she went to the room with the medicinal herbs to find a remedy for one of her patients, and as she was turning to leave, William walked in. The door closed behind him. They were alone.

He froze. Her eyes darted to the door and then back to him. She carefully put down the bowl of herbs she collected on a shelf, and for a moment, everything was suspended. Neither of them moved. His eyes raised slowly to hers.

Though he stood on the opposite side of the small room, the memory of his intimate caress seemed more real than the distance between them. She bit her lip, unable to stop the wave of sensation that overwhelmed her simply from being in the same space with him.

He was faring no better. He gripped the shelf behind him and dug his nails into the wood. She could see the telltale outline of his growing desire as he gritted his teeth and turned his eyes to the ceiling.

Their eyes met again, and she could practically hear the snap as his restraint broke and he moved forward with desperate intent.

When he was one step away, the door opened, and Brother Joseph walked in, oblivious, and then yelped when he saw them.

"I'm so sorry, I didn't realize, I was just collecting some herbs for..." He stopped and stared.

"I was just leaving," she said, grabbing her bowl of herbs and ducking out of the room before things could get any more awkward. What must he think? Granted they were to be married in mere days, but they shouldn't have been alone together, even by accident. If Brother Joseph said anything.... But he wouldn't, would he? After all, there was nothing to see. They weren't even touching. Nothing happened. Nothing at all.

A few more seconds, though, and God knows what he would have seen. She took a deep breath and practically ran back to the infirmary hall where Rosamunda gave her a friendly smile and wave.

As the rest of the week passed, she noticed that every time William left the dormitory, he took Brother Joseph with him, as if he needed extra protection from a chance encounter. She would have teased him about it if she wasn't doing the exact same thing with Rosamunda. No more solitary trips to collect herbs. Even when she went to the garderobe, she made sure Rosamunda stood right outside.

The day before the wedding, her mother insisted she stay at the castle. Now that the number of cases had diminished to a few dozen, her help was hardly necessary anymore, so she surrendered to her mother's demands. The day passed in a flurry of fittings, fussing, and frivolity that left her bored and exhausted. It was a relief when she found herself alone in her room for a few minutes with her sister, Alais.

"Has Mother given you the blood and sticky liquid talk yet?" Alais asked with a knowing smile.

"You know she gave us each that talk when we started to menstruate."

"Were you terrified?"

"Only until I started working with midwives."

Her mother, unlike most mothers, told her daughters the gruesome details of procreation at an early age, to terrify them into guarding their chastity until marriage. But Iselda had long since learned that her mother's version was misleading, if technically accurate. A man did press himself into the hole between a woman's legs and leave a sticky liquid, and something inside a woman did tear and bleed the first time. But she had long ago heard from the expecting mothers she assisted that the act could be pleasurable, irresistible even. Her own experience with William gave her a taste of what it might be like, and she could hardly think of anything else.

"She'll give you the talk again before the day is out, but with a few additions," Alais said. "But I wanted to talk to you first."

"Oh no. Alais, I love you, but I don't want to hear from you about marital relations. I already hear more than I'm comfortable with." Most mornings, and sometimes evenings as well. They were insatiable.

"What do you mean?" Alais stared at her, and then her eyes grew wide. "Please tell me you can't hear us."

Iselda closed her eyes and took a deep breath. "Your bed thuds against my wall."

Alais covered her mouth with her hand and stared. Leaning in, she whispered, "Why didn't you ever say anything? At the very least, we could have moved the bed."

Shrugging, Iselda said, "You were happy. And I…. Well, I was a bit jealous. I thought that saying something would be spiteful. It's not a nice thing to admit, I know, but it's the truth."

"I'm so sorry." Alais grasped her hand and squeezed. "I know you're moving rooms, so it's a moot point, but if I'd had any idea,

I would have done something about it."

"I know." She squeezed back. "So what is it you wanted to tell me? I know you're not going to let me go without having your say," she said with a wry smile.

"Mostly, I wanted to make sure you knew it could be pleasurable. Not all women enjoy it, but then not all women have husbands that are properly attentive. I also wanted to tell you to speak up for yourself. Ask for what you like and don't be shy if there's anything you don't like."

Iselda wanted to crawl under her bed and hide, but she promised she would listen. Alais seemed to misinterpret her red face. "I'm sure William will be kind and giving," she reassured. "He obviously adores you." Iselda offered a wan smile. "Oh, and don't be ashamed of your pleasure. The priests want us to feel sinful and abashed, but there is nothing wrong with finding joy with your husband."

"Are you done?"

"Yes."

"Thank heavens."

At that moment, there was a quiet knock on the door, and Carenza asked to come in. Alais gave her shoulder a squeeze and let Carenza in as she went out.

As soon as the door was closed, Carenza asked, "Has Mother come by for the blood and sticky liquid talk yet?"

"Not you too," Iselda said, rubbing her temples.

"Oh, is that why Alais was in here?" Carenza looked highly amused. "What did she tell you?"

Iselda sat down on her bed and stared at the floor. "She told me it can be pleasant, to ask for what I like, and not to be ashamed."

"All very sound advice, and suspiciously similar to the advice I gave her before her wedding. I know you've learned quite a bit from your work with the midwives. Do you have questions? I made Daniel explain everything on our wedding night, poor man. If there's anything you want to know but don't want to ask

William, now is your chance."

Was there anything? She was quite clear on the basic mechanics, and she already had some sense of how deliriously pleasant it could be. She did have one or two questions, but did she dare ask her sister?

She stared at her knees, unable to bring herself to look her sister in the face. "Is it possible to be too eager? I never thought I would want it like I do. But ever since we were in the cellar together, I can't stop thinking about it. I don't want to scare him or cause him offense."

"Is this your way of telling me more happened in that cellar than you let on?"

Iselda said nothing. She couldn't bring herself to divulge secrets that might bring shame on William.

"Fine. You don't have to tell me. You're marrying him tomorrow, so it hardly matters now. To answer your question, I don't think he'll take your interest amiss. From what I know speaking to other married women, as well as from my own experience, men appreciate enthusiasm. There's the occasional hypocrite that insists a woman should remain pure of thought even when he's making free with her body, but most men find a woman's desire to be an aphrodisiac."

Taking a deep breath, Iselda nodded slowly. She suspected as much, but it worried her that William was the voice of reason when she lost her mind. He wasn't disapproving exactly, but when the euphoria of their encounter began to subside, she couldn't help wondering what he must think of her wanton response.

"Any other questions?"

What do I do while he…does what he does? She didn't want to disappoint him. What would he expect? But she couldn't bring herself to voice the question aloud.

"No more questions."

Carenza nodded and patted her hand. "I'll leave you alone, then. I'm sure Mother has been buzzing around all day driving you mad."

She hugged her sister and let her go.

Alone at last, she opened her Hildegard to the chapter on birds. "The starling is hot and timid," she read. *Yes, I am both of those things*, she couldn't help thinking as she hid in her room trying to calm her racing pulse.

No sooner had she resumed her reading then her mother marched through the door without knocking.

"You had your final dress fitting?" she demanded.

"Yes, Mother."

"You've bathed and used the scented oils I gave you?"

"Yes."

"Rosamunda cleaned and filed your nails?"

"She has."

"And plucked your eyebrows?"

"Yes."

"Then I suppose the only thing left is for me to explain your wedding night."

Here it comes. Iselda wasn't sure what the correct response was. She tried a modest smile.

"Don't grin at me, young lady. This is serious."

She folded her hands in her lap and stared at the floor, keeping her face carefully blank.

"That's better. I've already informed you of what happens between a man and a woman," her mother said, pacing and avoiding meeting her eyes. "Since you marry tomorrow, though, I must enlighten you further upon this topic. What I told you was true but incomplete. Your husband will put his man parts into the hole between your legs and leave a sticky liquid, and you will bleed tomorrow, but there's a bit more to it."

Iselda nodded, not daring to look up. She followed the progress of her mother's feet back and forth, counting her laps and praying for this little speech to end.

"Your husband will most likely want to kiss and caress you before he puts his thing inside you. And when he enters you, he will move about for a while before the sticky liquid comes out. You must permit his attentions, even when he touches parts of your body you generally keep hidden. This is a normal and natural thing for a husband to do. Do you understand?"

She nodded, unable to form words.

"The pain and the bleeding will occur when he enters you for the first time. God seals women's wombs to preserve them from sin until they are wed. Your husband must break the seal to plant his seed in your womb. You will allow him to enter despite the pain. It is your duty. God willing, the pain won't last long. It didn't for me. And it will not be repeated after this first time."

Her mother paused and stared down at her as if expecting a response. But what was there to say?

"Um. Thank you for telling me?" she said in a small voice. *Please let this be the end.*

"Furthermore—"

Dear God in Heaven, there's more?

"—to ensure the succession, you must allow your husband the use of your body when he wishes so that he might plant his seed. You may deny him during your monthly flow when your body is unclean. Some say there are gnashing teeth within a woman's womb that make her bleed. He will not come to you during that time for fear of injury. At any other time, however, you must accommodate him. Do you understand?"

"Yes, Mother." *Please let this be the end. I can't take any more.*

"Good. I will have your dinner sent up. You should spend the rest of the evening in prayer and contemplation, so that you are ready, body, mind, and soul, for your duties tomorrow. Goodnight."

Her mother strode out of the room without another word.

Iselda sagged onto her bed in relief. Thank heavens that was at an end. There would be no more agonizing heart to hearts today.

This time tomorrow, she would finally be alone with William, and he would touch her again. She closed her eyes and imagined his hands on her body. Her own hands made their way to the parts of her body that hungered the most, one squeezing her breast and the other pressing between her legs. Just as she gave in to the temptation to lift her skirt to see what more direct contact might feel like, she heard a knock.

Sitting bolt upright and smoothing her skirts, she called, "Come in."

It was only Rosamunda with her dinner. She heaved a sigh of relief. "Thank you, Rosamunda. You've been wonderful through all of this. I can't tell you how much I appreciate all you've done."

Rosamunda blushed and curtsied. "Only doing my job, my lady."

"Well, thank you."

"My lady?" She was blushing even deeper now. What was on her mind?

"Yes?"

"I know it's not my place to discuss such things, but I've heard about what your mother told you when you were young. I wanted you to know it isn't all bad, my lady. I'm sure Lord William will be gentle and kind. You might even find you like it."

Iselda groaned. "Not you too. This is the fourth talk I've gotten today."

Now Rosamunda was as red as a holly berry. "I'm sorry, my lady," she mumbled, shuffling toward the door.

"It's all right," Iselda said, relenting. "I know you meant well."

"Oh! I almost forgot. Lady Maud asked me to give you this." She handed over a small bottle of golden liquid with a tiny scroll attached. "I'll leave you alone now, my lady."

Rosamunda fled the room before Iselda could even say good-bye.

Idly examining the bottle, Iselda wondered what it could be. Scent perhaps? That would be a nice gift. She pulled the scroll from the ribbon that held it.

A few drops of this in the right place will smooth the way and save you pain on your wedding night, as well as many nights to come. Use it well, and make lots of babies. I expect a grandchild within the year. Regards, Lady Maud

It took all her self-control not to throw the bottle at the wall. If one more person said one more word about her wedding night, she might have to strangle them.

Did William have to put up with this? She took a certain grim satisfaction imagining the humiliating conversations he might be having this very minute. What did a father say to his son on the eve of his wedding? Someday when she was feeling especially brave, she would have to ask.

For the moment, she prayed she wouldn't have to speak to her mother again until after the wedding.

CHAPTER FOURTEEN

WILLIAM DIDN'T MIND appeasing his mother as long as it didn't involve her interference with how he lived his life, so he let her plan the grand wedding she'd always dreamed of with no resistance from him. She'd been dropping hints about him returning to Arundel with his new bride, but that was an argument for another time. On his wedding day, he was happy to let her have her fun, and at night, he would have his.

He awoke early and took a bath, then let a manservant give him a shave and make sure every hair on his head was in place. He put on a plain shirt and breeches to eat a simple breakfast with his father, Michael, and Victor.

Michael threw an arm around his shoulder when he joined them and murmured confidentially, "Today is the day you kiss goodbye to your freedom. I'm glad it's you and not me. Lord knows I'm not ready to shackle myself to one woman for life, one pussy until the end of my days. Are you ready?"

Michael seemed to have forgotten that William had planned to forgo "pussy," as he so crudely put it, for life. After all these years of abstinence, having one woman promise to share his bed every night until the end of his days was unbelievably decadent.

"I am," William answered at full volume. "And don't get too hopeful that our parents will let you off the hook just because I'm walking down the aisle. Your day will come. Mark my words."

His father gave Michael a disapproving look before turning to William. "I'm only glad you've finally come to your senses and given up on this monk nonsense. I confess I'd given up hope this day would ever come. I'm proud of you, son. This alliance with Winchelsea will be an enormous boon to Arundel, and I'm relieved that you're finally getting down to business to produce an heir."

Of course, his father thought of this in nothing but political terms. What did he expect on his wedding day, love advice?

"Don't expect too much of her tonight," his father continued. "She's a highborn lady, not one of those peasant girls you liked to tumble in your youth. She likely doesn't know a thing about what happens between a man and woman. Be quick. Get it over with, and don't be surprised if she cries. She'll get used to it with time."

William stared at his father and shivered as he considered what his parents' wedding night must have been like. Thank God his wedding night with Iselda would be nothing like that. If anything, Iselda was likely to keep him up all night with her enthusiasm. How many hours until they were alone together at last?

"Victor, you're very quiet over there." His friend sat on the other side of the table trying to keep a straight face. "What advice do you have for me today?"

"Listen to your wife," he answered after a pause for thought. "Yes, that is the best and only advice I can give."

William wanted to ask for the story behind that advice. Clearly there was one, based on Victor's look of earnest entreaty. But he suspected it wasn't something he wanted to talk about in the present company.

"This has all been most illuminating," he said, grabbing a roll, "but I think I should go get dressed. I'll meet you back here shortly, and we can walk to the church together."

He went back to his room and donned the midnight blue hose and tunic that his mother had chosen for him. The tunic was ridiculous, the rich velvet embroidered with tiny gold stars draping in folds down to his knees and the gaping sleeves hanging as low as the hem. He missed the comfort and simplicity of his Hospitaller robes. It was hard to adjust to all this frippery, but for his wedding day, he supposed he had to oblige and play the part of a fancy noble.

He went back downstairs, and the men made their way out of the castle and up Church Street. It was an unseasonably warm day for March, and townspeople lined the road, excitement already building for the big event. When he arrived at the church, he was ushered into a small antechamber with Victor to await the ceremony.

"So I have to ask about the advice you gave me. I can't help thinking there's a story there."

Victor grimaced. "There is, but for my wife's sake, I don't want to say too much. I was…er…overly considerate on our wedding night. I wasn't listening to what she wanted. She was…offended. It all came out all right in the end, but I still regret not listening to her from the first."

William smiled. "Thank heavens de Veres aren't shy about what they want."

Victor raised an eyebrow. "Even Iselda? Good for her. I always thought she was a bit timid, but then you seem to bring out her feisty side. I didn't even know she had one before you."

"Feisty is the least of it."

"Oh?"

William grinned at his shoes. "I'm very much looking forward to being married."

"Please don't tell me anything I don't want to know," Victor said, clapping him on the shoulder. "The priest is waving at us. I think it's time."

William went out and stood on the steps of the church in front of the priest. The mothers were both dressed like queens, presiding over the event from their seats of honor at the foot of the steps.

A hush fell over the crowd, and Iselda appeared on her father's arm, walking up Church Street. He forgot to breathe. There were no words for the vision he saw before him. She was dressed in twilight blue with gold trim at the sleeves and hem. The scooped neck was just low enough to display her lovely shape to advantage. Her dark hair, which she usually kept covered, cascaded down her back to her waist. She seemed to glow as she joined him at the top of the steps, giving him a shy smile and looking into his eyes with deep love.

As the priest began to intone the Mass, William couldn't help thinking of the other vows he had once planned to take before God and man. Whatever fears he had about marriage, he was certain he made the right choice taking these vows instead. A life with Iselda would be infinitely better than a life alone.

With that in mind, he spoke his vows with all the solemnity and fervor that this sacred moment deserved. When he placed the ring on her finger, he was floating in some otherworldly realm. It was difficult to attend to anything at all except her. The only words he truly heard was the priest's pronouncement at the end that they were man and wife. It reverberated through him like the tolling of a bell. It was done. She was his, and he was hers, and life would never be the same.

As they emerged from the church after taking their first communion, the people of Winchelsea lined the streets and tossed flowers at their feet. He threw caution and propriety to the wind and kissed her, deeply and thoroughly, in the middle of the street. His parents would be horrified, he knew, but he wanted everyone to know exactly how much he loved this woman. The townspeople roared their approval. He would have to wait until later for more. He'd hoped the kiss would tide him over, but it only stoked his desire.

There was music and dancing in the streets, and wine and ale flowed freely, courtesy of the baron, Lord Martin. Back at the castle, there was an elaborate feast in the great hall. They sat at the head table, smiling, and chatting with one well-wisher after another, hardly able to take a bite as course after course of delicacies were served.

After watching Iselda interrupted three times in her attempt to eat an oyster, he picked it up and tipped it between her lips. The guests yelled and cheered. The only way to eat, it seemed, was to feed each other. It was the sort of thing that would have made him cringe if he was watching someone else, but he surrendered to the moment. If he was ridiculous, so be it. It was his wedding day, and he was in love with his wife.

There was music and dancing. Troubadours sang of love and longing. The earl and countess, or Daniel and Carenza as they'd now told him to call them, sang a touching duet about the bittersweet parting of lovers at dawn. As always, when they performed, their eyes locked on each other, and the passion of their marriage was plain for all to see.

At last, the festivities seemed to be winding down, and a group of the more drunken guests crowded around the table, demanding that the couple go off to their chambers to consummate. It was time to escape before people started trying to tear off pieces of Iselda's dress for luck. To dissuade them from getting too close to his bride, he swept her off her feet and carried her out of the hall, putting her down at the foot of the grand staircase. They ran up the stairs together, hand in hand, and escaped into the bedroom where they would be spending their first night.

Iselda was laughing the whole way up, but as soon as the door closed behind them, she went silent and still. Some invisible force connected them, drawing them together, even as she trembled at his touch.

She leaned back against the door as he leaned in, needing to feel her body pressed against his own. He paused and caressed her cheek. "Are you nervous?"

"No," she whispered, eyes wide. He kissed her forehead gently, and she squeezed her eyes shut. "A little."

"Did anyone speak to you about what to expect?" It was hard to imagine she didn't know the mechanics, given her work, but perhaps she'd heard unpleasant stories.

She laughed anxiously. "I got far more advice than I wanted, I assure you. I know what will happen, but…"

She stopped. He nuzzled her neck as he waited for her to finish, taking pleasure in the way her breath caught as his lips brushed her skin.

"Yes?" he prompted when it became clear she wasn't about to finish her sentence.

She rested her forehead against his, and her hands timidly explored his chest.

"Everyone talked about what you would do, but they were all very vague about what I was supposed to do, other than…allow you to…"

He could imagine what they might have told her. After his father's cold-blooded advice this morning, he couldn't blame her for being worried.

"Are you afraid I'm going to hurt you? I can't deny that there will be some pain this time, but hopefully it will be brief, and I promise to make up for it as best I can with pleasure. You remember how you felt that day when I lost control and touched you?"

She took a ragged breath. "Yes."

"I'll make you feel like that again only more and longer. I promise I'll be gentle, and—"

"It's not the pain I'm worried about. I know you'll be gentle."

"Then what is it, sweeting?" He kissed her forehead and her cheeks, brushing his hands softly against her sides.

She blushed a fetching shade of rose that reached down to the neckline of her dress. It was all he could do to keep his head and hold back from kissing the tender swell of her breasts. "I'm afraid of disappointing you," she said at last. "I want you so much, and I know you've been with other women that know how this works far better than I. I'm afraid I'll do something wrong or that I won't live up to your expectations."

There was only one response to that. He claimed her mouth with all the fury and passion he'd been holding back and let himself touch her with abandon. He grasped her buttocks and pulled her hips against his own, and she responded instinctively, opening herself to him, twining her leg around his. She moaned into his kiss as she grasped him every bit as tightly as he held her. He intended to seduce her slowly, gently, but he was drowning in the torrent of her ardor.

"Touch me. Take me, William. I've waited so long," she said in a soft, breathy voice that robbed him of the little control he still had.

He picked her up with her legs wrapped around his hips, carried her to the bed, and sank down on top of her, pressing against her through layer upon layer of cloth. She met each thrust with a counter thrust. Her tongue tantalized and teased as his own plundered her mouth the way he ached to plunder other parts of her.

He needed a moment of respite to collect himself. It was her wedding night. He wanted to spend it focused on her pleasure, so he reached beneath her skirts to touch her. Her body convulsed as he began to stroke, and he managed to roll to the side, allowing himself some much-needed distance.

In the brief time it took to bring her to her peak, he managed to regain some semblance of composure, though watching her face as she came nearly sent him over the edge again. She was transformed. The shy, prim Iselda gave way to a sultry and wild sensualist who held nothing back as she trembled and quaked with pleasure. It was the difference between an unopened bud and a rose in full bloom.

They lay panting on the bed together, still fully clothed. "Did I convince you?" he asked.

"Convince me of what?"

"That you couldn't possibly disappoint me." He traced a finger from her chin down her neck and over the fabric across one taut nipple to the ties on the side of her dress.

"But we haven't even…you know…"

"Oh, I know," he said as he tugged to untie the bow to loosen her side laces. Then he traced back across her breasts to the other side and tugged. "Did you know how to do anything that you did just now?"

"What do you mean? I didn't do anything."

"Oh, so you were laying still and silent that whole time? I imagined the wild woman who was writhing in pleasure at my touch?" He stood up beside the bed and offered a hand to help her up.

"Well, no, clearly not," she said, as he pulled her to standing.

He gathered up the skirt of her gown, and she gasped as he pulled it over her head, leaving her in her shift and stockings. He could clearly see the shape of her nipples through the thin linen, and he allowed himself a moment to touch and tease them through the cloth before pulling off his own tunic and shirt.

"This is one of our deepest instincts," he explained as he let her explore his bare chest with her soft, inquisitive hands. "We don't have to study this in a book. Our bodies know what to do even if we've never done it before."

A cloud of worry passed over her face. "Does that mean it's equally pleasant with everyone?"

He smiled and kissed her hair. "No." In fact, he could re-member a number of unsatisfying experiences. *Best not to think about that now.* "But I knew it would be pleasant with you."

"How?"

How indeed?

He stepped close and began gathering up her shift. "I suppose I suspected from our very first kiss. The way you responded to me drove me wild. It's been haunting me ever since. And then I knew for certain that night at the hospital. The way you melted for me... You have no idea how hard it was to let you go that night."

"I have some idea," she whispered right before he pulled her shift over her head.

He stepped back and gasped. She was completely bare to him except for her creamy woolen stockings, held in place with blue ribbons for garters. He drank her in, this spectacular woman who was his to have and to hold for life. He took in every detail, the decadent river of her hair swept over her shoulder, her lovely pink tipped breasts, her lithe form and slim hips, the dark triangle of curls he had touched but never seen, and her magnificent, breathtaking legs. *Dear Lord in heaven, thank you for my wife.*

HE KNELT DOWN and slid his fingers down her thighs until they caught the tops of her stockings. *My God, these legs.* He could spend a week doing nothing but admiring them—so long and perfectly formed. It gave him a thrill to think that they were hidden from the rest of the world under her skirts, and only he knew what beauty lay beneath. They were a gift, just for him.

He unwrapped her inch by inch, caressing and tantalizing as he slid each stocking down. Then he slipped them off one slender, shapely foot at a time.

Removed her clothes. Check. Only one to go…

She looked suddenly shy as he stood and raked her from head to toe with his hot gaze. "Do I please you?" she asked, her hands fidgeting as if she was resisting the urge to cover herself. "I know my breasts are small, and my mother always said I was too skinny like a boy, and—"

He cut her off with a furious kiss and placed her hand against his erection. "Do you feel what you do to me?"

The bold minx gave him a seductive smile and pushed down his hose, placing her hand directly on his cock. He made a strangled noise as she stroked him and said, "Now I can feel you better."

Oh, dear Lord.

Stepping quickly out of his hose, he backed her into the bed where she reclined and spread her legs to welcome him.

Take it slowly, William. Just because she's offering herself doesn't mean she's ready.

He lowered himself into her embrace and took a nipple in his mouth.

Pink.

Lapping his tongue gently over her sensitive skin, he made her squirm beneath him. Then he suckled her, and she gasped, as her breathing grew ragged. He let a finger drag lightly through the hot, moist folds between her legs, finding her sensitive bud again and stroking it ever so lightly. She moaned. He grazed her nipple with his teeth, and she whimpered in a way that sent a tremor of need through his whole body.

He repeated his treatment on the other breast, and her body arched toward him in need as he tantalized her. She was so wet and ready, he could hardly contain himself.

As he slipped a finger inside her, she ran her hands over his shoulders and back, caressing and exploring. When he added a second finger, she froze and then grasped, scratching at him in desperation. He could feel the reverberations of her response as she ground against his hand, hungry for more, so he quickened his pace.

"Oh, William," she moaned. "I'm…. I'm…" Whatever she was going to say was lost in a wail as she came against his hand, wide eyes fixed on his as her body trembled.

He made a low rumbling noise of appreciation in his throat as he kissed his way down her belly. Now that he'd watched her, twice, he wanted to taste her. He could not get enough.

"William?"

He arrived at his destination, and her body convulsed as he licked her salty cream. He had to hold onto her hips to keep her from bucking away. As he teased and sucked, feeding her mad frenzy, a memory popped into his head of that first dinner with their families when he ate the tender, salty flesh of perfectly prepared mussels while trying to ignore the way her décolletage enflamed him. And now, here he was, feasting on her shamelessly, giving in at last to his hunger and longing.

The pulsation against his fingers warned him that she was on the brink. Her back arched off the bed as a new burst of cream slicked her engorged nub and the entrance he longed to sink into.

Recovering from her release, Iselda demanded in a husky voice, "William, take me now."

"With pleasure, sweeting."

It was time at last. He could do this. He was dying to do this. Risks be damned. If she got pregnant, so be it. He had to be inside her.

"Do you want me to go slow or fast?" he asked as he nudged against her entrance. "Slow will hurt less but for longer. Fast will hurt more but be over quicker."

"Fast, please. I'm ready."

So he plunged in to the hilt, momentarily seeing stars. She was so tight around him. Every pulsation that passed through her drew him deeper. The urge to move was almost overwhelming, but somehow he managed to stay still long enough to ask, "How do you feel? Are you in pain?"

It took him a moment to focus his eyes on Iselda's face. Her eyes were large and round, and she was barely breathing.

"Iselda?"

At last, she began to breathe again. "It hurt, but it's already going away. I just needed a moment."

"May I move?" He wasn't sure he could stop himself, the need was so strong, but he held on as best he could until she whispered, "yes."

They began to rock together, slowly at first as she adjusted to him, then more quickly as she began to move with him. Soon her legs wrapped around his hips, and she strained against him with each thrust.

How had he lived nine years without this? No. How had he lived his whole life without this? Because nothing could compare to the way she felt beneath him. His conviction in the hospital that she was goodness and healing and sweetness and life came back stronger than ever. He wasn't making love. He was giving himself to her utterly.

Their movement became frantic as they let go of the last of their control and surrendered to their need. She moved with all the fury and desperation he'd dreamed of, and he sank into her again and again, making her cry out with each thrust. He could feel her release building and tried to hang on long enough for her to reach her peak.

He groaned as they gyrated in a frenzied dance. Black was creeping into the edges of his vision. Her pulsation around him intensified, driving him further over the edge. He exploded inside her, emptying himself as he pressed into her once, twice, three times, and it was done. As if from a great distance, the final waves of her fruition milked him dry. She trembled and arched and then went limp beneath him. He rolled to the side, boneless lethargy overtaking him. He managed to wrap his arms around her before closing his eyes and surrendering.

Made love to her. Check. Holy Mother of God.

He wasn't sure how long he lay there in blissful oblivion. When he opened his eyes, she was still curled next to him, her head tucked beneath his chin.

Never in all his youthful adventures had he ever felt anything like this. It was the most stunning encounter of his life. And it was thanks to the magical, amazing, seductive, loveable woman curled beside him. He kissed the top of her head and grazed his hand along her back.

"I love you, sweeting," he murmured into her hair.

"I love you too," she whispered against his chest.

CHAPTER FIFTEEN

ISELDA LAY IN silence in the dawn light, remembering the night before. The experience of making love to William exceeded all expectations, not that anything anyone said could possibly have prepared her. "Pleasant," they called it. Ha! It wasn't that she had a better word. If someone asked her to describe it, she supposed she would call it "pleasant" too. What else could one possibly say in polite company?

She draped one leg lazily over his hip and snuggled closer. It would be heaven to stay like this forever, but too soon he shifted. His eyes blinked open, and he smiled.

"Good morning, Wife." He kissed her forehead and ran his hand down her side, making her burrow further into his embrace.

"Good morning, Husband."

There was a quiet knock at the door, and she reluctantly got up and wrapped a robe around herself. When she opened it, Rosamunda was there with a heaping tray of breakfast.

"Good morning, my lady," she said giving Iselda an insinuating wink. "Sustenance for the newlyweds. Got to keep your strength up." She was giggling.

"Thank you, Rosamunda," Iselda answered, giving her a pointed look, taking the tray, and closing the door. The amount of food the kitchen sent up was absurd for two people. "Hungry? It looks like they sent up enough food for a week." She set the overflowing tray down on her dressing table.

William eased out of bed and pulled on his breeches. "Anything sweet?"

"It looks like there's pear tart, sweet buns, toast and marmalade, custard—"

He came up behind her and wrapped his arms around her, peeking over her shoulder. "Any ginger cakes?" he asked, kissing her shoulder. "I know you brought them by for my patients, but I think I ate more than I gave away."

She laughed. "I suspected as much, especially after you dined with us, and I saw how much you loved desserts. Did you notice I started bringing you extra after that?" Sure enough, she found a ginger cake hidden behind the sausages, and she turned and fed him a bite.

"Mmm, so good," he said, taking the ginger cake for himself. "Ooh, I bet it would be delicious with some of that custard on top."

She watched his boyish glee as he sat down and stuffed himself with sweet treats. She herself wasn't feeling very hungry. A pear tart and her usual mint tisane were all she needed.

"You're hardly eating," he said after washing down a sweet bun with some mulled wine. "Come over here." He pulled her onto his lap and spooned up a large bite of custard. "Say aah. Physician's orders."

She readily complied. How could she say no to custard?

"You've got a bit...right...there," he said, nibbling on the corner of her mouth, then pulling her into a languid kiss. There was a bit of a chill in the air, and she shivered. "Are you cold, sweeting? What do you say we go back to bed and warm ourselves up beneath the covers?"

"Excellent idea," she said, shedding her robe and climbing back into bed.

He stoked the fire and threw on another log before joining her. As he settled in beside her, she nestled into his warmth.

"So," he asked, tracing lazy circles on her back. "How does it feel to check off the last items on your list?"

"My list?" She propped her head on her hand to look at him.

"Twenty-eight suitors, twelve...activities." He teased her nipple playfully and gave it a punctuating pull, making her breath catch.

"How do you know about my list?" Her brow furrowed. She remembered telling him about twenty-seven suitors, but not the rest.

"I confess I pinched it while you were sick."

No! That was private.

He must have been alarmed by the look on her face because he hurried to explain. "You left it tucked inside your book of notes on patients. I made the excuse to myself that I was keeping it safe so that it didn't fall into the wrong hands, but the truth was I couldn't stop thinking about it once I'd seen it. I knew I had to be the one to help you finish it. I wanted to be the last name on your list, the last man you considered giving your hand, your heart, and your body to. And now you are mine, and I am yours, and our row of check marks is complete. How does it feel?"

"I don't know," she said, rolling onto her back and staring at the ceiling. She didn't want to be angry with him today of all days, and she did leave it in the patient book she asked him to look at. Mostly, she was mad at herself for being so careless. He was right. Anyone could have found it.

"Are you upset that I took it?"

"No. I mean a little, but mostly no." Turning back toward him, she twined her leg around his hip once again. "To be honest, I'm embarrassed," she said, tracing his collarbone with her fingers. "I started that list so long ago. I don't even know why I kept going."

"Why did you start it?"

She tilted her head to kiss him, trying to distract him. And it worked, but not only on him. As he kissed her back, everything slipped her mind, and all that mattered was lips and tongue and more, more, more....

"What were we talking about?" he murmured, nuzzling her neck.

"I forgot."

"Oh, yes. Your list." He scooted back, putting some distance between them. "I want to know. I've been wondering for a month."

"You are so irritatingly persistent," she said, touching the tip of his nose with her finger. He raised an eyebrow. "Fine. After Alais got married, mother wasted no time trying to set me up with a match. I was a practical girl. I didn't expect to fall madly in love. I wanted what my sisters had, of course, but I didn't think I'd get it. I'm not the sort of girl men pine for."

"They never saw you like this, or they would all have fallen at your feet. Luckily for me, your beauty was well hidden, or I might have missed my chance," he said, giving her a seductive smile that made her squirm.

"Well, none of the men my mother cajoled into visiting seemed to find me worth even a civil conversation. I made the chart in a fit of pique after a particularly disappointing afternoon with a castellan from Hampshire. It was amazing how rude he managed to be without deviating one hair from polite small talk. He was number three." *What an insufferable snob he was.*

"Idiot number three. Noted."

"The list was my adolescent fantasy of what a man might do if he genuinely liked me and found me desirable. Except that for seven years, no one did. Did you notice that not one of them managed to laugh with me *and* give me a heartfelt compliment? I could have one or the other, it seemed, but not both. And not one wanted to touch me. At least, until you."

He rolled onto her and pinned her to the bed. "I want to do more than touch you."

"Oh?" she asked, wrapping her legs around him and running her finger up his growing arousal.

"Mmmm," he murmured, as he kissed her neck. "If you're not too sore…"

She was a little sore, but how could she turn down more delirious bliss? She wiggled her hips beneath him and smiled. "I would like it very much if you did more than touch me."

The truth was she would do anything at all for him as long as he kept looking at her the way he was right now. What miracle made this gorgeous man find her irresistible? *Her.* She could only pray that whatever had addled his brain lasted for a very, very long time.

His skillful fingers drove her mad again. He was right about her body responding without lessons. She couldn't control her actions right now if she tried. He'd reduced her to nothing but instinct and sensation. She could barely think, let alone move on purpose.

She needn't have worried about her excessive eagerness either. He seemed to feed on her enthusiasm. The more her body responded, the more crazed his own response became.

There was something she wanted right now, something she needed, a hunger that consumed her whole body, and ... *Oh God yes THAT! Again and again and again...*

She was fire itself as he drove into her in a steady rhythm, each stroke an explosion of sparks, stoking the flame to even greater heights. She wanted to burn and burn until nothing was left of the old Iselda. From today forward, she would be something new, her imperfections blown away as ash, nothing left but the woman he saw and loved, the woman who filled him with passion as hot as a forge.

Soon she was consumed in blinding light, and she was insubstantial as a wisp of smoke as she floated back to herself and rested in her lover's embrace.

They lay there together for some time in quiet contentment.

"William," she murmured into his chest.

"Hmm?" His deep voice vibrated against her cheek.

"When did you realize you were in love with me?"

What she really wanted to ask was "why," but "when" seemed safer.

He tightened his embrace and kissed her hair. "I realized I was in love with you the day I saw your list. I couldn't stand the thought of your adding another name. When I realized that, I knew what I had to do. I went to speak with Brother Joseph about leaving the Hospitallers. He laughed when I told him—said it had been obvious to him for months. He was amazed it took me so long to figure it out."

Brother Joseph was a perceptive man.

"And you?" he asked, stroking the now-tangled skein of her hair.

Of course, it was only fair for him to turn the question on her, but the answer made her feel a bit sheepish.

"When you kissed me in the cellar."

He laughed. "I like to think I'm a good kisser, but I must be better than I thought."

"No, I didn't fall in love with you because of the kiss. That was only when I realized. Or really not so much when you kissed me as when I realized I had to tell you to stop."

He turned on his side to face her, dumping her abruptly onto the mattress. "You realized you loved me when you told me to stop kissing you."

"Yes."

"And here I thought you liked my kisses."

"I do." Of course, she liked kissing him, but that wasn't the point.

He watched her with a wounded expression for a long moment before cracking a smile and then bursting out laughing. "I'm sorry. You look so serious."

She grabbed a pillow and hit him over the head with it. He grabbed his own and retaliated immediately before pouncing on her and tickling her. But with three older siblings, she had had to become quite proficient at escaping tickle attacks, and after a moment's scrambling, she was straddling his chest with a triumphant grin, pinning his hands above his head.

In a heartbeat, his amused expression gave way to something

else. His eyes traveled to her lips and then her breasts and then her spread legs and then slowly back up again. An entirely different kind of smile spread across his face.

"I am entirely at your mercy, my lady. What do you plan to do with me?"

"I haven't decided yet." Then a mischievous thought popped into her head. "Perhaps I'll recite Hildegard's chapter on the medicinal uses of ginger. I have it memorized, you know."

"In our marriage bed? You wouldn't."

"'Ginger is hot and easily diffuses itself—'"

"Peace, woman! Or I'll tickle you some more."

"'It is injurious as food for—'"

He flipped her over with ease and covered her mouth with a kiss as he slid his hand between her legs and began to stroke. "I didn't say *where* I'd tickle you," he said with a devilish grin as she began to gyrate beneath his touch. "Consider this your punishment. Lettuce won't save you now."

"How...do you know...what...lettuce...is for?" she asked with difficulty between gasps and sighs.

He quickened his pace, the fiendish man. "I perused your Hildegard while you were sick. I had to know why you were sitting in lettuce. Some of what she has to say is quite reasonable, you know. But the lettuce is complete nonsense."

"What?" Really all she absorbed was "Hildegard...nonsense."

"Lettuce. Cured you of your lust, has it?" He made some minor change to his motion that made her moan uncontrollably. "I'll take that as a 'no,' which is just as well because I don't want your lust cured. I want you to be feverish with it. I want every wanton thought, every impure impulse. I want you to be as delirious with desire for me as I am for you. Come for me, sweeting. Let me watch you lose that gorgeous mind."

And she did. Completely. Punishment did he call it? If this was what happened when she quoted Hildegard in bed, she might have to make a regular habit of it.

As her mind returned from a land far away, she found him

hovering beside her, watching her with a smug smile.

"And now I want to know what objection you have to my kiss because you certainly don't mind my touch." He was grinning as he said it, but still…

"I didn't object to your kiss that night." He raised an eyebrow. "Really, I didn't! I wanted to keep kissing you more than I'd wanted anything in my life. But I wanted you to be free to live your life even more. That's what made me realize I might be in love."

He reached out to caress her cheek. Leaning close, he brushed his lips against hers, whisper soft. Then he leaned in again and kissed her with such tender devotion she was amazed she didn't melt into a puddle.

"And that is why I fell in love with you," he said.

"Because I stopped kissing you?"

"Because you were willing to let me go when you didn't want to, when you would have been entirely justified in making demands. You were willing to risk ruin rather than trap me, and, to my everlasting shame, I let you. It took seeing your list for me realize both how much I wronged you and how much you were giving up. That was when I knew I could never let you go. I don't deserve you, sweeting, but since I can't seem to live without you, I promise to do my best to be worthy."

She stared. Then she blinked. At last, she opened her mouth to say something, but nothing came out. Her mind was a blank. Words slipped away like water through fingers. The more she grasped, the more elusive they became. She hated it when this happened. It was always at the worst moments. Surely, she could come up with something to say after his beautiful profession of love. One word. Any word. No, not any word. What if it was the wrong word? Better to stay silent than say the wrong thing. But what was the right thing?

Never mind words. Words were useless. She would have to show him some other way.

Running her fingers through his hair, she pressed her lips

gently to his. He took a deep, shuddering breath. then pulled her tight against him, then rolled on his back so that she was lying on top of him. This was new. But then everything was new. She deepened her kiss, and he answered her with tender hunger.

His arousal grew as she tried to put all the words she couldn't find into the ardent movement of lips and tongue. As she kissed and nuzzled down his neck and along his shoulder he said, "I want you to take me, Iselda. I've had you twice. This time it's your turn."

"What do you mean? You know I don't know—"

"Don't worry. I'll tell you what to do. First, I want you to spread those glorious legs of yours and straddle me." He placed his hands on her buttocks and ran them along her legs, drawing her thighs apart and her knees up by his sides. "Oh, yes. Just like that." His voice was ragged as he ran his hands up and down the backs of her thighs.

"Now sit up so that I can see you," he said. So she did. Earlier, when she pounced on him for tickling her, she felt bold and playful, but now, in the exact same position, she was exposed, spread wide, provocative.

"So beautiful," he murmured as he slid his hands up her sides and then down again, resting them on her hips.

"Now up on your knees," he instructed, directing softly with his touch. A moment later, the smooth insistent tip of him pressed right where she wanted it. "Now lower yourself slowly, and take me in."

As she did, he filled her, inch by inch. It was the strangest, most thrilling sensation. Somehow, this way he penetrated deeper, touching her in new ways from within. When he was fully sheathed, her eyes rolled back in her head, and she moaned his name. One tremor and then another shook her before she looked down and saw his face.

With lips slightly parted and eyelids heavy, his eyes bored into her with a look of ecstasy and desperation. Everything inside her clenched at the sight, and he cried out as she tightened around him. "Move," he whispered. "Please."

Guided by his hands, she began to move her hips tentatively at first and then with more confidence as she found a rhythm. Soon instinct and need took over, and she rode him mercilessly, taking her pleasure as he bucked beneath her. What was this delectable man doing to her, and what was she doing to him?

She would never have suspected she had such a passionate nature. Lust was heat, an imbalance of the humors akin to a fever or a quick temper, but she had always been cool and tame to a fault. Hadn't Alais always teased her about her excessive modesty and bookishness? Even her mother seemed to think she was a cold fish. But William had ignited her. She burned like a torch. No, like a bonfire, growing ever higher. Nothing seemed to quench her. She could not get enough of him.

Was there some secret pocket of heat that could only be accessed through the sex act? Perhaps it had hidden within her for years, waiting for the right touch to release it. William's touch. Skilled physician that he was, perhaps he knew things about her body that she did not. Though perhaps it wasn't learning but simply experience of the world she did not possess.

Whatever the cause, she trembled as pressure and heat built within her. Needing even more, she grasped his hands and brought them to her breasts, which he cupped and caressed as she undulated. The wave of building heat grew stronger, and her whole body quaked as euphoria exploded within her, shaking her to her core. As she writhed and strained, prolonging the moment of ecstasy, he went stiff beneath her, thrusting upward with a groan.

She collapsed onto his chest as he spent himself. The furious heat of moments before died down to a warm tingle that filled her head to toe. He folded his arms around her and lay still. He didn't bother to withdraw, and she felt every small twitch as he recovered himself. In his arms, listening to his heart beat within his chest, the connection between them erased all barriers. For most of her life she was so alone. She had a loving family, but she was convinced she was a disappointment in comparison to her sisters. No one truly understood her. But she was alone no longer. William knew and understood her as completely as another person could—body, mind, and soul. Together, they could face anything. The future unfurled before her, warm and full of promise. *Please let this contentment last forever*, she thought to herself as she dozed off.

CHAPTER SIXTEEN

S O FAR, WILLIAM couldn't have been happier with his marriage. Granted, they were less than one full day in and had barely made it out of bed. But then why would he want to leave a bed that had Iselda in it? Reality would intrude at some point, and they would have to figure out their new life together. For now, though, he was happy to pretend nothing outside their bedroom door existed and revel in his newfound bliss.

Then there was a knock at the door. "Iselda? William? It's Carenza," she called through the door. "I need your help. It's little Charles. He has a terrible fever, and his cough is scaring me. I hate to bother you today of all days, but I'm so worried."

"We'll be there in a minute," William answered as he hastily pulled on his clothes.

Iselda was up and dressed in no time, wearing one of her practical, high-necked dresses that hid her beauty. Knowing now what was underneath, he was grateful for her modesty. If she wore something more provocative, he'd never manage to concentrate properly on his work.

Together, they met Carenza right outside the door and hurried after her to the nursery. The little boy lay limp and pale in his bed, hardly moving except for his labored breathing. "We need to move him away from the other children," he said, looking at the other beds in the nursery and hoping it wasn't already too late.

Carenza nodded. "I'll ask Elaine to see to it."

The poor child was burning up, but then children's fevers were always worse than adults'. "He's very feverish. We need to bring his humors back into balance. I hate to bleed young children, but we may need to. First, though, I'd like to try giving him the remedy we've been using at the hospital. I'll go down and get some. It will be faster than making it from scratch. Iselda, do whatever you can to cool him down. I'll be back shortly."

He made his way swiftly from the castle down to the hospital. Clouds were threatening rain as he walked down Castle Street, and the first few drops fell right as the hospital came in sight. Slipping in the side entrance, next to the examination room, he walked straight into a stranger.

"Who are you, and what gives you the right to barge in here like you own the place?" demanded a man with white hair and a wizened face, wearing Hospitaller robes.

"I'm Broth—" He stopped himself. "I'm William. I helped build this hospital from the ground up. Who are you?"

The man looked him up and down with disdain. "Ah yes. William. I'm glad you've come. I'll thank you to take your personal belongings from the scriptorium and be gone."

Was this the man sent to replace him? William did his best to keep his irritation out of his voice as he said, "I'm on an urgent errand from the castle. The earl's son is ill with the same sickness that has been going around. I was only headed to the kitchen to fill a bottle with the remedy we've been using. I assure you I'll collect my belongings as soon as I am able."

The old man barred his way. "I'm not aware of the earl's son being a patient here in the hospital."

William bristled. Who did this man think he was? "He's not. He's up at the castle under my care, and he needs the remedy urgently."

The man continued to bar his way. "Hospital resources are only to be used on hospital patients. My concern is the people under my care here. Why should I give my remedies to a private physician for a child that isn't a patient here? Now go get your books out of what's supposed to be my scriptorium, and don't show your face here again."

Brother Joseph popped his head into the hall momentarily and then ducked back out again upon seeing the new Hospitaller, whose name William still didn't know because the man hadn't deigned to introduce himself.

With very little choice, William went to retrieve his books. He suspected the old codger would have refused to give them back if he had refused to take them. As he was carefully placing his books into a burlap sack for transport, Brother Joseph sneaked into the office and handed him a flask.

"It has the remedy," Brother Joseph whispered. "Don't let Brother Xavier see it. He'll have my hide."

"Thank you," William whispered back, clapping his friend on the shoulder.

"I should go. It's good to see you. I wish I had time to speak at greater length." With that, Brother Joseph slid out the door and disappeared.

When he finished packing his books, he headed out into the hallway as quietly as he could manage, hoping to avoid Brother Xavier. The flask was hidden in his sack with his books. Unfortunately, the old man strode out of the examination room and into the hall just as he was passing. The man didn't say goodbye, instead giving a disapproving growl.

As William exited without a word, he heard the man mumbling something under his breath of which he only caught, "...shameful, allowing a woman to practice the healing arts in a hospital..."

William shook his head with a sad smile, thinking he would have to warn Iselda to stay away now that the hospital was under new leadership.

BACK AT THE castle, he went to the nursery only to find little Charles had been moved. A servant directed him to the correct bedchamber, and he rushed to the child's side to give him a swig of the remedy.

"I'm glad you're here," Iselda said as he administered the brew to his drowsy patient. "My mother says she has something urgent to discuss with me. I don't know what it is, but I should go see her now that you're here. Do you mind?"

"Not at all." He sat down with the boy and touched his forehead. "His fever is lower. Whatever you did worked."

"Cool damp cloths and plenty of water to drink. Simple, but it did the trick."

She kissed him on the cheek before heading out the door, and even such a chaste gesture set him aflame. Those soft lips and those impish eyes and that lithe body…. He needed to cure Charles quickly so that he could concentrate on important things, like taking his wife back to bed.

As she walked out the door, he couldn't help picturing her wearing nothing but her creamy woolen stockings with the blue bows for garters.

Mm. Yes, it was good to be married.

He settled into the chair at the side of the room where Iselda had been sitting. It still smelled faintly of her. The boy was asleep again, having barely woken for his remedy.

Tempting as it was to ruminate on memories of last night and this morning, he reluctantly pushed such thoughts away. He was in a child's sick room, after all. But that brought him to what happened at the hospital.

He'd never imagined that his separation from the hospital would be so absolute and abrupt. After all, he'd continued to work there for weeks after leaving the order. All that had changed was his clothes. He never expected the new person to push him out like that, nor could he believe the attitude the man was taking toward his primary benefactors.

Refusing to treat the earl's son? Did he not realize who provided most of the gold to build and run the place? The old man was in for a rude awakening if he thought he could shun Lord

Daniel and Lady Carenza without consequences.

Nonetheless, it hurt to be pushed so unceremoniously out of a hospital he'd put so much time and effort into. He'd overseen its construction, and negotiated its funding with the earl and the baron as well as the Order. He'd personally gone out into the community to tell the people of Winchelsea about the services available for their use and worked to convince the local healers that the hospital was there to help them, not replace them. He considered half the town his patients. He'd put his heart and soul into that place. And this Brother Xavier had the nerve to treat him like an interloper?

Well, if he wasn't wanted here, perhaps he should go away. Iselda was open to going to Arundel. Maybe, if she liked it, they could stay, and he could build a hospital there, this time as its sponsor rather than its manager. He'd have to speak to Iselda about it when she was done with her mother.

⇛⇚

WILLIAM DIDN'T SEE Iselda again until dinner. Whatever business her mother had with her had kept her occupied all afternoon. Carenza came in to relieve him from his vigil with Charles, and he found himself at loose ends for the first time in years. It was an odd feeling, and he wasn't sure he liked it. After instructing a cook in the kitchen on the proper preparation of little Charles's remedy, and practicing with a sword for an hour in the yard, he settled into the library with volume one of his Galen and read, trying not to let himself be distracted by torrid fantasies about Iselda.

As the hours dragged by, he found himself almost as distracted by his anger about Brother Xavier as he was by thoughts of Iselda. Why did the man have to ruin today of all days? Everything had started out so well.

When he went to the hospital, he was so preoccupied with

Charles that he'd brushed off the interaction with Brother Xavier, but now the memory was like a bruise that turned tender and purple hours after the injury. He ached for his old work and the sense of purpose it gave him. Of course, he'd known things would change when he left the Order, but not so abruptly or completely.

He'd never been more grateful for the arrival of dinner. Idleness did not suit him at all. He practically pounced on Iselda when he ran into her outside the great hall.

"Where have you been all day?" he asked, trying to sound interested instead of desperate.

"I'll tell you about it later," she said, looking almost as irate as he felt.

As he sat down at the table, his mother had a worried smile on her face. "Ah, the happy couple," she said. "How are your preparations going for the journey to Arundel?"

William stared at his mother. "We don't have any immediate plans of going anywhere." Even though he planned to broach the subject with Iselda, he had no intention of letting his mother bully them into it.

He turned to look at Iselda and she was staring down at her plate intently, and her face was red. "Sweeting, are you all right?" he murmured in a low voice.

"They all think we're leaving with your family in three days," she murmured back. "My family included."

Three days? No wonder she looked miserable. He had no intention of uprooting her so quickly.

"I'll miss you so much," Iselda's mother gushed.

"Mama, I told you three days isn't enough time. I can't wrap up my…my charity work," she said, with a glance at his mother— "in such a short time."

"None of that matters now that you're married," her mother said, waving her concern away. "After today's purchases, you should have everything you need for the journey. The dresses will be ready the day after tomorrow, and I've already asked

Rosamunda to get rid of all those dowdy, high-necked wool dresses you wear. From now on, you need to dress like a proper lady. There's nothing to prevent you being ready in three days."

Iselda's eyes went wide, and the blood drained from her face. "Mother, I can hardly do charity work here or in Arundel wearing what you ordered for me today."

Her mother waved away her objections. "But you won't have time for charity work, dear. Isn't that right, Maud You'll be too busy with courtly pursuits, playing host for visiting nobility, learning to manage the household, attending tournaments, musical entertainments, etcetera."

Iselda was stiff as a board by the end of this little speech.

"Oh, yes, Isabella," his mother said. "She'll be far too busy. And I must thank you for arranging everything today so that she will be ready to depart in time."

That was enough. It was time to intervene. "Mother, she's a highly skilled healer. It would be a terrible waste of her talents to force her to give it up for the sake of courtly frivolity, not to mention that it will make her miserable. I won't have it. I—"

"You," his mother said in a sharp voice, "will be far too busy for this healing business as well. You've had nine years to indulge in your little hobby. You're a married man now and the heir to Arundel. It's high time you came home and fulfilled your responsibilities to this family."

"Iselda and I are not your pawns, Mother," he said, putting down his eating dagger with too much force. "Neither of us is going to jump on command. We're done here," he said, offering his arm to Iselda, who gave him a grateful look and followed him back to their room.

They sat down together on the bed, and she sighed. "What are we going to do? You know they are going to conspire to make it impossible to stay."

"We can't let them win. My mother has gone too far this time," he said putting an arm around her.

"She went too far last time too," she said, staring at her knees.

"That's what worries me. God only knows what scheme they will concoct this time to get their way. William, we were planning to go anyway. Perhaps it would be for the best if we give in, at least for now. If we're miserable, we could always leave."

He stood up and started pacing. "You can't be serious. We can't give in. They're practically kidnapping us, and you want to let them have their way?"

"We have to pick our fights. In the grand scheme of things, I care more about my work than where I am. My mother made very clear earlier today that she won't allow me to continue my work here in Winchelsea. I feel like I might have more luck swaying your mother than mine."

He sat down beside her and sighed. "I was planning to speak to you about going to Arundel before all this madness this evening. The hospital here has a new manager, and he made it clear today that I am not welcome. Without the hospital, I have nothing to do here. I would have to build a private practice from scratch. In Arundel, I could sponsor a new hospital and do some real good."

"I'm so sorry about the hospital. I know how much work you put into it. It's horrible that you've been pushed out by a stranger." She took his hand and kissed it, and he melted. At least he still had her, whatever madness might be waiting outside their door.

"So we're going to Arundel with your parents?" she asked.

He took a deep breath. "Yes, it seems so. Are you sure we're not giving in to their manipulation?"

"We're picking our battles, not giving in."

The look of determination in her eyes warmed him down to his toes. He took her in his arms and kissed her softly. "At least we'll be together, sweeting." He kissed her again, reveling in the warmth of her body against his own, her small, perfect breasts pressing against his chest. "You're wearing stockings," he said, looking down at her slim ankles emerging from her practical shoes.

"It's cold. Of course, I'm wearing stockings," she said, laughing.

He knelt down in front of her and took off one shoe, then the other, leaving her in her stocking feet. "I like you in stockings," he said pushing the skirt of her dress up over her knees and then bunching them high on her thighs, exposing the length of her legs. Running a hand up each leg, he parted her knees, smiling as he heard her gasp. "I want to watch you come, sweeting."

And he did, and it was every bit as gratifying as he hoped.

CHAPTER SEVENTEEN

ISELDA KNEW HER wedding would bring change, but not so much so quickly. It wasn't William's fault. He'd done his best to defend their independence, but the reality was that this wedding bound them closer to their parents, as opposed to giving them more freedom. Before they married, they were of little use to their families, but now they were at the center of an important political alliance with all the weighty expectations that came along with that—a future earl and countess.

She only had one more day left to say her goodbyes and prepare for the journey to Arundel. Wrapping things up with her patients was easier than she anticipated, since she had always partnered with midwives and healers in her work. She needed to check on Charles, who was recuperating nicely. Then she needed to pack up her apothecary workshop. At midday, the healers and midwives she worked with were throwing her a goodbye luncheon at The Bird's Nest. The afternoon would be spent with Rosamunda, packing for their journey, and in the evening, there would be a goodbye dinner with her family.

It was going to be a busy day to say the least. She was tired thinking about it, though perhaps her exhaustion had more to do with how she'd spent the previous night than with what she had planned for the day. She and William couldn't get enough of each other, and she was still getting used to sharing a bed. How was a person supposed to sleep through all the little noises and movements, especially when the other person in bed made her ache all over with wanting? No matter how much pleasure he gave her, it was never enough. She always wanted more.

Shaking herself, she made her way to the room where little Charles was staying and opened the door to find Daniel tickling him as he cackled while Carenza stood to the side, looking on adoringly. Charles coughed a few times between giggles but otherwise seemed to be happy and healthy.

"More tickles, Papa," Charles demanded when Daniel took a break.

"I see my patient is doing better this morning," Iselda said, coming inside. "Can Aunt Iselda tickle you for a moment?"

"Auntie Zelda," he squealed. He gave her a daring look and then stretched, inviting her to take advantage.

"First, I'm going to tickle your neck," she said, as he wriggled beneath her fingers. The fever was gone. His coloring was good, and his energy levels were clearly back to where they should be. "Then, I'm going to tickle your tummy," she said, pulling up his night shirt and tickling before bending down to listen to his chest. The rattle from previous days was mostly gone. "Then I'm going to do this," she said, blowing a raspberry right above his bellybutton. He cackled in delight, curling up to defend his belly and pushing her face away.

"No Auntie Zelda! No more tickles! Too much." He squirmed away, still laughing. As soon as he recovered, he turned to them and said, "Now…more tickles." He looked expectantly from one adult to another, not sure who would oblige.

"He's fine to return to the nursery today," she told Daniel and Carenza. "I'll leave you to your tickle time."

From there, she made her way up to the tower with her apothecary workshop to pack. Normally, it was where she created distillations, tinctures, medicinal oils and more using the specialized and unique equipment she'd had made things she couldn't entrust anyone else to put away safely. The straw-filled crates she requested were here, and she began the work of dismantling everything and packing it away.

When she was about halfway done, there was a noise at the door.

"Iselda?" It was William. "So this is your secret lair. I had to ask for directions three times on my way here, or I would have been here sooner to help."

"Thank you for coming. I wasn't expecting you. If you have other things you need to do…"

He shook his head. "I'm packed. I only lived here seven months, and for six of them, I lived like a monk."

She laughed.

"I've been curious about this place. I've heard about it but never seen it. We could use a setup like this at the hospital," he said, opening tiny drawers at random in the large square chest where she kept supplies. "When we build a new hospital in Arundel, I'll be sure to consult you on setting up an apothecary workshop. You use this for distillation?" he asked, pointing to a copper contraption that dripped its contents into a white glazed ceramic jar.

She nodded and began disassembling it. It was so odd having anyone up here with her. It had always been her private space. She'd had the occasional visit from a servant, but that was all. Since becoming engaged, she'd hardly visited it. And now, being alone up here with William was oddly intimate and almost improper. She half expected a flustered Brother Joseph to walk in the door and send them scurrying.

"How long have you had this space?" William asked, sniffing at the remnants of some dried herbs she'd powdered with her mortar and pestle last time she was up here. "Galingale, oregano, and celery seed?"

"And a little bit of white pepper. I mix it with honey for a phlegmatic stomach. I got it from Hildegard, but I tested it with my patients to make sure it worked. I recorded my findings here," she said, handing him a vellum scroll. Their fingers brushed, and she tried to ignore the tiny shock that shot through her.

"Impressive," he said, examining it. "And how long have you had this lab?"

She smiled, remembering. "My brother, Charles, set it up for me when I was thirteen. He noticed my interest in herbs and remedies and cleared the rusty old armaments out of this room so that I could use it. I hope someday you'll get to meet my brother. He lives in Ireland now, but he comes to visit every few years with his wife and children. His son, Thomas, is my father's heir."

"Not your brother?" he asked, looking up from the jars he was packing in straw.

"No. My brother has some health difficulties that make it impractical. I've given him remedies to use, but some wounds never fully heal. And he doesn't want to inherit. He's happy to pass the title along to his son."

William finished packing the jars and closed the crate. "An unusual man. Although I suppose I nearly gave up my right to my father's title myself. I look forward to meeting him someday."

They worked largely in silence for the next hour, broken only by the occasional question from William. Every so often, he would brush up against her, making her wish they could abandon their work and head back to their bedroom.

"I think we're done," she said at last, looking at the bare tables and shelves. "I still have some time before my goodbye supper at The Bird's Nest. What should we do?"

"How long do we have?" he asked lightly, taking her hands, his gaze darkening with desire.

"I don't need to leave for another hour or so—Oh!" He lifted her onto her apothecary workshop table and kissed her furiously. "Here? Now?!"

Heat was already building between her legs, but she was so surprised she hardly knew how to respond. "How would it even work? There's no bed."

"Let me show you." He lifted her skirt until it was high on her thighs, and she wrapped her legs around his waist, startled by how quickly he could turn her into a bonfire of need. She opened to him, inviting his touch, and oh, how he touched her.

Within minutes, she was pure fire, all vestiges of concern for propriety or even conscious thought burnt to a crisp. All she wanted in the world was for his fingers to continue to spark her flame until her body went up in smoke. And when it did, that was not the end.

He opened his breeches and thrust into her with a groan, and she gasped. He filled her so quickly, it was like an explosion of light within her. Something about the angle at which they joined made it feel like he was penetrating deeper, and she wanted all of him, every last delicious inch. This was no gentle lovemaking. This was raw lust, and she loved it. She loved that she could do this to him, make him so wild and ravenous. He thrust into her again and again, each stroke resonating within her like a church bell. She bit his shoulder as she came again, shuddering and quivering against him, and he cried out in his final throes.

"Oh, dear Lord in heaven," she whispered as conscious thought returned. "I'm surprised the entire room isn't scorched after that."

He looked at her, his eyes still smoldering. "So am I." He smiled deviously. "And by the way, that is what I ached to do to you that day in the dispensary when Brother Joseph interrupted us. I would have, too, if he hadn't shown up in the nick of time. I can't keep my hands off you, sweeting."

She grinned. "Please don't. I like your hands on me."

He made a low rumbling "*mm*" sound. "If you want to go to your luncheon, you had better leave now, or I might have to have you again."

At that moment, there was a knock on the door, and both of them rushed to make themselves presentable.

"My lady?" a man's voice called. "I'm here to take the boxes down to the cellar for storage."

"Come in," she called, smoothing her skirts. The servant came in and kept his eyes down as he went about his business. It was hard to know whether he suspected what they had been up to. "William, thank you for your help packing. I should go to my luncheon at The Bird's Nest. I wouldn't want to be late."

"Of course, my dear," he said with an overly formal bow of his head, gesturing toward the door. "I'm supposed to meet Brother Joseph for a pint. I'll see you later."

THE LADIES AT The Bird's Nest outdid themselves. There were savory and sweet pies, roast goose with black currant sauce, fresh bread, goat cheese, roasted root vegetables, and an enormous bowl of custard for dessert.

Her friends and patients beamed as she entered and gasped in delight at the spread.

"Adelaide and Madeleine will be here soon," said Caterina. "Esther can't make it and asked me to give her regrets. Josela went into labor two hours ago, and Esther has her hands full. Griselda will join late. Old Mistress Olivier has a phlegmatic stomach again. She said to thank you for the remedy you made. It's very helpful."

After a quick grace, they began passing the food. "Thank you for all of your help with the residents here that got sick," Jane said. "I don't know what we would have done without you. I'm glad we were finally able to get rid of that miasma that was causing all the trouble."

Iselda piled her plate with a little bit of everything. "Of course. You know how much I care about your residents and the work you do here. I'm going to miss you all terribly."

"We're going to miss you too," said Adelaide, putting down two large jugs of wine on the table. "Now we'll have to do all the work ourselves without your assistance."

"Or filling in for us when we couldn't get there in time," added Madeleine, who was carrying a mysterious bundle wrapped in bright green fabric. "You all remember the story about Valeria's fifth child."

"Less than an hour in labor! Thank heavens you got there in

time, my lady," Caterina said to Iselda.

"Oh, and do you remember Giselle?" asked Adelaide. "A day and a half in labor, poor woman. The baby was breech, and we all had to take turns. Iselda was there at the end and made sure mother and baby came out fine."

"You're all too kind," said Iselda. "You did all the real work. I only helped."

The entire table burst out laughing. "That may be the line you feed your mother," said Caterina, "but we all know the truth. Your husband is the only one in Winchelsea that knows as much as you, and I reckon you have him beat too. By the way, how is married life, *hmm*?"

Heat burned her cheeks. "My husband is very kind and attentive," she said so quietly they all had to lean in.

"Kind and attentive! You hear that, ladies?" said Madeleine. "You'll be needing our services in no time. Or at least you would if you were staying. If they don't have any good midwives over there, you come back to Winchelsea when it's your time, and we'll take care of you."

"Well, I'm not pregnant yet," she objected.

"Oh? Have you had your monthlies?" Madeleine asked. Iselda's cheeks heated again as she stared at her plate. "You're young and healthy. If he's attentive, it won't be long before you start swelling with his babe. Mark my words."

Her monthlies were another week away. She wanted children, but she wasn't sure she was ready in her first month of marriage. A bit more time with only her and William would be ideal.

"You come out with us all the time. Since when are you shy about these things?" asked Caterina.

"Since it was me that you were talking about," Iselda answered.

"Look, ladies! You're making her blush," said Jane. "He must be very attentive indeed." She waggled her eyebrows.

The rest of the meal proceeded in a similar vein—a mix of

teasing and reminiscence, and Iselda thoroughly enjoyed it, despite her blushing. She was going to miss these women. They were the opposite of everything she'd been raised to be. With these ladies, propriety flew out the door, replaced by refreshing honesty and directness. Iselda could only hope she managed to make one or two new friends like this in Arundel.

The lunch was over too soon, and she said her goodbyes. Madeleine handed over the green bundle. "A gift from all of us," she said. It was a beautifully made leather bag with lots of tiny pockets for storing herbs, a larger pocket for storing a flask of remedy, and a large main pocket for storing bandages and other supplies she might need for healing.

"Thank you all," Iselda said, tears forming in her eyes. "This is beautiful, and so useful! It will be so functional when I make house calls in Arundel. I love you all."

They all replied at the same time in a cacophony, returning the sentiment. With many hugs and even a few tears, she said her goodbyes and headed back up to the castle.

The afternoon was dull, spent with Rosamunda packing. She did manage to sneak a few of her plain, high-necked gowns into the bottom of her trunk, thwarting her mother, so it wasn't a complete waste of time. Nonetheless, she was relieved when dinnertime arrived. She changed into one of her new dresses, a blue one with a scoop neck that was barely high enough not to feel scandalous. Rosamunda said she looked gorgeous, and Iselda did her best to believe her.

Her sisters cheered as she came into the room, and she found that William was already there waiting. She hated being the center of attention, but it couldn't be helped.

After they all sat down to eat, Carenza proposed a toast. "To my littlest sister, the smartest of us three and the first one to leave Winchelsea. I wish you a safe journey, and I hope you'll come back to visit us frequently."

"I-I will." Having everyone stare at her was making her tongue tied. William put his hand on the small of her back and rubbed gentle circles. His gentle touch leached away her tension. It was amazing how safe he made her feel.

"It's only one day away by ship. I'm sure we'll be back often," William added as everyone raised their goblets.

"To Iselda!" Goblets clinked, and everyone drank.

"To our friends in Arundel," her father proposed, looking at Lord Arundel and Lady Maud. "Here's to a long and fruitful alliance between our families. Take good care of my baby girl for me, will you?"

Iselda felt her face turning hot and wished she could leave the room, but William took her hand and gripped it tight. Why did her father have to talk about her like she was an infant? And in front of her in-laws too!

They all drank, and Iselda took a deep quaff.

"To our alliance," said Lord Arundel. "May we all prosper from it." First, he nodded to Daniel, as earl, and then turned to her father.

At that moment, the servants arrived with the first course, and conversation was replaced with the sounds of eating and idle chatter. Iselda was relieved to have the focus off of her.

For the rest of the meal, Iselda was content to sit and listen, watching her family and wondering about her in-laws. What would they expect of her? How could she carve out time to do the work she cared about without shortchanging her duties as the future baroness? Would they be supportive of her work? She guessed not, given their attitude toward William, but at least they hadn't forbidden it, as her mother had a few days earlier.

At the end of the meal, as they were serving themselves dessert, Carenza cleared her throat. "Alais and I got a present for you, Iselda. I hope you like it." She handed over something heavy and rectangular in a cloth bag.

Iselda opened it and gasped. "Hippocrates! How did you get this? It must have cost a fortune. Thank you so much!" She got up and hugged her sisters.

"We paid a scribe to reproduce the copy at the abbey," said

Alais. "We commissioned it a year ago and planned to give it to you on your birthday, but I'm glad it was ready in time for this."

"Your father and I have a gift for you too, though it's already packed away. We got you an emerald necklace, and I stitched you a tapestry. We added it to one of your trunks, and it's already on the ship."

Her mother smiled expectantly.

"Thank you for the generous gift," Iselda managed to say as she stood up and kissed her mother and then her father on the cheek. Looking up at her entire family, she said, "I'm going to miss you all terribly."

"We'll miss you too," said Carenza. "You were always the kindest and wisest of the three of us. Alais and I will do our best to stay out of trouble while you're away, but don't stay away too long. We need you to keep us in check."

Iselda laughed. "You don't need me, but I won't stay away too long. I love you all too much."

At last, Iselda made her exit with William, and she yawned as they climbed the stairs.

"Sleepy, sweeting? You've had a long day."

"And a long night," she murmured.

He laughed. "I promise to let you get plenty of sleep tonight in preparation for tomorrow's journey."

When they went to bed, he made sweet and tender love to her, and then she fell into a restless sleep, wondering what her new life would be like.

CHAPTER EIGHTEEN

WILLIAM WAS GRATEFUL the journey to Arundel was uneventful. The English Channel could be unpredictable this time of year. They left in the wee hours of the morning before dawn, changed from ships to river craft at Worthing, and just as the sun was setting, the familiar outline of the town came into view as they made their way up the river Arun. William had only been home twice since joining the Hospitallers, but some landscapes never fade in the mind's eye. He dreamed of his hometown regularly, the rolling hills of the town rising up from the river, crowned by his father's castle.

How often had he made love beneath just such a sunset, taking advantage of the romance of the moment to seduce a woman? Even now, the sight made him long for time alone with Iselda, who stood beside him, shoulders tensed as she braced herself for her new home. If they were alone, he knew the perfect way to dispel all that tension, but alas, they were not. Nonetheless, he wrapped his arms around her from behind and nuzzled her neck, trying to ignore his mother's smug smile from the other side of the deck.

"What do you think?" he asked, murmuring in her ear.

"It's beautiful—very different from Winchelsea but still somehow familiar. I suppose all towns have certain things in common. I'm glad we aren't too far inland. I don't think I could be happy away from the sea."

He nipped at her ear, unable to resist, and was satisfied to hear her sharp intake of breath. "Almost home," he murmured, tickling her ear with his lips. "And then I can help you relax properly."

"*Mm*," she said, leaning into his embrace. "But won't we have to be introduced to the household staff and join your parents for dinner?"

"Say you have a headache and need to rest. I want you, sweeting."

He pressed his growing arousal against her to prove his point. It was embarrassing how much he wanted her, and the desire was relentless. Having her seemed to make him want her all the more instead of sating his hunger.

"Don't be silly. I must make a good first impression. Someday I'm going to be running this household. If I'm going to gain the servants' loyalty, I must show them the respect they deserve when we meet. We'll have plenty of time alone together after dinner."

Unfortunately, she was right, but he was not feeling particularly patient. Maybe he should plead illness and insist she tend him. That way it wouldn't look like she was avoiding her responsibilities, and he could still bury himself between her legs and take her until she fell apart in his arms. And then maybe he'd have her some more, touching and licking her until his cock was ready to—

"Your mother is coming over here," she said, straightening and stepping away.

Well, that killed his burgeoning ardor.

"Have you made me a grandchild yet?" his mother asked with an all too knowing smile.

Iselda cleared her throat and turned bright red.

"Mother, please don't—"

"It's too soon to tell." Iselda spoke at the same time as he.

His mother smirked and looked from one to the other. "It

won't be long." A wave of terror swept over him at the thought, but he shoved it away. "But William," she continued, "Don't even think about stealing Iselda until I'm done with her today. She's mine until tonight."

"As you wish, Mother." *Archangel Raphael's wing tips.* He would have to be patient. There was no gainsaying his mother. Though he had to admit his ardor had cooled considerably with her mere presence.

"In fact, I'd like to borrow her now. Go see what your brother is up to." She nodded toward Michael, who was standing astern, joking with a sailor.

Recognizing defeat, he made his way reluctantly over to his brother.

"…and the friar said, 'I'd rather undo ten virgins than one married woman.' And the blacksmith said—"

William cleared his throat. The sailor stopped in the midst of his joke and made an excuse to go to something with rope on the other side of the ship.

"He was about to finish," Michael complained.

"Are you telling me you haven't heard it before?" Even William had heard it before, and he'd been a monk at the time.

"Of course, I have, but that's not the point."

"And the point is?"

"I have to entertain myself somehow. Some of us don't have a pretty girl hanging on our every word and making bedroom eyes at us."

William stiffened. "Leave Iselda out of this. You had your chance with her, and from what I saw, you couldn't have been more insulting if you tried."

"It was only because I didn't want to marry her. I didn't want her to get the wrong idea. She's a pretty little thing. I wouldn't have minded taking her to bed. But marriage? No, thank you."

It took all of William's self-control not to punch his brother in the face. He had to settle for grabbing his arms and shaking him.

"You will not speak of my wife that way ever again. Do you

understand?"

His brother looked genuinely scared. William wondered what his own face must have looked like. He couldn't remember the last time he'd scared another man like that. But Iselda did things to him.

"Christ's teeth, William. I won't say another word about your wife. I promise."

Releasing him, William let his arms drop to his sides. "See that you don't."

Michael shook his head. "I thought you'd be more fun after leaving the Hospitallers and lying with a woman, but you're as uptight as ever."

What was there to say to that? William sighed. "I'm guessing you're happy to be home?"

With a noncommittal shrug, Michael said, "It won't be the same now that you're home and married. Everyone had written you off, and they thought I would be the next earl. The ladies like an heir. But now, unless you have nothing but daughters, I'm out of the running."

William hadn't thought about how his marriage affected his brother. He should have, but he was so concerned with his own fate and Iselda's that he forgot about Michael. "I'm sorry, Brother. I never meant to take anything away from you."

"Eh," Michael said with another shrug, "I didn't want to actually *be* earl. I mean, I like the attention and all, but Papa wanted me to learn about trade and port business and grain stores and defenses and all kinds of boring shit. Now I'm off the hook. I can focus on tournaments and let you do all the hard work. Thanks, Brother," he said, clapping William on the shoulder.

William laughed. Perhaps he'd done his brother a favor after all. He couldn't say he was looking forward to all of it any more than Michael, but he knew from his hospital work that he had a talent for it. Running a hospital was like running a town on a smaller scale. You had to keep everyone fed and housed. There were supplies to be purchased, funds to be raised. Though in truth, while he didn't mind doing all these things when it had to do with medicine, he rather dreaded taking on all of Arundel.

"Fine. I'll do the boring shit and leave you the tournaments. I never liked tournaments anyway."

The ship was docking, and it was time to disembark. He took a deep breath, drinking in the familiar sights, sounds, and smells of home.

HE BARELY SAW Iselda until dinner time. His mother kept her occupied from the moment she interrupted them on the ship, not relenting for a second. His father hadn't been much better. As soon as they landed, his father drew him aside to point out improvements he'd made to the port and to give him a tour of the new custom house. What he was supposed to gain from watching a bunch of notaries do their scribbling, he wasn't sure. When they returned to the castle, his father made him sit with him as he debriefed with the marshal on security matters and the steward on household matters. Then there was a pile of correspondence to go through that his father asked his help with.

"You see?" his father said as they were wrapping up responses to the last of the letters. "It isn't a dull life. There is plenty to occupy a man's interest. You'll hardly miss medicine at all."

"Father, about that—"

"Oh dear, we're late for dinner. You had better go change quickly."

And he was dismissed without another word. It was not going to be easy to plant the seed of building a hospital here, but he was determined to make it happen.

He was the last to arrive at dinner. Iselda looked spectacular in green silk, wearing the emerald necklace from her parents. She also looked petrified. His mother sat by her side and kept whispering things in her ear. Iselda dutifully nodded and said nothing. She shot him a panicked look as he came in, and he swept to his spot beside her, anxious to come to her rescue.

"Mother, I love the new tapestries in here. How long have

you had them?"

Iselda's hand found his beneath the table and squeezed. He gave her a chaste kiss on the cheek.

"Are you trying to change the subject to rescue your wife from me?" his mother asked. Of course, she saw right through him.

"Yes." There was no point in denying it.

"She's doing fine. Lady Isabella did her job, giving her daughter a good education in how to run a household, even if she did let her run a bit wild and read more than was good for her."

The wan smile on Iselda's face said it all. "Mother, you've terrified her enough for one day. Tell me about the tapestries and release my bride from your talons."

His mother sighed and shook her head. "Despite what you may think, I'm not torturing the girl. All I've done is introduce her to the household she will one day run. There's a tremendous amount to learn, though men never seem to give these things any thought.

"She'll have a staff of fifty servants to manage. She'll have meals and entertainments to plan, correspondence to maintain, improvements and repairs to oversee, visiting nobles to welcome. I plan to share the responsibilities with her now so that she has a comprehensive understanding when the time comes for her to take them on. You wouldn't want me to throw her to the wolves, would you?"

Taking a deep breath, William tried to remind himself of the reasons he came back.

"Obviously, I don't want to see her thrown to the wolves. All I ask is that you relent for this evening."

His mother stared at him, eyes narrowed, and he thought, not for the first time, that under her graying hair and wrinkling skin, she was pure steel.

"Fine. The tapestries are two years old. Are you happy?"

He spent the rest of the meal engaged in small talk about the weather, their neighbors in Portsmouth who were hosting a tournament the next week, improvements to the castle—anything to allow Iselda some peace to eat her meal.

As soon as he could get away with leaving the table, he made his excuses and escaped with her to his room. Their room. It wasn't only his anymore, he had to remember. And technically, it had been a guest room for the last nine years. Still, it was the room he'd spent his childhood and youth in, and it took some mental rearranging to think of it as a shared space. He would have to encourage her to redecorate, make it feel like hers as well.

"Thank you for coming to my rescue," she said as soon as they were out of earshot of the great hall. "It's been a very long evening."

She clung to his arm, and his desire for her came roaring back. Without thinking, he turned and backed her into a wall, kissing her ferociously. There was a tentativeness to her kiss back that gave him pause. "What's wrong?" he asked.

"The servants will see."

"Why does that matter?" They were discreet, he knew. He'd never been particularly stealthy about his liaisons, and they'd never betrayed him.

"I need them to respect me."

"They already respect you because of who you are," he said, confused by her concern.

She stiffened and put some space between them. "I want them to respect me because I have earned their respect, not only because I have a title. I want their loyalty, not their blind obedience."

At that moment, there was a movement down the hall. One of the servant women stared at him, eyes filled with disdain, and then she turned and was gone. He knew those eyes. Was it possible his parents didn't know about him and Maribel? If they did, they would never have given her a job in the castle. Suddenly, he understood Iselda's concern all too well. It was a long time ago, but kissing Iselda in full view of the servants could open old wounds. It was a mistake.

"Who was that?" she asked.

He shook himself. "Who?"

"The servant woman you were looking at. I think we made her uncomfortable."

He shook his head. "I'm not sure. She had a familiar face, but it's been so long."

Coward.

"I'm sorry for making you uncomfortable. Let's go to our room," he said and led her down the hall.

Opening the door, he took in his room. Every vestige of his youth was gone. The furniture had all been replaced. The narrow bed of memory was gone, replaced by an enormous, canopied monstrosity that took up most of the room. His desk and shelves had disappeared, replaced by a tall wardrobe. He wondered if his childhood treasures were still hidden behind a loose stone in the west wall or if that too had disappeared. The strangeness of it all was another reminder of how ill-adapted he was to his new life.

As soon as the door closed behind them, he apologized again. "It was inconsiderate and unwise. It won't happen again."

"Thank you," she said, folding her arms.

"Forgive me?" he asked, wrapping his arms around her.

After a moment, she uncrossed her arms and wrapped them around his waist. Then she snuggled against him, her head tucked beneath his chin. She was so sweet, so trusting.

It wasn't in her nature to resist for long. And here he was hiding his past from her. But there was no need for her to know details, was there? He'd already confessed in general terms. Did she really need to know the specifics? Telling her about Maribel could only hurt her, and she didn't need that right now on top of everything.

"What did my mother do to you today?"

"Exactly what she said," she murmured into his chest. "I met the entire household, and she began instructing me in how to run it. This week, I am to observe. Next week she plans to start assigning me responsibilities. I do know what I'm doing, you know," she said, looking up at him. "My mother did teach me how to run a household for a nobleman. I can do the work. It's only that…"

She tucked her head beneath his chin again.

"Only what?"

"I don't like being in charge of people. It ties my stomach in knots. And the looks on their faces when they met me…. They tried to hide it, but some of them clearly pitied me, and a few obviously loathed me. Why would they have such strong feelings upon meeting me for the first time?"

Oh dear. Was it possible he was at fault? He'd been gone from Arundel for nine years, but what did the servants know about his life during that time? Before he left, he did many things he wasn't proud of. Maribel was the least of it. Did they pity her because they doubted his fidelity? Did they hate her for marrying the man who wronged more than one servant in this household without taking responsibility?

All of this was conjecture. He needed to find out the truth before he troubled her with his suspicions. In the meantime, he should soothe her worries and help her rest.

"Sweeting," he began. "I don't know the answer, but I will try to learn more. Tonight, though, you should let it go. Relax. Rest."

She turned her face up to him with a mischievous smile. "Will you help me?" she asked, cupping his cheek with her hand.

For the fifteenth time today, he thought, *Dear Lord in heaven, thank you for my wife.*

CHAPTER NINETEEN

ISELDA AWOKE IN a strange bed to the distant crowing of a cock just before dawn. William's arms folded around her, holding her body against his own. Oh, how she wished she didn't have to get out of bed!

Knowing she shouldn't, she snuggled closer to her husband. He stirred in his sleep and started to fondle her breast. Now, she wanted to get out of bed even less, but the thought of Lady Maud's disapproving glare if they were late for Mass made her gently nudge his hand away and start scooting toward the side of the bed.

He reached out and pulled her firmly back. "Where do you think you're going?" he murmured into her hair.

"We can't be late again. Your mother will have our heads."

He groaned. "Just a little bit longer. I like it here." Beneath the covers, he began pulling up her shift until he bared her to the waist, stroking her skin and sending ripples of delight all through her. His hand made soft circles on her belly, dipping lower each time until he grazed the curls between her legs.

She gasped, heat and need pooling in that woman's place, even as all the reasons this was a bad idea paraded through her mind. In the week they'd been here, they'd only been on time to morning Mass twice. It wasn't seemly. They were supposed to set an example for their subjects, and Iselda felt the subtle weight of disapproval from everyone in the church every time they tried to sneak in late. No one except her mother-in-law would ever come out and say anything, but the looks and murmurs conveyed enough to make her wince and redden.

Every time, she swore she wouldn't let it happen again, but then he went and did exactly what he was doing now, dipping his finger into her drenched folds, and making her lose all ability to form words.

"Don't worry. I'll handle Mother," he said as she began to shudder from his ministrations, her breath growing ragged.

Rolling her onto her back, he settled between her thighs, rubbing his thickness against her, nudging at her entrance. Why did all her best intentions go out the door every time he touched her? Nuzzling her neck and covering it with kisses, he entered her slowly, each stroke filling her a bit more, making her moan.

"William," she gasped, digging her fingernails into his back, and angling her hips to take him deeper, despite her better judgment. And it was heaven!

How had she lived her whole life without knowing what pleasure there was to be had in the meeting of flesh? She, who had spent years studying the body's every nuance in her work as a healer, had never suspected such sensations were possible before their marriage. With each passing day, her hunger for her husband deepened. He was her solace in this new and strange place where everyone was unfamiliar, and she fell all too willingly under his spell when she ought to be tending to her new duties.

But with each thrust, those duties seemed farther away. All the reasons to get out of bed vanished from her head, as she surrendered to the steady rhythm of William's love. He covered her in kisses as the blooming sensation within her grew and grew. Soon, she wrapped her legs around her husband's hips and cried out as bliss coursed through her, obliterating all conscious thought. Moments later, William pulsed within her, filling her with his seed, then collapsing by her side.

She smiled to herself at the thought that even now, a child

might be conceived from their joy. Perhaps William had overcome his reluctance around having children. He certainly seemed enthusiastic about engaging in acts that would lead to one.

Patting her belly, she gazed adoringly at her husband. "Soon I'll be round with your child if we continue like this."

He stiffened beside her and offered a strained smile. "That would be wonderful, sweeting."

So his reluctance was as strong as ever. Perhaps they should take precautions, at least until he accustomed himself to the idea. "If you wish for us to wait—"

"No, love. You want children. My family wants children. I won't let my fears stand in the way."

It was a sweet thing for him to say, but she truly didn't wish to make him miserable. Despite his words, everything in his expression said otherwise.

"We *can* wait. I would like a family, but it doesn't need to be right away. I still have many childbearing years ahead of me, and there's no need to rush."

He chuckled grimly. "My mother has other views."

Lady Maud was formidable, and truth be told, Iselda was a little bit scared of her. But this of all things should be decided between a husband and wife. "I don't care what your mother thinks. I—"

They were interrupted by a knock.

"My lady, do you need assistance getting dressed this morning?" Rosamunda asked through the closed door. "Lady Maud asked me to be sure you are on time for Mass today. May I come in?"

William launched himself out of bed, stumbling over his own feet in his rush to pull on clothes.

"Just a moment, Rosamunda," Iselda called out, straightening her shift, and pulling a robe around her. They were going to be late *again*, and have to endure Lady Maud's keen-eyed, wrathful glare *again*.

William hurriedly poured water from a pitcher into an ewer and splashed it on his face, running wet hands through his hair to tame it. With a strip of rough linen, he rubbed his teeth clean, then turned to open the door.

Rosamunda bustled in the moment the door cracked open. "Lady Maud will have my hide if I don't get you to church on time this morning, my lady."

"I'll go hold her off," said William, making a quick exit. "Come as quickly as you can."

As soon as the door closed, Rosamunda pulled off Iselda's robe and shift. With practiced motions, she slipped clean garments over Iselda's head. "I'm sorry to interrupt, my lady," she mumbled as she tightened the ties on the sides of Iselda's green surcotte. "But Lady Maud insisted. I know it isn't your fault. You were always an early riser before you married."

It might not have been Iselda's fault, but Lady Maud would most certainly lay the blame at her feet. "You need to manage your husband just as you manage your household," her ladyship had said the day before after they were late for Mass the third time in a row. "You must always keep the upper hand. It should never look like you are managing him, but never, ever relinquish control."

"Don't worry, Rosamunda," Iselda said, trying not to wince as her maid pulled a wooden comb through the tangles William had made of her long, dark hair. "Get me ready as quickly as you can, and hopefully we'll be at the church before the priest starts services."

Her own family back in Winchelsea went to Mass at Nones in the family chapel after breakfast rather than attending Matins at the town church at the break of dawn. It made for a much more relaxed morning routine, but Iselda had to accustom herself to the way things were done in Arundel.

She tapped her foot impatiently as Rosamunda braided and pinned her hair, fixing a silk veil in place with a silver circlet.

"I'm sorry, my lady. I'm going as fast as I can."

"I know." It would be a wonder if she didn't have her dress on backwards at the rate her maid was working.

"Finished," Rosamunda said after pushing in one final hairpin.

Iselda tore out the door and walked as quickly as propriety would allow down the stairs to the entrance hall where William was in the midst of an argument with his mother.

"For the last time, Mother, it's my fault. I kept her back."

"Then why is it that you are here, and she is not?"

The blood drained from Iselda's face. She wanted to run back upstairs to her bedroom and hide for the rest of the day, but she didn't dare.

William looked up and noticed her on the staircase, eyes widening as he took in her no doubt pale visage. "She's right here, Mother, and she heard every word you just said."

"*Hmph.*" Lady Maud looked Iselda up and down like a fire-breathing dragon considering how to roast its prey. "It's about time. Come. The priest won't dare start without me."

Attended by guards, they walked the short distance to the enormous stone cathedral with its soaring tower. Morning light filtered in through the tall, pointed, stained glass windows as they hurried up the long aisle to their pew at the front of the church. The air was redolent with incense and judgment as the eyes of a hundred or more townspeople followed their progress to their places.

Lord Arundel was already there, waiting for them. "Good. You made it just in time," he murmured to his wife.

"Barely," she answered, darting an accusatory glance at Iselda.

The priest peered out at them and nodded before proceeding to the pulpit and beginning to intone in Latin. The familiar ritual played out as it had every day of her life. There was something soothing in reciting the prayers and engaging in the call and response as she had thousands of times before. Though the enormous cathedral was far more forbidding than the small family chapel where she was accustomed to taking Mass in

Winchelsea, every syllable was the same. It was such a relief that something in this new place was recognizable, or at least it was until the priest began his homily.

"Lust is one of the seven deadly sins." He looked pointedly at Iselda, who quickly dropped her gaze, her cheeks heating. Was it written on her face what she and William had been doing earlier? "We must guard ourselves against the temptations of the flesh lest we become mere animals, our souls lost to perdition."

He continued to enumerate the myriad dire consequences of succumbing to the temptations of the flesh and went on at length about how women were vessels of sin and how men must guard themselves against temptation. "For Eve led Adam astray in the Garden of Eden. But for lust, all of mankind would still live in innocence in an earthly paradise."

Iselda wished the floor would open up and swallow her. How was it possible that something that felt so right, an act that led to the blessing of children, could be so terrible for the soul? But amidst her embarrassment, there was a little flicker of angry resistance. How dare the priest blame women for lust as if men were not participants? Were men not responsible for their own souls? And what right did he have to look down on her in condemnation when all she had done was try to conceive a child, her sacred duty as a wife?

She shifted in her seat, cheeks aflame with indignation. Sensing her discomfort, William laid a soothing hand over hers. Taking deep breaths, she focused on his touch and let her mind drift away from the priest's dire threats of fire and brimstone. What she truly needed to soothe her aching soul was a chance to engage in charitable acts. She missed her work serving the poor and comforting the ill. If only she could find an excuse to get away!

How was it that her life as a wife had been reduced to nothing but procreation, the drudgery of managing household concerns, and playing hostess to visiting nobles? And apparently, she was in grave danger of perdition from her enjoyment of the first. There was no winning as a wife. She was damned no matter what she did.

As she ate her holy wafer and drank the consecrated wine, she was seething with indignation, and her mood had barely improved by the time services were over.

William placed her hand in the crook of his arm for the walk back to the castle. "I'm sorry about Father Jerome. I should have warned you about his favorite topic."

"That was so humiliating. He stared at me the entire time, as if it was all my fault that lust existed in the world."

Leaning in close, William grinned and murmured, "Well, you do inspire some rather sinful thoughts in that dress."

She made an indignant noise in her throat. "That's it. I'm changing as soon as we get back. I want my old high-necked gowns. The ones my mother bought are nothing but trouble."

"You'll do no such thing," her mother-in-law said behind her. "We're entertaining Lord Saul and Lady Edith today, and I won't have you dressed like a dowdy peasant."

Christ's teeth! How much did she overhear?

"Of course, Lady Maud." Why did she cave so easily to her terrifying mother-in-law? There had to be some way to assert herself and do what she so craved. "I...I was hoping..."

"Yes?" her mother-in-law snapped impatiently.

"I was hoping I could take the afternoon to do some charity work." There. She'd said it. Lady Maud was going to say no, but at least she'd voiced what she wanted.

"Of course not. We're going hawking with our guests."

Oh dear. Iselda had forgotten about that. She hated hunting. It went against every healing instinct she had. And worse yet, she'd be forced to make small talk with strangers for hours on end. It was torture!

Seeing the look on her face, William intervened. "Tending to the misfortunate is our duty, Mother. Surely, you can spare us for an afternoon."

Lady Maud pursed her lips. "Not you too. I expect you both

to join us on this outing, and I won't hear another word."

"But—" William began.

"Enough. You think I don't know what you'll really be up to? I want grandchildren as much as anyone, but you have plenty of time in the dark of night to make me one. Your days belong to *me*."

Iselda wanted to die on the spot. Accustomed though she was to the frank talk of midwives, she never dreamed she would hear such words from Lady Maud. She closed her eyes and struggled to compose herself. But even in the midst of her embarrassment, a spark of resistance began to grow into a flame.

"No, they do not," Iselda said quietly but firmly. "We will do our duty, but I must insist that we be allowed some time to ourselves. I propose a compromise. Give us the morning to do as we please, and we will join for hawking in the afternoon."

With a sharp intake of breath, Lady Maud came to an abrupt halt and narrowed her eyes at Iselda who held her gaze and did not relent even as her face burned up. After a long moment of tense silence, Lady Maud spoke. "You have the morning. You will join us for luncheon, and your afternoon is mine."

Had Iselda just won an argument with her mother-in-law? And was that tilt of Lady Maud's lip amusement? Grudging respect?

They resumed their walk back to the castle and soon arrived. Resisting the urge to flee, Iselda walked calmly up to her room on William's arm, leaving her in-laws behind. Hastily, she changed from the gown she was wearing to one of her old high-necked gowns, ignoring the heated look William gave her as she disrobed.

At last, she was free to explore Arundel and get to know her new subjects!

"Come. Let me show you around and introduce you to the local healers," William said, offering his arm again. "You look too lovely for me to let you go off on your own."

Iselda laughed. "Even in this old thing?"

"Especially in that old thing. I believe you were wearing that when I first fell in love with you."

Turning toward him, she placed her hands on his chest and smiled up at him. "Oh? And when was that?"

He kissed the top of her head. "I do believe I was yours from our first argument."

She pulled back, surprised. "But that was the day we met."

"Yes, it was." He kissed her softly on the lips. "Now let's go before my mother changes her mind."

"Yes, let's."

Life in Arundel was looking more promising by the moment. She had a loving husband and the freedom to do her work. What more could she want?

CHAPTER TWENTY

PERHAPS MOVING TO Arundel so soon was a mistake. They were going to have to go eventually, but if they had truly set their minds to it, they could have argued for more time in Winchelsea. William knew exactly how trying his parents could be, and yet he'd allowed Iselda to convince him this was for the best. After the way their day started, he was seriously questioning whether they had made the right choice.

At least they were now free for a few hours, and he could finally show her around the town. They had been cooped up in the castle all week. It would be a relief to be amongst the common folk once again. He missed the days when he was simply Brother William. While he'd reveled in his position in his youth, now the distance between him and his people rankled. Farmers and shopkeepers were much better company than nobles, he'd found, not that he would ever dare to say so aloud in front of his parents.

Morning mist still hung over everything as he led Iselda out the castle gates, giving the surrounding countryside an other-worldly quality as if it was inhabited by fairies. And Iselda looked like a fairy queen, even in that conservative dress. Somehow all that dowdy cloth made him all the more aware of the loveliness that lay beneath it. Her healer's bag was slung over one shoulder, and William carried a large basket of food to share with those they visited.

"Where shall we start?" Iselda asked as they ambled downhill on the curving road to the river Arun and then up to the town.

"We'll start with Master Quentin. I spent countless hours in his company when I was young, eager to learn all his secrets. He's a very learned man when it comes to the healing arts. He studied in Paris and was the personal healer to my grandmother, who was King Henry I's widow before she married my grandfather. He's served our family for countless years and knows everyone in the town."

Rays of sun pierced the fog as he led Iselda up the road. The half-timbered houses and shops he remembered so well stretched along the hillside, which was capped by the church. Townsfolk went about their morning business opening up street stalls, feeding livestock, emptying chamber pots into the drainage ditch, hanging laundry out to dry. The ones who saw them bowed their heads in deference as they passed. Once again, William longed for his humble Hospitaller robes. Now he fully understood why Iselda preferred the gowns she did. There was a peace in anonymity that he would never experience again as long as he stayed at Arundel.

Was he imagining things, or was there a touch of animosity and disapproval in some of those gazes? Were the townsfolk still angry with him for his youthful indiscretions? He had hoped the years would have wiped away memories of all of that, but it seemed some memories lingered. Well, he would have to grin and bear it. He could not undo the past. All he could do was live better in the present.

He turned down a familiar alley, his feet following a route they had traversed a thousand times in his youth. He stopped in front of Master Quentin's apothecary shop, taking in the familiar edifice. It was smaller than he remembered, and the building was dilapidated compared to the neat storefront in his memory. The daubed walls were chipped in places and needed a fresh coat of paint. One of the wooden shutters was askew, hanging from a single hinge. Had Master Quentin fallen on hard times, or was he merely too old to take care of the place?

Opening the door beneath the wooden sign painted with a mortar and pestle, he led Iselda into the shop and breathed deeply. The unique scent of herbs and elixirs filled his nose, bringing up memories of a simpler time when he was a mere boy, trailing at the heels of the local miracle worker. Narrow shelves filled with small clay pots of remedies covered the walls, just as he remembered, though they were dustier now, and some were covered in cobwebs. Master Quentin was getting on in years. Perhaps he needed help with the shop. Shouldn't he have an apprentice to take care of such things?

"Master Quentin," he called out. A minute went by, and there was no response. "Master Quentin," he called out again. "It's William. There's someone I want you to meet."

Rustling noises came from the back room, and moments later, an old man whose spine curved like a snail's shell came shuffling into the shop, leaning heavily on a cane. A few wisps of white hair still graced his mostly bald head. His scraggly white beard reached his waist. But his eyes were keen and sharp. They snapped to William and widened. Then they flickered to Iselda briefly before returning to him and narrowing.

"Well, my lord, it took you long enough," Master Quentin said in his thin, reedy voice. "I hear you've been in town a week, and this is the first time you come to visit me?"

William beamed at him, grateful beyond words to see the cranky old man again. "My apologies. My parents wouldn't let me get away."

"And I'll wager she has something to do with it too," Master Quentin said, glancing at Iselda again and pursing his lips.

"Master Quentin, I'd like you to meet my wife, Lady Iselda. I think you two will get along quite well. She's very skilled in the healing arts and used to keep her own apothecary workshop in her family castle back in Winchelsea."

The man bowed his head in solemn greeting.

Iselda smiled kindly and nodded in acknowledgement.

"A healer, eh, my lady?" he said with a wink.

Iselda blushed and stammered, "Well…I…er…"

"A very skilled one," William said, intervening. "She knows her herbs and remedies as well as any physician I've ever met."

"I see," his old friend said, straightening to the best of his ability and looking down his long nose at Iselda. "When a patient is suffering from an imbalance of humors should one treat the affected body part first or treat the body as a whole?"

"According to Galen, one should ensure the whole body is empty before subjecting any part of it to strong remedies. And one must consider the whole body in treatment. Otherwise, one risks drawing the body's superfluities to the affected region and fixing them there."

Pride swelled in William's chest at her easy recital of the ancient healer's advice. What an amazing woman he'd married! Master Quentin appeared to think so too, judging from his slight smile. From him, that was high praise.

"Well said, my lady," said his wizened teacher. "It seems you know theory as well as practice. As for you," he said, turning to William, "I'm glad to see you've given up your wandering ways and settled down. I know you wanted to be a monk, but I never thought you were suited for it. You always had an excess of heat. You need a wife to bring you into balance."

William sighed. "You're right. It took me far too long to realize it." Leave it to Master Quentin to find a medical explanation for his past transgressions and to view his current marriage as a prescription for his health.

"What brings you to my shop today, my lord? You both appear in excellent health. Surely you didn't come just to visit with an old man like me."

"Of course, I came to see you."

The elderly man gestured to stools around a table in the center of the room near the hearth, and they all sat.

"If I may be so bold, I see that your shop isn't as tidy as it once was. Don't you have an apprentice to help you out?" William wanted to assist him if he could. Perhaps he could send a servant down to help with tidying and repairs.

His teacher's eyes got watery. "I haven't taken an apprentice since young Timothy. He died of a tooth infection three years ago. I did everything I could to save him, but nothing worked. I haven't been able to bear to take on another since."

"I'm so sorry," said Iselda, reaching out a hand and placing it atop Master Quentin's. "That must have been a terrible loss."

William's heart swelled at the sight of his wife comforting his former teacher. "A terrible loss indeed," he echoed.

"Timothy was talented," his master said. "Almost as talented as you. And much better behaved. Everyone loved Timothy." He looked off into the middle distance.

"Unlike me," William said carefully.

Master Quentin gave him a penetrating look. "You've noticed that have you?" he asked lightly. "You'll win the townspeople back, my lord. I can see you've changed for the better. And this young lady you've married will certainly help."

Iselda furrowed her brow. "What exactly did you do to offend them?"

William's face heated at the thought of his youthful transgressions and how casually he'd treated the young ladies he seduced. "We'll talk about it later," he said quickly. "Master Quentin, we were hoping to distribute food and blankets to families in need this morning. Are there any particular families you would recommend we visit?"

His mentor mentioned several families who would benefit from a visit.

"Thank you. We should take our leave," William said, rising. "It was wonderful to see you. I promise we'll be regular visitors. May I send someone from the castle to help with repairs to your shop?"

The old man waved him away. "I've done fine by myself for three years. Don't bother yourself, my lord."

"It was a pleasure meeting you," Iselda said, squeezing Master Quentin's hand. "I look forward to getting to know you better."

"As do I, my lady," he said, patting her hand.

They took their leave and started their visits. The butcher's wife had just had twin girls, and they cooed over the babies and shared provisions. The longing in Iselda's eyes as she held one of the twins made William's heart ache. He would give her the child she wanted. It was only a matter of time before she conceived, given his ardor, but his fear for her well-being was almost paralyzing. Even though her sisters had both survived giving birth, even if Alais had had a hard time of it. The de Vere women were strong. Nothing bad would happen to Iselda, would it?

Iselda handed the tiny infant to him, and his heart dropped to his stomach. He'd never held an infant before. They were the province of midwives. Were all babies this tiny and fragile? All this time he'd been worrying about Iselda, but what about the child? How would he keep such a helpless and precious creature alive in a world so fraught with peril?

"You're shaking," Iselda whispered. "Should I take her back?"

William gulped and nodded.

They took their leave of the family with well wishes. As soon as they were outside Iselda asked, "Can it be that you've never held a newborn babe before?"

"That was my first time. I was terrified I was going to break her," he confessed.

Iselda laughed. "Trust me. Babies are more resilient than you think. They aren't made of Venetian glass."

"You would know far better than I. You've probably held dozens of babies."

"Hundreds," she corrected with an amused smile. "In my work with Winchelsea's midwives, I'd be surprised if there was a baby in town I hadn't held at some point or other."

A lump formed in William's throat. He was so proud of his amazing wife. And look what a mess he was after holding one little baby!

"We should keep going," Iselda said, blushing prettily at his gaze. "We don't have very much time left before we have to return to the castle for that awful hunt."

Together, they made the rounds of four villagers and three farmers, taking turns treating their ailments and injuries. Iselda's knowledge of medicine continued to astound him, and her quiet, patient way with people was an inspiration to watch. They all warmed to her, whereas several of those they visited were quite wary of him.

Was it because he was a lord, or were there still lingering memories of his past behavior that were coloring people's views of him? He didn't dare ask. It would only make others uncomfortable, and he was certain they would lie and tell him what they thought he wanted to hear.

When the basket was empty, they wended their way back up to the castle. Iselda's back grew straighter, and her gate stiffened as they approached the castle.

"You're dreading the hunt?" he asked, planting a soft kiss on the top of her head.

Her shoulders sagged. "Is it so obvious?"

"We could try to beg off," he suggested, knowing she'd turn him down.

"It's our duty. We already promised to go. Your family expects it of us, and our guests will be offended if we don't join. Besides, I've had enough of your mother's condemnation for one day."

She was right, of course, but that didn't stop him from wishing to whisk her away, preferably to the privacy of their room where they could spend the afternoon in more pleasant pursuits.

Of course, his mind would go there. Back in his ancestral home with a beautiful wife, he found he could hardly think of anything else. It was as if his years with the Hospitallers never happened. How was it possible he'd ever contemplated being a monk?

Iselda's maid was waiting in the entrance hall as soon as they went inside. "My lady, I'm so glad you're back. Lady Maud is quite anxious for you to join the hunting party for a midday meal, but first I'm to see to it that you change into your hunting clothes."

So much for getting Iselda alone. His ever-vigilant mother had taken precautions this time to make sure they didn't dally. Their brief respite was over, and they were back to playing lord and lady, engaging in the dull and empty pursuits of the nobility. He made his way to the great hall, dreading the afternoon ahead.

CHAPTER TWENTY-ONE

ISELDA RODE CAREFULLY with a hooded merlin perched on her leather gauntleted forearm, wishing she was her sister, Carenza. While Iselda had learned the art of falconry at her mother's insistence, she had never particularly enjoyed it. The predatory birds made her uneasy, as did the business of killing small animals for sport. Meanwhile, her sister was fearless and fierce, much better suited to this sort of thing than Iselda.

Lady Edith rode at her side, wearing a hunting outfit that exposed a great deal of flesh, despite the icy wind that chilled Iselda to the bone. Surely, one needn't show that much bosom to hunt for hares and grouse.

"Lord Saul loves to hunt," Lady Edith enthused, ignoring Iselda's silence. "Since we were married two months ago, we've gone hunting almost every day. Such a delightful pastime, don't you think?"

Concentrating on maintaining balance with the bird, Iselda couldn't summon a response. Fortunately, Lady Edith didn't seem to need one.

"It was such a lucky thing Lord Saul was in the market for a wife when my first husband died. I wasted no time with mourning. I couldn't afford it, not with such a valuable keep to maintain and no heir to take it over. Fortunately, Lord Saul already has two sons, and he was willing to take me on. More than willing, if you catch my meaning," Lady Edith said, turning to wink at Iselda.

These were details Iselda absolutely didn't want to know, but she didn't dare interrupt the woman.

"Oh, I see you're blushing! Surely, we married women can talk openly of such things," Lady Edith continued, hardly taking a breath. "You're lucky to have such a handsome husband. My first husband was a toad and forty years my senior. I did my duty, of course, and we had three daughters together. He never did give me a son. They always blame the woman when there's no son, but I think it's the man's fault. Don't you?"

Actually, Iselda did. Based on the evidence she'd collected from women who remarried and had children with both men, it appeared to be the man rather than the woman who influenced the sex of the children. "Well, I—"

"But women take the blame for everything, don't they?" Lady Edith asked before Iselda could get more words out. "Even in the Garden of Eden, it's Eve's fault for eating the apple. Never mind about the serpent. Or the fact that God had told Adam it was his job to keep an eye on the tree. So what was he doing, just standing there, and watching it happen? Yet, the priests blame Eve. And tell me, is it written anywhere that she *forced* him to eat the apple? He knew the rules. But he ate it anyway."

While Iselda tended to agree, she was worried about what Lady Maud might think of this conversation. Her mother-in-law rode just ahead, chatting with Michael, but every so often, her sharp glance darted back to Iselda. Perhaps it was best to remain silent and focus on not upsetting the bird on her arm.

Lady Edith didn't seem to mind. "Men are simple creatures. If one understands their appetites, they are easy to control. Wouldn't you agree? Show a bit of flesh and they are easy enough to lead about by the nose. When I married Lord Saul, I—"

"Here we are," Lord Arundel announced, interrupting a sentence Iselda didn't want to hear the end of.

They were in a large, open meadow where the birds would

have good visibility. Their party of seven plus the falconer and three servants came to a halt. William sidled up on his horse and quietly asked, "How are you doing?"

"I'm fine," she lied. She would rather be just about anywhere else.

He nodded and returned to the group of men after a sharp glance from his mother.

"Our guests should go first," said Lord Arundel. "Lord Saul?"

"I must defer to my lady. She does so love the hunt," Lord Saul answered, giving his wife a heated look.

"As you wish," said Lord Arundel. "Lady Edith?"

The castle falconer went to beat the bushes in the nearby forest to scare up the game as Lady Edith rode a short distance from the group and took the plumed, leather hood from her goshawk. With a whistle from Lady Edith, the bird took flight and began to circle. Soaring in the sky, it was a thing of beauty, and Iselda could almost understand the appeal of the sport. Then the falconer made a call from the nearby bushes, and the goshawk dove. It disappeared from view for a short while then reappeared with something bloody and feathered in its talons, making a gift of its prey to Lady Edith.

After giving her goshawk a bit of meat, she handed off the bloody game bird to a servant and replaced the goshawk's hood. Much to Iselda's chagrin, Lady Edith retreated to her side as her husband took a turn.

"I like a man who can hunt," said Lady Edith, confidentially. "Is there anything more appealing than watching a man conquer nature and kill prey for you? The deadlier the hunter, the better, as far as I'm concerned. A man who can provide meat for his household is a man worth keeping. Does your Lord William like to hunt?"

Iselda thought back to William tenderly binding up a burn on the arm of a young farmer's wife earlier in the day. Thank heavens she had married a healer, not a hunter!

"I'm sure he does. Don't all men?" Lady Edith said before

Iselda could reply. "It's such a primal instinct. Oh, look! It's his turn. Your man has rather nice arms, doesn't he? If I was ten years younger…"

Iselda's lips pursed into a thin line as she followed Lady Edith's gaze. William looked so confident as he sent his red-tailed hawk soaring into the sky. She'd never seen him hunt before. Somehow, she had expected him to be as awkward and reluctant about it as she was, but instead, he was a natural, utterly at ease as he chatted casually with his father while the hawk circled.

What did Iselda truly know about her husband? She'd met him as a physician and a monk, and now he seemed to have transformed into someone else entirely. This was who he'd been before he joined the Hospitallers, a handsome young lord at ease with the casual deference everyone showed, attracting the eyes of every lady in the vicinity. What would such a man see in her?

Her merlin seemed to sense her unease, shifting from leg to leg on her hand and turning its head. Lady Edith continued to ramble on by her side, but Iselda barely heard her as she struggled to stave off a sudden wave of self-doubt. She was invisible Iselda again who no one wanted to kiss, the awkward and shy girl always living in the shadow of her bolder siblings. William, the physician, was someone she was safe with, cherished by, but this man before her? What did they have in common? He was a stranger, and a danger to her heart.

William's hawk returned with a hare, and he accepted the bloody gift as if it was his due before handing it off to a servant. Then he turned to her, and the full weight of his smoldering gaze fell on her. She swallowed, her throat suddenly dry. How had she convinced herself she could hold such a man's interest?

His brow furrowed as he looked at her, and he rode to her side. "Are you all right, sweeting? You look rather pale."

Suddenly, he was her William again. The stranger disappeared and was replaced by her attentive husband. But which man was an illusion? Which was the true William?

She shook herself, trying to shed the sliver of unease that

entered her heart. The merlin ruffled its feathers and rearranged itself on her hand. "It's nothing. I don't know what's come over me."

"Do you need to return to the castle? Lord knows I wouldn't mind an excuse to cut this short."

It was sweet of him to pretend, but she wouldn't deprive him of his fun just because she was feeling uncomfortable. "No, thank you. I'll be fine."

"Well then it's your turn, my lady," he said with a gallant sweep of his arm.

Iselda squared her shoulders and rode out to an open space. Carefully, she lifted the leather hood that covered the merlin's eyes. It gave her a dubious look before turning away. It seemed this bird didn't trust her any more than she trusted it. She whistled to the merlin which clutched her leather glove with its talons and took off. With a sigh of relief, Iselda lowered her hand and looked up.

Higher and higher it flew until it was hardly visible in the gray, winter sky. It was foolish to hope it wouldn't catch anything, but she didn't particularly want to be presented with a bloody animal carcass.

Think of Carenza, she told herself as she stretched her arm, freed of the bird's weight, at least, for the moment.

The falconer sounded his signal, and the bird plummeted. It would have been a majestic sight if she didn't know what came at the end of it. She wasn't squeamish. In her work as a healer, she saw bloody wounds with some regularity. But it bothered her to intentionally inflict injury on a living creature.

Too soon, the merlin returned with two baby rabbits in its talons. Iselda winced as she saw what it was carrying. Jesus wept! Did it have to be *babies*?

As soon as the tiny creatures had been taken away, William was by her side. "I think that's enough for today. You are too tenderhearted for this sport." Turning to his parents, he said, "I'm taking Lady Iselda back to the castle. She's feeling unwell."

Lady Maud pursed her lips and narrowed her eyes but said nothing.

Lord Arundel shrugged and said, "We'll see you at dinner."

"It was a pleasure, Lord Saul and Lady Edith. We shall see you anon," William said with a bow of his head to the guests. They both handed off their birds to servants.

She turned to leave, trying to look regretful when she felt anything but.

As soon as they were out of earshot, he turned to her and asked, "You obviously hated that. Why ever did you agree to go?"

"It's my duty, especially after her agreement to give us the morning to ourselves," she said, looking resolutely ahead.

"You don't have a duty to make yourself miserable."

"I'm alone here. The only friend I have is you. I cannot refuse a perfectly reasonable request for my attendance on an outing, no matter how much I may dislike it."

He thought all the rules could be bent, that she would be given the same leeway he had always received. But he was a man, his father's firstborn son, and this was his home. He didn't understand what it was like to be a woman in a strange place, under constant scrutiny by her in-laws and the entire town. How could he?

"I knew when I came here that my life would be different. I need some time to adjust. That's all," she said to herself as much as William.

"I'll have a talk with Mother. There won't be any more hunting for you, I promise."

"No, please don't," she said quickly. "The last thing I want is to give your mother another reason to think me weak."

He halted so that he could look her in the eye, and she signaled her horse to stop. "You are anything but weak, love, as anyone would know who has seen you in action as a healer. I know my mother is difficult, but you can't let her bully you like this."

He had a point. She might gain more respect from Lady

Maud if she stood up to her more. "Please don't speak to your mother. I promise to do so myself. I will let her know that I don't wish to be included in future hunting expeditions."

"Are you certain?"

"I'm certain."

She smiled, quelling the butterflies in her stomach at the thought of having such a conversation with her mother-in-law.

He smiled, and it was a balm to her weary heart. "Have I told you how much I love you today?"

Her smile widened. "Yes, but you are welcome to tell me again."

His murmured words of love as they made their way back almost succeeded in distracting her from the growing unease she had in her new life.

CHAPTER TWENTY-TWO

WILLIAM WAS ON his way to the kitchen to steal some sweets before dinner when he ran into his father, who beckoned him over. It had been a month since Iselda had had her little talk with his mother. She had resolutely refused to tell him what was said, but since then, things had improved, at least marginally. But his parents' demands on their time remained unrelenting. As he walked over to his father, he wondered what new form of torture he was about to be subjected to.

"Are you ready for our trip to London?" his father asked him.

"What trip?"

"The one we're leaving for tomorrow to attend the king's tournament. Michael is competing."

Come to think of it, his father had mentioned something about this. He'd just forgotten.

"It's an important opportunity to curry favor with the crown. This meeting isn't only important for Arundel but Winchelsea as well. They need the king's support to resist the Church's attempts to encroach on their lands."

"I understand, Father, but we just got back from visiting Bournemouth. Must we embark on another journey so quickly? I've hardly seen my wife this week." He was going to lose this argument, he knew, but he was obliged to try.

"Don't worry. She'll be coming with us. We want the king to

meet the future countess."

Oh no. Iselda is going to hate this.

"Iselda's mother was a lady of the court before she married Lord Martin," his father added. "I'm sure he'll want to reminisce with Iselda about old times."

William closed his eyes and took a deep breath. Was it worth arguing with his father? No, it was not. There was no avoiding a visit to the king. "I'll let Iselda know. When are we leaving?"

"Tomorrow morning at dawn. The journey should take us four days."

William nodded and left without another word. What was there to say?

He found Iselda in their room, seated at his old desk, which he'd had a servant drag up from the cellar. She was answering correspondence. "Has anyone told you about the proposed trip to London?"

She turned to him with a little frown and a furrowed brow. "You're going away again?"

"We both are."

"We both…why?"

He put a hand on her shoulder and sighed. "To meet the king, apparently."

Sitting up straight, she stared at him. "King Henry?"

"He's sponsoring a tournament that Michael plans to compete in."

She shuddered. "I hate tournaments. So many unnecessary injuries."

"I couldn't agree more, but my father is adamant. Apparently, he thinks the king will want to reminisce about the days when your mother was a courtier."

"That's absurd. My mother was a lady-in-waiting for Queen Eleanor, and everyone knows the king has locked his wife away. I hardly think he'll want to be reminded of the past."

Yes, she was taking this about as well as he expected.

"I'm sorry, sweeting, but we have to go. My father is right.

We can't pass up an opportunity to be introduced. It's too important to Arundel and Winchelsea."

She nodded sadly. "I suppose it can't be avoided. I'll go speak with Rosamunda about packing."

⇒⟫⟩✕⟨⟪⟸

FOUR DAYS LATER, Iselda's hands were shaking as they stepped down from their coach at the tournament grounds. William wished he could spare her this agonizing day, but it was too late. And his father was right. This was a part of their responsibilities as the future baron and baroness. They couldn't avoid it without creating problems for their families.

It was beginning to fully sink in how much his life had changed with marriage. Before they'd wed, he imagined they would carry on much as they had before but with each other for company. He'd expected to practice medicine and maintain ties to the hospital in Winchelsea, and he thought she would be able to keep doing visits to her patients, though perhaps less frequently. When it became clear they were moving to Arundel, he'd thought he would be able to maintain autonomy for themselves so that they could practice their vocation. He'd been full of enthusiasm for the idea of building a new hospital.

After spending two weeks with his father, though, he was realizing how foolish his expectations had been. Neither here nor in Winchelsea would it have been possible for them to live as before. They were political figures now. Their responsibility to lead was irrefutable. He'd seen firsthand exactly how much his father had to shoulder. Michael had been of no help. It fell to William, as the eldest and heir, to see to the needs of the town.

They made their way past the stalls of vendors selling their wares. The tournament participants were to wear red and yellow. There were ribbons, flowers, hats, and flags for sale in those colors. He and Iselda were already dressed in red to show their support for Michael. There were vendors selling food as well—ham sandwiches, pork pies, sausages, sweet treats—and wine flowed freely from every stall.

The wooden palisades of the tournament grounds came into view with billowing banners with the king's coat of arms. Knights and their horses were milling about, making final preparations for the day's events. Squires ran back and forth carrying out their assigned tasks and attempting to stay out from underfoot.

Iselda's shaking grew more pronounced as they approached the central platform where King Henry II was holding court. Ignoring the glares from his parents, he pulled her aside. "It's going to be fine," he said, pulling her into a hug and kissing her forehead. "We practiced. You know what to say."

"Yes, I know what to say," she said, her voice trembling slightly. "Let's get this over with. I don't want to prolong things."

"Take a deep breath." She complied. "And another. I love you no matter what, and tonight I'm going to make love to you until you forget everything that happened today, good, or bad."

"William!" Ah, there was that fighting face he loved so much.

"Pretend he's one of your patients. Imagine he's covered with itchy purple spots, and your job is to put him at ease."

She laughed, and some of the tension leached out of her as he held her.

"Are you ready?"

She took another deep breath and nodded.

They returned to his parents who gave him another disapproving look before leading them up to the dais. The king had the solid build of an active man, even though white streaked his reddish blond hair. He was wearing a full-length robe of red brocade embroidered with yellow and gold. Though he was not wearing his crown, power and authority radiated from the man. He needed no outward trappings to indicate that he had the divine right to rule.

"Your Majesty," his father said with a deep bow. They all followed suit. Iselda curtsied deeply and gracefully, with no hint of fear or awkwardness.

"Harold! What a pleasant surprise. I thought you were still in Winchelsea. I take it your son is competing today?"

"He is indeed," said his father, beaming.

"My son, John, is too," said the king with a frown. "I'd rather he didn't. I think he's too young, but I didn't feel right forbidding it. How old was Michael when he started?"

His father shook his head. "Too young. My heart was in my throat every time he entered the lists. But he proved my fears baseless. I've lost count of how many tournaments he's been in, and he has yet to suffer any serious injuries, thanks be to God."

"Thanks indeed, and may He continue to be merciful toward you and your family. Who is this you've brought with you? There seems to be a family resemblance, if I'm not mistaken."

His father smiled broadly. "This is my oldest son, William, recently returned from nine years abroad. And beside him is his new bride, Iselda. She is the youngest daughter of Lord Martin de Vere. Her oldest sister is married to Daniel, Earl of Winchelsea, whose troubadour verse you find so entertaining."

The king perked up upon hearing the word "troubadour." "Yes, I heard about the earl from my friend, Lord Giraut. He sang me a fascinating song by him that was all woodworking meta- phors. *Joining tongue to groove, my words a perfect fit, I smooth and then improve each verse with whetted wit.*' I quite liked that phrase. He also sang me one about a peach that I don't think I should quote in present company. I hear his wife is quite talented as well. Perhaps it runs in the family?"

He looked straight at Iselda, and William saw her subtly tense. "Your Majesty," she said in a remarkably even voice. "I-I'm afraid I do not share my sister's talent, but I certainly share her good wishes toward you. Perhaps they might visit so that you could hear their verse yourself?"

"I would be delighted to see them," he said.

"I will be sure to let them know," she said with a curtsy.

"And you," he said, turning to William. "I don't believe we've met before. I don't recall your face. It's rather surprising, given what a friend to the crown your father has been."

"I met you on several occasions, but I was a child at the time. I've been away for the last nine years." William decided not to mention the Hospitallers. It was too much to explain.

"I see. Well, I'm sure your father is glad to have you back. It seems you've made a fine alliance through marriage. I look forward to seeing more of you."

"And I you, Your Majesty," William said with a bow.

"It was good of you to stop by, Harold," the king said. "Perhaps I'll see you again before the tournament ends. Good luck to Michael!"

"Thank you, Your Majesty."

Everyone bowed and curtsied, and they took their leave.

As soon as they were out of sight, Iselda grasped his arm tightly. "Did I say the right thing? I stuttered, but only a little, I think. Did I sound nervous? I was so anxious, I thought I might pass out."

"Shh. You did very well, sweeting," he said, taking her in his arms. "You barely even looked nervous."

"Really?" she asked, looking up at him with those big, beautiful, brown eyes. "I wish we could go home now instead of sitting through the tournament."

"I know, but we have to stay for Michael."

"I know." Her shoulders slumped in resignation.

"Let's go get some food and wine. That should distract us from this mockery of warfare for a few more minutes."

He led her over to the stalls where they bought an assortment of dried fruit, some nuts, a small loaf of hard brown bread, and some chunks of soft white cheese. They also bought a wine skin to take back to the family for sharing. By the time they found their seats in the stands, the jousting had already started.

As he watched, he couldn't help thinking of all the lance injuries he'd seen in the Holy Land and in Spain. Bruises and broken bones were the least of it. He'd once seen a man decapitated by a lance. It struck him in the neck just so, finding a chink in his armor. Before William saw it, he didn't know that was possible. Now, sitting at the tournament, all he could think of was his brother lying dead from a lance through the neck. He shivered despite the heat.

"Are you all right?" Iselda whispered.

He shook himself and nodded. "I don't like tournaments. It's bad enough that men go to war. Must they also play at it in their leisure time?"

"I couldn't agree more," Iselda said. "I can hardly watch. When I was a girl, I saw a man impaled in the shoulder during a joust. I've avoided tournaments ever since."

He squeezed her hand. "Do you need distraction?"

"Yes, please."

"So do I. Tell me about something in Galen you disagree with."

"Other than bloodletting?" she asked with a hint of a smile.

"Yes, let's steer clear of blood for the moment. There must be some herbal remedy we can argue about."

She looked at the sky in thought for a moment as hooves thundered and a loud crack sounded. The crowd roared in cheering, and he kept his eyes carefully averted. "Galen says mint is useful for preventing conception, and I can assure you it is not. I've known many women that eat mint leaves daily to freshen their breath and get pregnant as often as those who don't."

"It isn't fair to choose an example having to do with reproduction. You know my knowledge can't compete with yours in that area." He watched her smile grow at the compliment.

"He also says radishes help with hair loss. I've known many a man who took Galen's word for gospel and ate radishes every day attempting to recover their head of hair. Not one succeeded in even slowing the pace of their balding."

William laughed. "I'll grant you that anyone claiming a hair loss remedy is selling a dream to the unwary. As hair loss remedies go, radishes are relatively harmless, though. Perhaps he suggested them as a cure to steer gullible men clear of more dangerous options. I've heard of remedies ranging from bear fat to pigeon droppings. I think Galen, in his infinite wisdom, put forward a harmless placebo to placate vain men."

Rumble rumble rumble crack! went the knights on their horses as he steadily kept his gaze on Iselda. She flinched at the crack sound, and he realized he had done the same. The audience erupted in applause once again.

"Let's never do this again," she said in his ear.

"I wish I could make that promise, sweeting," he said, enjoying the excuse to tickle her ear with his lips. "This is the fourth tournament I've been obliged to attend since we came back. It's an important place to meet with other nobles and transact business, or I would have refused. I promise to keep you out of it as much as possible. But when the king is in attendance…"

"I know," she said, looking him in the eyes.

"All right, you two lovebirds," his mother interrupted. "It's time to turn around and watch. Michael is up. It looks like he's jousting with the king's son, John."

They turned reluctantly to see Michael in position on the right and a slim youth who looked barely strong enough to hold a lance on the left. And yet John's form was perfect as he lowered his lance into position to face Michael.

As the starting flag dropped, they charged. The horses galloped at each other with alarming speed. Then *crack!*

Oh no. Something was wrong. Michael didn't fall cleanly from the saddle. The horse dragged him some distance before he came loose.

Meanwhile, John was bleeding heavily from his shoulder.

The referee called for the physician on duty who staggered onto the field, obviously drunk. Without thinking about what he was doing, William tore through the crowd in the bleachers, Iselda following close behind. They ran around the palisades to enter the field and reach the two injured men. They reached Michael first. He was groaning in pain but was at least conscious.

"I'll be right back," William told his brother. "John is badly injured."

His brother nodded.

William and Iselda went running to John and shooed off the drunk doctor. Taking off John's armor as he groaned, William examined the wound. It was in the soft tissue and muscle right below the shoulder. Thankfully, it missed anything vital.

The referee came over and asked them to clear the field. Two men came with a stretcher and carried John off to a tent. They found Michael there too, awaiting treatment.

Iselda opened her bag and offered him tweezers to remove the splinters of wood still lodged in the wound.

As William removed splinters from John, Iselda went over to Michael. A few minutes later, she returned to his side. "Michael has a dislocated hip," she said quietly. "I think you had better set it. He's likely to struggle, and I'm not strong enough to hold him still."

Nodding, William removed the last of the splinters from John's shoulder. Iselda produced a needle and thread. *God bless Iselda.* Taking great care, he stitched up John's wound and then applied lavender oil and honey, also from Iselda's bag, and accepted a bandage from her to bind up the wound.

She disappeared for several minutes and came back with two steaming mugs. "It's an infusion of white willow bark for the pain." She gave one to John and the other to Michael.

"Thank you," John said, his voice strained but steadier than it had been. "I'm glad you were here and didn't let that drunk treat me."

"Of course, my lord," William said. "I must tend to my brother now."

Enlisting the aid of a nearby knight to hold Michael still, William maneuvered Michael's leg to the proper position, ignoring his screams, and popped the joint back into place. Immediately, the screams stopped.

"I feel better," Michael said in an awed voice. "I was so scared

I would never walk again, but you fixed me. You're a miracle worker, brother."

"You're not all the way fixed yet. It will take several months for you to recover. You'll need to take it very easy on that leg while it heals. I'm afraid this tournament is over for you, and you shouldn't ride a horse again until you are fully healed."

Iselda handed him a steaming cup. "Drink this. It will help with the pain."

Michael nodded and drank obediently.

At that moment, the king strode into the tent, and William and Iselda bowed. Michael bowed his head, the most he could manage for the moment.

"John, are you all right?"

"Yes, thanks to this physician. He cleaned the wound and stitched and bandaged me," he said, gesturing toward William.

"It's a mere shoulder wound, Your Majesty," William added. "He should make a full recovery in a matter of months."

The king turned and looked at him. "William, isn't it?"

William nodded.

"You have my eternal gratitude for this. I had no idea you were such a skilled physician."

Smiling, William said, "I spent the last nine years learning from the Hospitallers. I've treated more than my fair share of battlefield injuries in my time. Your son will be fine. But I don't deserve all the credit. My wife is a skilled healer as well, and it was thanks to her preparation that I had everything I needed at hand to help him."

She dipped into a deep curtsy and said, "I believe in being prepared, Your Majesty. I packed my bag with the necessary supplies for wound treatment before we left for the tournament."

William beamed at her. What a clever woman he'd married!

"You both have my profound thanks for what you did today. I will not forget it," the king said, helping John rise. "Harold," he said, as William's father rushed into the tent. "You must be very proud of William. He treated my son's wound most admirably, and your daughter-in-law helped," he said.

Bowing, William's father said, "Your Majesty, I am your humble servant. I am glad to hear that William has been able to assist your family."

"I must get John to a place where he can rest. I bid you farewell. You have my deepest gratitude."

Everyone bowed and curtsied as the king and John left the tent.

"Perhaps your medical skills have their uses after all," his father said, giving William and Iselda an assessing look.

"Does this mean you'll support my proposal to build a hospital in Arundel?"

"Don't push it," his father replied. "Let's get Michael home. I think we're done here."

William gritted his teeth. What would it take to convince his father to relent if even saving the king's brother wasn't enough? One way or another, he was determined to get his way on this, whatever it took.

CHAPTER TWENTY-THREE

THE EARL FROM Portsmouth and his wife just left, and Iselda was exhausted. After two months in Arundel, being a proper lady and spending her days making visits, attending events, entertaining, and managing the household, she felt like she could sleep for a week. It didn't help that her monthlies were three days late. She'd started to feel twinges of nausea, but she wasn't sure if she was imagining things. If possible, she wanted to wait until seven days had passed before saying anything to anyone. She'd seen enough women get excited over nothing in her work that she didn't want to get everyone's hopes up.

The only bright spot in the last month of drudgery was William. He'd been relentless in his pursuit of two things: a hospital for Arundel and her. Given the frantic pace of her social schedule, she was starting to pin her hopes on the hospital too. It would be a way for her to engage with medicine without having to make patient visits in the field, an impossibility with her mother-in-law watching her like a hawk. As for William's pursuit of her, she'd been all too happy to oblige. She lived for the evening hours after dinner when they were alone together, and he would make her body soar.

Of course, all that lovemaking had consequences. Everyone wanted them to have babies, herself included, but it was so soon. It would have been nice to have a few more months with William before their family grew.

She retired to her room to change for dinner and was met by a maid whose name was escaping her. "Where's Rosamunda?"

"I'm afraid she twisted her ankle, my lady. She can't make it upstairs to tend to you and asked me to take her place." The woman kept her eyes down as she curtsied.

"Oh dear! I'll have to go check on her. I hope she's staying off the ankle and keeping it elevated. I should check for a break. Can you take me to her?"

The woman looked startled and confused. "As you wish my lady, but you needn't trouble yourself over a servant's health. We can take care of her needs."

"Of course, I'm going to trouble myself. I'm a healer, and she's the only friend from home I have in this place. It's my duty to see to her." She couldn't let Rosamunda go through this alone.

"As you wish, my lady, but perhaps first you should change for dinner? I can help you with your hair. If we're quick, you can see her before you dine." The woman lifted her eyes and the tiniest of smiles appeared on her face. It was a beautiful face, if somewhat melancholy. She had beautiful cheekbones and full, luscious lips. Her womanly curves filled Iselda with envy. But there was a furrow in the woman's brow that appeared to be permanent, and she had dark circles under her eyes. There was a sadness in her expression that made Iselda's heart ache for her.

"Of course," Iselda said after a moment's thought. "Can you remind me of your name?"

"I'm Maribel, my lady."

"Maribel. What a lovely name," Iselda said with a smile, moving to her wardrobe to pick a gown for the evening.

"Thank you, my lady."

Maribel helped her shed the linen gown she was wearing and exchange it for a red satin gown with a low-cut neck and gold trim. She fastened a gold belt with jewels around her hips and let the chain dangle down the front from the clasp. William always liked this dress.

"If you don't mind my asking, my lady, how did you convince William to marry you? We all thought he would never marry. Even before he left, he showed no signs of ever settling down." Maribel was more interested in the question that she was letting on. Iselda was sure of it.

"His mother played a trick on us and threw us together."

"Ah," Maribel said with a little laugh. "That explains it."

"But the trick didn't work. We ended up falling in love despite his mother's machinations."

Something in Maribel's face closed. Iselda couldn't put a finger on it. Outwardly, her expression remained the same, but a door shut behind her eyes.

"Love," Maribel mumbled as she began combing out Iselda's hair. "I don't believe in love."

"No?" Iselda prompted, hoping to hear more.

"No." Maribel said no more as she pinned up Iselda's tresses.

Suddenly, there was a commotion outside the door, and a servant girl, aged eight or nine, came running in.

"Mama, mama," the girl said, hiding behind her mother. "Ronald is chasing me with a poker again."

Maribel put the last pin in Iselda's hair and turned to her daughter. "Posy, you know better than to interrupt me when I'm working as a lady's maid. My sincere apologies, my lady," she said to Iselda. "I'll get her out of your way."

At that moment, William came in and stopped short. He and Maribel locked eyes, just as they had that first night in Arundel. It was the same woman, Iselda was sure of it. What was between them? They were acting almost like guilty lovers, even though that wasn't possible. Or was it? Was there something between them in the years before he'd left? An unwanted spear of jealousy pierced her. She dug her nails into the palms of her hands trying to wish it away.

William's eyes traveled to the little girl and widened. He blinked several times and shook himself. "My apologies for interrupting. I was about to change for dinner."

"We're done," said Iselda, trying to keep her voice even. "Maribel was about to take me to see Rosamunda. I'm told she twisted her ankle and can't make it upstairs."

William nodded and swallowed, still with a guilty look on his face that he was obviously trying to disguise.

Maribel gave him a warning look and said, "Come, my lady. I'll show you the way."

As soon as they were out the door, Maribel paused and whispered a few words in her daughter's ear. Her daughter's shoulders slumped, and she curtsied grudgingly. "I'm sorry, my lady, for interrupting. It won't happen again," little Posy said to the floor.

Iselda bent down so that her eyes were level with Posy's. "Don't you worry about it. Now be good and listen to your mama." Posy smiled, and Iselda stopped breathing. She knew that smile. And those eyes. Oh God, she knew those eyes.

Posy curtsied again and hurried away. Iselda stood up, trying to convince herself she was mistaken.

"I apologize again, my lady. She's cheeky, like her father."

"Her father?" Iselda asked as lightly as she could.

"I was married to a miller. He died three years ago," Maribel said without looking at Iselda. "His son by his first wife inherited, so I entered service here. It keeps us fed and a roof over our heads."

Maribel led Iselda through one hallway after another, then down two flights of stairs. "Here she is, my lady," Maribel said at last.

During her visit with Rosamunda, Iselda could hardly keep her mind on what she was doing. Her thoughts wandered as she examined Rosamunda's ankle. Fortunately, it was a sprain, not a break, so she prescribed rest and elevation to bring down the swelling and made her excuses as quickly as she could.

Did William know he had a daughter? Was he hiding it from her? He definitely recognized Maribel, and he hadn't said a word. Before they were married, he admitted he slept around in his youth, and he mentioned a woman who got pregnant and died of complications. He never mentioned other children, though.

It wasn't so much the existence of children that troubled her but the fact that he was hiding things from her. When he first saw Maribel, why didn't he admit they had a history so that she didn't have to find out by accident? And why didn't he admit he had at least one child already? Were there more?

And then there was Maribel herself. Iselda didn't like to think of herself as the jealous type, but the woman was gorgeous—with a beauty entirely different from her own. The guilt in William's eyes worried her. Clearly, they had a history, but was some ember of their passion still alive? Why else would he avoid speaking to her about it?

Then another thought struck her. What did his parents know? Did they bring her here knowing full well what she would be confronted with?

She'd never been so lonely in her life. There was no one to talk to about this. No one at all. She needed a friend, someone like the healers she'd worked with in Winchelsea who would listen and speak their minds.

Yes, that's exactly what I need, and I have an excuse to speak with one.

She had every reason to speak with a midwife, perhaps more than one. She could find someone she trusted not only as a midwife but as a confidante.

It was time for dinner, and she rushed to the great hall, arriving just in time to take William's arm and let him lead her in. "You look beautiful, sweeting," he said for her ears alone.

"We need to talk," she murmured in return. "But not now."

He gave her a concerned look as they took their seats.

After grace and passing around food, Lord Arundel said, "My dear, can you help me talk our son out of this preposterous proposal to build a hospital here in Arundel? He persists in pushing for it despite my warnings that it would be costly and impractical."

"Oh dear," Lady Maud said. "You aren't still going on about

that are you, William? You must see what a waste it would be, and I'm not very warmly inclined toward the Hospitallers after they stole you for nine years. You should listen to your father and give it up."

William took a tense breath in and out. "It would be good for the town's prosperity. We already have our fair share of travelers coming to town and spending their coin at our shops and taverns on their way to the nearby ports. This would only increase it. We could become a center of medical learning, perhaps start a university of medicine—"

"A university? Have you lost your mind?" Lord Arundel said. "You have enough responsibilities here at home without these foolish dreams about impractical projects."

Iselda could hear William's teeth grinding. "Foolish dreams? Impractical projects? I've built five hospitals from the ground up, and every one of them has benefited the towns where they were built. The only foolishness here is your pigheaded grudge against the Hospitallers. What I'm proposing would benefit everyone in Arundel."

"Don't you disrespect your father like that," his mother said in a voice that could freeze sunshine.

"I've had enough of both of you," William shot back. "If you can't see sense, I'm taking Iselda back to Winchelsea. You can't cut us off from our life's work and expect us to stay."

Lord Arundel and Lady Maud recoiled as if his words were a physical blow. "Well now, perhaps we've been rash," said Lady Maud, gesturing furiously at her husband. "If it means that much to you, of course we can discuss it."

Lord Arundel cleared his throat. "Yes, of course."

"I don't want to discuss it. I want to take steps to make it happen. I have explained the costs and benefits in agonizing detail. I have talked you through every step of the process, Father. There can't possibly be anything further to discuss."

If Iselda wasn't so upset with him, she would have been entertained to see his argumentative tendencies turned on someone else. For better or worse, she had married a highly tenacious and stubborn man, both characteristics she admired.

"Are you saying that if you get your hospital, you'll commit to staying permanently? We won't have to worry about your changing your mind and moving away?"

William turned to Iselda then looked at his mother. "I need to talk it through with my wife, but yes, that is what I will offer if she agrees."

Oh no. Did it all depend on her now? Why would he put her in that position? There was only one answer. She couldn't deny him now that he had publicly offered. But she was in no mood to give him anything right now, even if the conclusion was foregone. "We'll tell you tomorrow," she said.

"You gave me tournament grounds. I don't see why you can't give him a hospital, which is much more useful for the town, especially after what he did for me and Prince John," Michael said.

Everyone turned toward him.

"Well, it's true," Michael continued. "You built me tournament grounds without demanding anything in return. Why can't you give him what he wants without strings attached?"

For the first time ever, Iselda wanted to hug Michael.

"This is different," said Lord Arundel. "You didn't abandon us for nine years then come back making demands."

"And I'm not the heir. For Christ's sake, give him what he wants before he moves to the Holy Land again. He deserves it, and God knows I don't want to be the next earl."

No one had anything to say to that, so they ate. And then all too quickly, dinner was over, and Iselda was alone with William as the family departed the great hall.

"I'm sorry for putting you on the spot that way," William said, taking her hand. "If you don't want to agree, I'll tell them I changed my mind."

She couldn't care less about that at that moment. Without preamble, she asked, "Did you know you had a daughter? Were you hiding it from me?"

"What?" He stopped dead.

A servant came in to clear away the meal.

"Let's go to our room," she said, nodding toward the servant. "We'll discuss it there."

She could feel the panic radiating from him as they walked in silence. When they got to the room and the door closed behind them, he immediately turned to her.

"I swear I didn't know. In fact, you might have known before me. I didn't know until I saw the girl this evening. I didn't keep anything from you. I promise."

Against her better judgment, she trusted his word. "Could there be others?"

He sat down on the bed and put his head in his hands. "I don't know. It's possible."

"Probable?" She asked, stepping closer.

"Fine, yes, probable." He squeezed his eyes shut and pressed them with the heels of his hands.

"In the castle?"

"Yes, some of the women I slept with worked in the castle. I thought they all left. I doubt any others are still here besides Maribel, but there are siblings and parents that still work here who remember. I'm sorry I didn't warn you. I know this isn't what you want to hear, but I was trying to spare you."

A wave of nausea swept through her. She ran to the chamber pot and vomited.

"Are you sick?" He came running to her.

She shook him off. "No, just pregnant," she said before her brain caught up with her mouth.

He sat down hard on the floor. "Pregnant?"

She heaved again. Her head throbbed. "Yes. I didn't plan to tell you this way. I planned to wait a few more days to be sure, but...well..."

William sat in the middle of the floor looking like someone hit him in the head with a brick. Had she broken him with her news? With everything else happening, it wasn't an ideal evening to tell him something life changing. *And yet,* she thought, *if I have to cope with it all at once, why shouldn't he?*

A moment later, she found herself in the air. William had scooped her up and carried her to the bed.

"What in heaven's name are you doing? I can still walk, you know. And we aren't done with our conversation about your daughter."

Ignoring her, he put her down gently on the bed and took off her shoes. He helped her take off her dress and tucked her beneath the covers. "William, I'm not an invalid."

Still ignoring her, he began to head for the door.

"Where are you going?"

"Don't move a muscle, sweeting. I'm going to get you mint tea and ginger cakes," he said, still very much in a daze. And with that, he disappeared.

Clenching her fists beneath the blankets, she tried to figure out what she was going to do with him. Clearly, her news had knocked all sense out of his head. The conversation they were having was completely lost in his newfound daze.

He had to do something about his daughter now that he knew about her. It wasn't right for her to be a servant in the castle where her father was lord. And what if there were others? Perhaps a midwife would know? With a potential heir on the way, he couldn't recognize them as his own, but he could at least make sure they were well cared for.

She sighed and turned on her side. How had her life turned upside down so quickly? A month ago, she was in Winchelsea with a family who loved her, a husband who adored her, and work she cared about. Now she'd lost her work and family, and her husband was hiding things from her. It didn't seem possible that things could go so wrong so quickly. She was still desperately in love with William, but for tonight she needed some space.

Closing her eyes, she let herself drift off to sleep, hoping her anger and frustration would ebb by morning.

CHAPTER TWENTY-FOUR

WILLIAM WAS FRANTIC as he badgered the cook into baking cakes and brewing a mint concoction he described. Iselda was pregnant. All those fears he'd pushed away came roaring back. If someone had threatened her with a knife, he couldn't be more anxious for her safety. So many things could go wrong in childbirth. And before the birth too. His stomach churned at the thought, and he took it out on the poor cook, badgering her to rush when he knew full well baking took time.

He was going to be a father. No. He already was a father. Iselda was furious and rightly so. What a way to find out. He'd been honest with her before the wedding, but being confronted with the reality in such stark terms was something else entirely. "Were there others?" she asked. Probably. How would he find out, though? He didn't think a grand tour of his past conquests would sit well with Iselda, or with him for that matter. Not to mention that they probably didn't want to see him any more than he wanted to see them.

"How much longer?" he asked the cook for the fourth time.

She gave him a look. "Let me get you some wine, my lord. You look like you need it."

He didn't argue.

She poured wine into a tankard instead of a goblet, and a bit of it sloshed on the table as she set it down in front of him. "Now, my lord, would you like to tell me why I'm up baking ginger cakes at this hour?"

"I just found out my wife is pregnant. Her stomach is upset. Evidence shows that ginger cakes help."

"Ah," said the cook, pouring herself a modest amount of wine in a goblet. "Congratulations, my lord," she said, raising her cup.

"Congratulations? Do you know how many ways she could die? Women die in childbirth all the time, and some of them don't even make it that far."

The cook looked him in the eye and raised her brow. "Women die of lots of things. Childbirth is only one of the many dangers she faces in a perilous world."

"Yes, but it's a danger that's my fault. How could I live with myself if the child I put inside her was the cause of her demise? I impregnated her with my irresponsible lusts."

The cook rolled her eyes and got up to tend to the boiling mint concoction in a cauldron in the hearth.

"Wouldn't be the first time," she mumbled just loud enough for him to hear.

The words hit him like a blow. This cook, whose name he didn't remember, already knew about his youthful misdeeds.

"What is your name, good woman?" he asked, his emotions running too high for him to address what he'd heard her say.

"Gilda," she answered. "I've been working in these kitchens for thirty years, my lord. My whole family works here in the castle. Except my niece, Daisy. She married a nice farmer and moved to the countryside with him. I believe you and she were acquainted?"

Daisy. Oh no. Does that mean she…? Blood drained from his face, and he took a long, deep drink from his tankard. Then he screwed up his courage to ask the thing he didn't want to ask, but for which he desperately needed the answer. "Mistress Gilda, I was reprehensible in my youth. I make no excuses. I know that I wronged Daisy, but by any chance, did I…did she…? Was there a child?"

"Are you pretending you don't know, my lord?" she asked, poking at the oven to check on the ginger cakes. "Whenever you or your brother gets someone in trouble," she continued, "your parents have the steward find them a husband out of town and offer a generous dowry." She looked him in the eye. "I can see what you're thinking plain as day. Don't you go poking where you're not wanted, my lord. The farmer gave her and her son his good name, and you'll do neither of them any favors if you try to interfere."

"But—"

"Leave them alone. You hear me? You've done enough damage already. They're respectable now. Let them stay that way."

He nodded slowly. "I spent nine years as a monk in penance. I won't interfere where I'm not wanted." Though he was going to have a talk with his mother. How could she?

"You just focus on the wife you have, and don't you stray from her."

"I wouldn't." Seeing her look, he said it again. "I really wouldn't. She's everything to me. And now she's…she's…" He paused and took a long drink. "She's pregnant."

"Your wife knows my name at least," Gilda said, ignoring his distress. "Very nice woman you married. Smart too. She gave me a salve for my bunions that worked wonders."

Yes, Iselda was nice and smart and bothered to learn people's names. It was all too perfect to last. He picked up his tankard to take a drink only to find it empty.

"Your ginger cakes are ready," Gilda said, pulling a tray out of the oven and easing the cakes onto a plate. "And here's your brew, though I can't say it smells too appetizing," she said pouring the cauldron's contents into a teapot. She put everything on a tray and called in the hall for a servant to carry it up.

"I can carry it up myself," William insisted.

"Yes, you could, but it would be an insult to those of us hired to make the castle run. Let us do our jobs, my lord."

Acquiescing to the inevitable, he made his way upstairs with a young boy trailing after with the tray. When they reached his door, he took the tray and eased inside as quietly as possible. Sure enough, Iselda was asleep.

He set the tray down on her dressing table and absently took a ginger cake as he watched her sleep. What a mess he'd made of everything. At least he could make it up to her. He would make sure she didn't have to lift a finger while she was pregnant, and she would have the very best care to be had.

He ate another ginger cake. Tomorrow he would have a talk with his mother. He needed to know how many children he had, and by whom. While he appreciated what Gilda said about not interfering where he was not wanted, he needed to be sure there weren't others like Maribel who had fallen on hard times. He agreed with Iselda. His own daughter shouldn't be cleaning the castle he lived in.

Eating one more ginger cake, which he was determined to make his last, he closed his eyes and let a plan coalesce in his head. The hospital. Yes, that would solve all of his problems. He would set up a wing dedicated to maternal health and hire the very best midwife he could find to run it. Meanwhile, she could also see to Iselda and ensure everything went smoothly. He would establish an apprenticeship program so that any of his children who wished could learn medicine. His daughters could learn from Iselda and from the midwife. His sons could learn from him. Their mothers could work for the hospital if they needed employment. It was perfect. It solved everything.

He drifted off in his chair, dreaming of dormitories, examination rooms, and apothecaries.

THE NEXT MORNING, he woke up with a terrible headache and a crick in his neck to the sound of Iselda vomiting. In his rush to her side, he tripped over his own foot and fell hard on the fresh rushes that covered the wood floor, scraping a hole in his breeches and skinning his knee. "Ow," he cried out.

Iselda's head shot up at the sound, and she stared at him. If looks could kill, he would be bleeding to death on the floor. So she hadn't forgiven him. Not that he really expected she would.

He crawled over to her and tried to soothe her by rubbing her back, but she shook him off. "Go clean your knee. You're leaving bloody spots on the floor."

He looked back. Sure enough, he was. This was not an auspicious start to the day.

"I got you ginger cakes. There are three left. And I have a stomach remedy here. It's cold, but it should still work." He poured water into a basin and dipped a rough linen cloth. Then he dabbed at his knee, cleaning the scrape.

"Three *left?*" she asked, her voice dripping with disdain. "How many did you eat?"

"Only three." He stripped off his breeches, bound a cloth around his knee, and put on a new pair.

"*Only* three. I suppose I should be grateful you saved me any at all," she said, shaking her head. She got up and came over to the dressing table for a ginger cake. It took all his self-control not to help himself to one as well.

"I'm sorry, sweeting. I'm sorry for everything. I'll make it up to you. I have a plan. The hospital is the key. The hospital solves everything."

She took a sip of the tepid remedy and made a face, then went running for the chamber pot again.

"In what way does the hospital solve everything?" she asked when she finished retching.

"There will be a midwife and an apprenticeship program, and my children can learn the healing arts, and—"

"Children? So there's more than one?" She was on her knees, curled in a ball, forehead to the floor next to the chamber pot, and it broke his heart.

"I found out about one more last night. I have a son whose family wants nothing to do with me. But maybe, if I could convince him to become my apprentice, I could—"

"If his family wants you to leave him alone, then you should respect their wishes. And from where I stand, the hospital solves nothing except your own boredom. Build a hospital if you want, but don't pretend it's going to magically solve all our woes," she said, still speaking to the floor.

At that moment, there was a knock at the door. "My lady, would you like my assistance this morning?" It was Maribel. *Wonderful.*

He opened the door and slipped into the corridor. "Iselda isn't feeling well this morning. She should return to bed. I'll make her excuses to my mother." He shifted from one foot to the other, unable to meet Maribel's eyes.

"Yes, my lord." She turned to go.

"Maribel, wait," he called after her. "I need to speak with you." He looked up and down the hall to make sure no one was in earshot. "Your daughter," he said quietly, "I'm her father, aren't I?"

Maribel looked at him in silence for a long moment then said, "Yes, but if anyone asks, she was my late husband's. As far as anyone knows, she is legitimate. You will not ruin that for her."

He looked at his feet and nodded. "I understand. I spoke to Iselda. Would Posy like to become her apprentice and learn healing? I don't want to interfere, but I don't feel right relegating her to scrubbing my floors. You either for that matter."

"It's a respectable job, and I'll thank you to stay out of my business. You disappeared for nine years, leaving me to deal with the consequences. Now you're back and think I'm a charity case? I have kept Posy fed and clothed with a roof over her head for eight and a half years without your help. I made sure she had legitimacy in the eyes of the church and law. I'll speak to her about your wife's offer of an apprenticeship. I won't deny her the opportunity to learn useful skills, but I don't want you anywhere near her. You made your choice when you left."

A servant with a pile of firewood came walking down the hall, and they both stood silent until he disappeared into one of the bedrooms.

"I know it doesn't help, but I'm sorry. If I could go back and do things differently, I would. I had no idea you were expecting. If I'd known, I would have…" He trailed off. What could he have done? Marriage was out of the question, especially since she wasn't the only one.

"You would have what?" she asked, eyes narrowed.

"I don't know, but you wouldn't have had to manage on your own."

She was silent for a long moment.

"I need to go see my mother," he said, finally. "Can you stay with Iselda? She shouldn't be alone while she's so unwell."

She nodded and turned toward the door, then paused. "William," she said, dropping formality for a moment. The intimacy of it brought him up short. "Thank you for the apology. It's nine years too late and not nearly enough to compensate for what I've been through, but I appreciate it."

He nodded and turned to go find his mother. Maribel had enough to do without having to further assuage his guilty conscience.

His mother was in the entrance hall, dressed for Mass and tapping her foot.

"William, dear, where's your wife?" she asked as soon as she saw him. "And what's wrong with you? You look like you've seen a ghost."

"Can I speak with you privately, Mother?" he asked, looking around at the servants.

She pursed her lips and headed for the great hall. He followed, closing the door behind them. "What is it, William? More about this hospital of yours?" She sat in the closest chair and patted the one next to it, so he'd sit beside her. Obediently, he lowered himself into it.

"No. Iselda is unwell this morning. She told me it's because she's expecting."

His mother clapped her hands and sighed aloud, triumphantly. "I knew it was only a matter of time. It's a good sign if she's sick. It means it's probably a boy. I couldn't keep anything down for the first few months when I was expecting you and your brother."

Ignoring her ridiculous superstition about the sex of the baby, he said, "I need you to let her rest. I know you've piled her up with a busy social calendar, but I don't want to overtax her."

His mother waved away his concern. "She'll feel right as rain by the afternoon, you wait and see."

"I mean it, Mother. I'm not going to budge on this. Let her rest." Some things could not be negotiated.

"Fine, if you insist. But you hardly need privacy to tell me she's expecting." His mother gestured at the closed door.

"No, but Iselda's pregnancy isn't the only thing I wanted to discuss."

"Oh? Then what else?"

"I'd like to discuss my *other* children." He stared hard, watching her reaction closely.

"Your other children? What other...? Oh." He saw the realization dawn, her face falling. "Is this because of Maribel's girl? I knew I was taking a risk when I agreed to let them work here. I couldn't very well have them out on the streets, though. Who knows what she would have said and to whom if we hadn't made sure she was in our employ?"

Red hot fury made it hard to see straight. "Maribel's girl. Daisy's boy. Were there more, Mother? How could you hide this from me?"

"You're acting like we cast them out into the cold. We made sure they found husbands that could care for them. Unfortunately, Maribel's husband died young, but we couldn't have our flesh and blood begging on a street corner, so we brought them here."

He ran his hands through his hair and groaned. How could she say it so blithely, as if she were discussing the dinner menu or new tapestries?

"There were three, if you must know," she continued. "Carolina had a boy. None of them will thank you for your interference all these years later. You had best leave well enough alone. We did you a favor. Them too. They were lucky we found them husbands, or they would have been far worse off. We pitied them, even if they were shameless harlots."

At that, he stood up and started pacing. "How dare you, Mother! I was the shameless one. How could you hide the consequences of my actions from me like that? Why am I only finding out I'm a father nine years later?"

"Because you ran away," she challenged. "You disappeared."

"Would you have told me?"

"No." The look on her face was fierce and unapologetic.

"Have you done this to Michael?" His voice was low and dangerous. He knew his temper was barely leashed.

"Only once. Conveniently, his current mistress is barren."

"I'm assuming he doesn't know?" He stopped pacing right in front of her and leaned in.

"And you won't tell him." Her eyes flashed fire.

"If you won't, I will." He wanted to throw things, break things, as his mother stood before him, completely unruffled.

"No, you won't. I assume you've spoken to Maribel. Did she want you in her daughter's life? Did speaking with her about it accomplish anything other than causing you both pain?"

Did it? The thought brought him up short. Everyone knew the truth except him, but was he better off knowing? Was anyone better off with him knowing? He took a deep breath.

"That's what I thought," his mother said as he started pacing back and forth.

"Fine, I won't tell him. I still think he should know, but it isn't my place. Just make sure his wife doesn't find out before he does when he marries."

His mother softened. "Is that what happened? Did Iselda see little Posy?"

He nodded, looking down at his hands. Tears prickled behind his eyes, but he held them back.

"Oh, my foolish boy," she said, reaching out and taking his

hand. "You made some mistakes a long time ago, but you're not that man anymore. She'll see that with time. Be a good husband and a good father, and she'll forgive you. She's a sensible girl, kindhearted too. And anyone with eyes can see she's madly in love with you. Give her time, and she'll forgive you."

He nodded slowly. *Be a good husband and a good father. I can do that.* Plans swirled in his mind. He would find her a midwife and make sure she didn't have to lift a finger. He'd give her free rein to redecorate the nursery. There were medical texts he could procure to keep her entertained during her confinement, and in the meantime, he'd build a hospital and give her a wing. She'd have the finest care, entertainment aplenty, and not a worry in the world, he'd make sure of it.

CHAPTER TWENTY-FIVE

"**I** NEED YOUR help," Iselda said to Maribel. "I'd like to meet the local midwives so that I can choose who I want to have with me during the birth. To do that, I need to escape the castle and my overly solicitous husband. He keeps telling me he'll find one for me, but he doesn't know the first thing about midwives. I want to pick someone I trust."

Maribel laughed. "I understand, my lady. When he's determined to do a thing, it isn't easy to talk him down."

"He's smothering me. I can hardly leave the room without him panicking and insisting I go back to bed. I'm pregnant. I'm not an invalid." The man was being ridiculous. He'd taken it upon himself to take care of her every need but hadn't consulted her about what those needs might be. After a lifetime of dedication to her work, he expected her to come to a complete stop and not to lift a finger. How was she supposed to live like this?

"He's scheduled to go to Portsmouth today for a hunt. I want to take advantage of his absence and go into town to meet midwives. Can you make arrangements?"

Nodding, Maribel said, "Where would you like to meet them, my lady?"

"Where would you recommend?"

Maribel looked thoughtful. "If you were anyone else, I would recommend the Riverboat Tavern. The food is excellent, and it's right on the water. You can sit at a table out front and watch the world go by."

That sounded perfect. What a relief it would be to be outside with the rest of the world!

"Then I will go to the Riverboat Tavern."

"But my lady—"

"Look in the bottom of my trunk. You'll find three plain, high-necked dresses, and a practical pair of boots. I'll wear the green linen one, if you can get out enough of the wrinkles to make it presentable. With my hair in a plain wimple and my gray hooded cloak, no one will look twice at me. Believe me. I have years of practice at being invisible."

She could hardly wait to put on her old clothes and feel like herself again.

"I find it hard to imagine a woman as beautiful as you being invisible, my lady," Maribel said with a tinge of something— discomfort, irritation, jealousy? No, not jealousy, surely. Maribel might envy her a bit for having married William, but the woman couldn't possibly envy her looks when she herself was so gorgeous.

"You're too kind, but believe me. I can disappear. William is the only man who has ever found me attractive."

"That can't be true."

Iselda sighed. "My parents tried twenty-seven times to find me a match, and not one of the young men took any interest at all until William. Believe me when I say men hardly notice me."

She grabbed a ginger cake from the tray that sat on her dressing table. For the last week, she'd practically lived on them. Too many foods she once loved now tasted spoiled and rotten. Especially meats. She couldn't tolerate chicken or, worse yet, the sausages that seemed to be so popular here.

"Have you considered that they might be intimidated by you? You are so smart and kind. And there's something about the way you carry yourself, almost like a nun, as if you live on a higher plane than us mere mortals. It's daunting."

Iselda stuffed her mouth with ginger cake, probably looking quite like a mere mortal and certainly uncertain what to say. She had no intention of daunting anyone. In fact, she didn't quite believe she was capable of it. "You're too kind," she murmured after swallowing, as blood rushed into her cheeks.

THREE HOURS LATER, she was dressed in her plain clothes and following Maribel through the narrow, winding streets to the tavern. It was the same as it always was when she was dressed like this. People's gazes slid past her as if she was invisible. For her, it was a relief to go unnoticed again. She hadn't realized how on edge it made her feel to be the center of attention all the time at the castle. Becoming anonymous was like slipping into a warm bath. For the first time since leaving Winchelsea, she was at ease.

She almost wished she had brought the beautiful bag her friends from Winchelsea gave her, but today was not about making patient visits. Today, she was the patient, and a choosy one at that.

Sending Maribel off to find the first midwife, she ordered watered wine, which arrived in a goblet covered with a toasted piece of bread with sauteed mushrooms on top. Though she couldn't stomach meat, she had an almost insatiable craving for vegetables, and she was excited to sample the tavern's offerings.

She had just finished her mushrooms on bread when Maribel arrived with the first midwife. They both curtsied to her, and the other restaurant patrons started to stare. Gesturing quickly, she invited them both to sit. "No ceremony, please. I don't want to attract attention. I went to great pains to sneak out of the castle, and I don't want to ruin it all by making a scene."

The midwife's eyes went wide, and she wrung her hands in her lap.

"My apologies, my lady," Maribel said in a low voice. "I will warn the others not to curtsy."

"Thank you. Please help yourselves. I ordered plenty of food for sharing." She gestured to the server, who took the newcomers' drink orders.

"Now," she said, offering an encouraging smile to the midwife, "What's your name, and how long have you been a midwife?"

The woman looked at Maribel as if asking permission. Maribel nodded. "My name is Julieta, and I've been a midwife for three years. It came naturally, you see. I was the oldest of ten siblings, and I assisted the midwife with all of my mother's births from the time I was five. It would be such an honor to work with you, my lady."

Iselda smiled. "And how many children have you birthed as a midwife?"

Julieta began to chew her nails then realized what she was doing and put her hand down. "I don't know, my lady. I didn't keep count. I usually attend at least one birth every week or two. I could tell you all their names, but don't ask me about numbers, my lady."

She didn't expect the woman to be literate, but Iselda worried that the woman couldn't even count the babies she'd birthed.

"And what was the most difficult birth you ever handled as a midwife?"

"Oh dear." Julieta went back to wringing her hands. "It was recently. The baby was the wrong way. We couldn't turn it, and it died. The woman pulled through but only barely. There was some tearing and a lot of blood. I'm sorry, my lady. I shouldn't speak of such things in front of you."

Iselda put a comforting hand on Julieta's shoulder. "It sounds very difficult. I'm sorry for their loss." Any experienced midwife would have a story of a birth gone wrong, but this particular story suggested Julieta lacked the necessary skills. A breech birth shouldn't have been a death sentence if the midwife knew the proper procedure. "I think I've learned what I need. Thank you for coming to speak with me, Julieta. I appreciate your taking the time."

The next midwife talked so much and so fast, Iselda could hardly get a word in edgewise. The third one tried to sell her an amulet. Fortunately, the fourth one looked promising. She was an older woman with white streaks in her dark hair and a canny look in her eye as she sat down across from Iselda. "My lady, if you think this disguise of yours is fooling anyone, you are sorely mistaken. Everyone can tell you're a noble in disguise, but they're too deferential to put you on the spot," she said, then popped a piece of bread in her mouth.

Iselda liked her already. The woman was observant, forthright, and unafraid—all important traits in a midwife.

"What's your name, and how long have you been a midwife?" Iselda asked.

The woman smiled and narrowed her eyes at Iselda. "My name is Alba, and I've been a midwife for thirty-six years. I attended your husband's birth as well as this one's," she said, nodding toward Maribel. "I've attended over a thousand births in my time. I won't pretend I haven't lost some, but everyone in this line of work does from time to time. God's plans for us are mysterious."

Iselda nodded. There was no guarantee of safety. She understood that. "Tell me about a difficult birth and how you handled it."

Alba sighed. "I was attending a young woman recently where the afterbirth wouldn't come free. Fortunately, I had a supply of rue with me. I boiled some water to make an infusion and had her drink it. Meanwhile, I continued to massage her belly in the hopes that it would work its way free of its own accord. In the end, I was successful, and she survived."

Oh, yes. This was the woman. Iselda always kept a supply of rue with her when she assisted at births for this very reason.

"Very impressive. I think you are the midwife for me."

Alba smiled. "I'm very flattered, my lady, but I should warn you your husband doesn't think much of me."

"Oh? And why is that?"

Clearing her throat, Alba said in a low voice, "There was a woman of whom he was fond in his youth that died on my watch. He's never forgiven me for it."

Oh dear. "Luisa," she murmured.

"He's told you, then." Alba's head bowed and she crossed her arms. "Luisa's death was tragic, but there was nothing I or anyone else could have done to prevent it. She was about six months along. First, her ankles got horribly swollen. I recommended wrapping them to force the liquid out and told her to rest. Then two days later, she got a terrible headache and her vision blurred. She was gone by the next day."

Ah. Now Iselda understood. She had seen two cases like this in her time with the healers in Winchelsea. She knew it was a death sentence. There was no cure.

"I'm sorry that he blames you," Iselda said. "I've seen such cases, and there is nothing to be done. Whatever the cause may be, once it starts, it's too late."

Alba nodded gravely. "You know something of midwifery?"

"Yes. I've assisted at one hundred and fifty-three births, sixteen of which I managed myself because the midwife wasn't able to come in time. I've also read every text I can find on the topic of pregnancy and childbirth in Latin or Greek. I do not claim to be a midwife, but I know a great deal."

Laughing, Alba said, "Then you know much more than I did when I started as a midwife. It's a rather unusual interest for a noblewoman."

With a broad smile, Iselda said, "I suppose I'm a rather unusual noblewoman." She helped herself to a roasted carrot. "Maribel, would you mind giving me a few minutes alone with Alba? I have some personal questions I'd like to discuss."

"Of course, my lady," Maribel said and wandered off toward a man playing the lute in front of a crowd in the street.

"Well, my lady, what can I do for you?" Alba asked when Maribel was out of earshot. "I doubt I can tell you anything you don't already know."

Iselda looked around to double-check that no one was listening. "I want to know about William's children. I know about Posy. He knows I know about Posy. He let slip that there's also a boy. I suspect there are others, but he won't tell me. He had a conversation with his mother about it, but I can't get either of them to say a word. As a midwife with such a history with this town, you must know the truth. Are there others?"

Alba examined her in silence for a long moment. "I have to keep my confidences like anyone else."

"You don't have to tell me who they are. I only need to know how many and whether any of them are in need." She didn't need to know who their mothers were or even their names. Mostly, she needed to assuage her conscience and gain assurance that they were not suffering in poverty.

"I suppose I could tell you that much. He has two sons in addition to Posy. Both have been accepted as the legitimate children of the men that married their mothers. They are not in need and will not welcome any interference." She gave Iselda a thoughtful look. "I must say you and Maribel seem to be getting on well, considering her history with your husband."

Iselda laughed. "She's furious with him and makes it known in a thousand tiny ways, though she is always outwardly polite. At the moment, I'm not too pleased with him either. She and I commiserate."

"Oh my. I bet he doesn't like that."

"No, he does not. But he has no say."

"Speaking of your husband, he appears to be walking this way."

Iselda's head whipped around, and sure enough, William was striding down the street making a beeline toward her.

"What are you thinking coming down here by yourself? And in your condition? And what in heaven's name are you doing speaking with this woman?" He was spewing steam like a cauldron as he came to a stop in front of her table.

Iselda stood up and took him none too gently by the arm. "I

am not here alone. Maribel is right over there," she said in a low, icy voice. "There is nothing about my pregnancy that prevents me from leaving the castle and enjoying a bit of fresh air, and this woman is going to be my midwife."

"Never," he hissed.

"She is far and away the most qualified and experienced in town. She knows her remedies, and I trust her. Luisa's death was tragic, but it was not Alba's fault. I asked her about Luisa's symptoms, and I'm sorry to say that no one could have saved her. I've seen other women die the same way. It's terrible, but some things are beyond our healing powers."

A crowd was beginning to gather around them. "Let's go back to the castle and discuss it there, in private. I'll go get Maribel."

They walked in frigid silence the whole way back to the castle. Maribel stayed well back from them, no doubt unnerved by the hostility between them.

When they were finally in their room, alone, with the door closed, William erupted.

"I can't believe you would deceive me like that, waiting until I was out of the castle and then sneaking off. How could you?"

Iselda stared him down, furious. "First of all, I didn't deceive you or sneak off. I walked out in full sight of the servants and the guards. Yes, I did it without consulting you, but since when have I had to ask your permission to go do something on my own?

"Second of all," she said, pointing a finger at his chest and jabbing. "*You* have practically kept me prisoner here ever since I told you I was with child. I'm sick of it. You can't cage me up and expect me to be happy about it. You've acted like you know better than me, but you are no expert at childbirth. It so happens that I am. I swear to you, William, with God as my witness, I am not on the verge of death."

"Iselda—"

"I'm not done." His face was bright red, but she didn't care. "How dare you try to choose my midwife for me! I am far more qualified than you to make this decision, and even if I wasn't, I should be able to choose whom to entrust with the health and safety of my own body."

"Iselda—"

"From here on out," she said, pointing to the floor. "I am going where I want when I want, and if you try to stop me, so help me God, I will get on a ship back to Winchelsea so that I can have this baby among people I love and trust and who love and trust *me*."

He sat down hard on the bed, eyes wide, and took a shuddering breath.

"I love you and trust you," he objected.

"Do you? Because you have an odd way of showing it. You haven't trusted me with the truth about your children. You don't trust me to leave the castle on my own or to choose my own midwife. Apparently, you didn't trust me enough to go to Portsmouth and leave me on my own for a day. One day! I love you, William, but you are driving me mad."

"I'm sorry for caring too much," he said quietly through gritted teeth. "I'll leave you alone. I can see you need some time to yourself." He got up and left without another word.

Good. He should be sorry.

But then why did she feel so awful? No, she was not going to take the blame for this. The problem was his. She had done nothing wrong. His behavior was completely unacceptable.

Nonetheless, as she sat down on the bed, tears started to flow. What if she had pushed him too far? She still loved him with all her heart, and the thought of going back to Winchelsea without him was terrifying. She wasn't sure she had the strength to carry out her threat.

There was something else, too, that she didn't bring up. He hadn't touched her since she told him her news. Did he find her repulsive now? What would happen as her belly grew? Would he seek solace with an old lover? She didn't think Maribel would have him, but that didn't mean there weren't any others. She only knew about the three that got pregnant, but presumably, there were more. He was the heir again and as handsome as ever. He could have his pick, especially now that he had done his duty and gotten her with child.

She took off her practical boots and her plain dress and went through the motions of dressing for dinner, though she had never been less inclined.

Maribel knocked. "My lady, would you like help getting ready?"

Reluctantly, she opened the door and let Maribel in.

"I'll be quick, my lady. I can see you need time to yourself."

Iselda sighed. "I'll be fine. I'm angry at him, and I know he's angry at me. But I don't need his approval to live my life."

Maribel chuckled. "No, you don't, my lady."

"I'm worried I've damaged our relationship beyond repair."

"No, you haven't, my lady," she said, pinning up Iselda's tresses. "And even if you did, I can personally attest that there is life after William. But he loves you, and you love him. You'll figure it all out."

Iselda shook her head. "I'm sorry. I shouldn't be burdening you with this. You've had enough drama with William for a lifetime."

"That I have, but I think he's met his match in you. You may be quiet, but you're smart and feisty enough to hold your own with him, something I've never seen anyone else do. I hope you make peace with him soon for both of your sakes. Don't you dare surrender, but if you can negotiate a truce, I think you'll both be happier for it."

Negotiate a truce. Yes. That was exactly what she needed to do.

CHAPTER TWENTY-SIX

WILLIAM TORE THROUGH the castle in search of someplace to vent his spleen. He had no particular destination in mind. He wandered the corridors in search of inspiration. Then he remembered his brother's sword pell. Maybe whacking at it in the training yard would help him feel better. He had to do something. Beating a piece of wood was better than taking it out on a person.

Striding out to the yard, he nearly ran down his mother.

"Good heavens, Boy. Watch where you're going." Her voice was sharper than usual, and her face looked drawn.

"Mother, are you all right? You seem a bit pale."

She grimaced, her hand going to her belly.

"You're unwell, aren't you? Let me examine you. Can you tell me your symptoms?"

"Nothing for you to worry about, Son. It's a woman's complaint. I've sent a servant for Alba. She'll have me fixed in no time."

Alba again. Why did all the women in his life insist on trusting that fraud?

"I assure you, I am well versed in all forms of medicine. I am perfectly capable of assisting you."

"Some things a mother doesn't wish to discuss with her son. Alba has helped me with this before, and she can take care of it today."

It shouldn't come as a surprise that his mother trusted her. After all, Alba birthed her children, himself included. But Iselda should know better. Iselda… A thought occurred to him.

"Mother, would you consent to letting Iselda see to your needs instead of Alba? I trust her medical knowledge much more than I trust that of that old bat."

His mother gave him a dubious look. "All right. Iselda can see me, but I'm still calling for Alba." He turned to go, but she put a hand on his arm. "William, what has you all worked up? When you ran into me you looked ready to take someone's head off."

William exhaled and clenched his fists. "Iselda and I had a fight. She says I'm practically keeping her prisoner—"

"Well, you are."

"And she wants Alba to be her midwife. Why she would trust that woman, I have no idea."

Looking at him with that motherly "you've done something foolish" face, she said, "I was wondering how long she was going to put up with your nonsense. I knew she had a spine, despite all her shyness. I'm glad to hear she's finally standing up to you."

He couldn't believe what he was hearing. "I thought you of all people would share my concern for Iselda's safety and well-being while she's carrying our child who may turn out to be the heir to Arundel."

"I do, and that's why I think you need to ease up on her. The way you've been acting would drive any woman mad. And I think she's very wise to have chosen Alba. The woman's been delivering babies for over thirty years. There's no one better in Arundel. I know you have a grudge against her because of what happened to that woman Luisa, but no one can save everyone. Haven't you lost people as a physician?"

He had, but not because of his own incompetence. Some people were too far gone to be saved. But that was completely different. "That's beside the point."

"Son, I can't stand here and argue with you all day. I need to go lie down." She winced, and he immediately felt guilty for delaying her.

"I'll walk you back to your room."

She nodded.

"I have a proposal for you. I'll listen to Iselda and to Alba, and I'll see what they recommend. If there's a difference, I'll consult you. If not, I hope you will put away this ridiculous grudge once and for all. Does that sound fair to you?"

William took a deep breath. It meant a lot that his mother was willing to consult him if there was disagreement and that she was willing to see Iselda. Taking the minor risk that Alba might have the right answer seemed acceptable when weighed against the risks to his mother's health if she relied on Alba alone.

"All right. If that's what it takes for you to see sense, then I'll agree to it."

He left her at the door to her room and went to get Iselda, who was in the midst of having her hair done when he came in. *Dear Lord in heaven, I have a beautiful wife,* he thought, looking at the curve of her neck as it met her collarbone. He missed her. He wanted her, but her delicate condition made him hold back. What if something he did hurt the baby?

Wombs were something of a medical mystery, prone to wandering about within the body and causing all kinds of trouble. It would be disastrous if her womb wandered while she was expecting. Pregnancy was supposed to calm the womb and make it stay put, but what if amorous attentions had the opposite effect? Certainly, the Church didn't approve, but then they didn't approve of any sex that wasn't explicitly for the purpose of procreation, and even then, not on saints' days or the sabbath. There were so many reasons for him to stay away, both moral and health related.

Nonetheless, his body craved hers fiercely. If he could only touch her, their connection would be renewed, and harmony restored. If he could take her in his arms and kiss her neck, trace her collarbone with lips and tongue…

No. None of that. He was here for a reason, and he had best get to the point before he lost control of himself.

"Iselda, my mother is ill. She says it's a feminine complaint and refuses to see me about it. She wanted to see Alba, but I've gotten her to agree to see you. Can you go examine her?"

"Of course," she said, her voice all concern, the hard determination in her face when he came in melting to something softer. "I'll see to her immediately. Are you done?" she asked Maribel.

"Let me tuck this last piece in… There, my lady. That should do." She rushed out the door, and he found himself alone with Maribel, who was looking daggers at him.

"My lord, you're being a fool," she said, hands on her hips. "You love her, and she loves you. Stop treating her as if she was made of Venetian glass, and give her the respect she deserves. Watching this little farce play out makes me grateful you ran away when I was pregnant with Posy. You would have driven me mad."

She spun on the spot and strode through the door.

Was he treating her as if she was made of glass? He supposed he was. There was a reason they called it being in a delicate condition. But then he thought about all the pregnant women who were servants and farmers, like Maribel and Daisy. They worked just as hard during their pregnancies as they did before and after. They had no choice. And somehow their children were born healthy. Was he perhaps a tad overprotective?

He could understand why Iselda chafed at the restrictions he was placing on her. He thought he was doing it for her own good, but perhaps he wasn't as clear as he should be on what was best for her.

Iselda came back, interrupting his reverie. "I just learned about your little bet with your mother. You should be ashamed of yourself. Alba and I agreed on the treatment, by the way. Your mother has an ailment of the bladder, and we're giving her an infusion of crushed saxifrage and instructing her to drink plenty of water. She should start feeling better within the next day or two. I'll stay with her tonight to make sure it doesn't get worse. These types of ailments can get serious very quickly if they spread to the kidneys. I've asked for her dinner and mine to be brought to her room. You'll have to dine without me."

He'd forgotten all about dinner. Were his father and brother back from the hunt yet? Was there any point in his going downstairs to dine? If they came back, they would want to know where his mother and Iselda were, so he decided to make his way down after all.

The great hall was empty, except for a handful of his father's men, and he consumed his meal in silence. He'd lost the bet about Alba. He couldn't fault saxifrage for a bladder ailment. Even the Greeks agreed with that. Perhaps Alba knew a bit more than he gave her credit for.

It gave him pause that Iselda said there was nothing that could have been done for Luisa. All these years, he'd been so certain the right treatment could have saved her. What if she was right, and it was no one's fault? Did he spend nine years of his life blaming himself for a tragedy no one could have averted?

He froze with his eating dagger in midair, the speared piece of venison dripping sauce onto the plate. His mind spun, trying to re-imagine the last nine years from this new perspective. If he was wrong about Alba, then it was all for nothing. His self-exile was meaningless if not actively harmful, given the women he left behind. If he was wrong, this whole fight with Iselda was pointless, and he owed her an enormous apology. Could he truly be wrong?

At that moment, Michael and his father threw open the doors and made their boisterous way to the table. "You should have seen the buck we caught, William. It was enormous. We're having the antlers mounted so that we can hang them on the wall." Michael was beaming with pride, and his father was beaming at Michael.

"You didn't ride, did you?" William asked, giving Michael a

worried look.

"Only a little, and I feel fine."

William shook his head in disapproval.

"Too bad you decided to turn around," his father said. "It was an excellent hunt. You would have enjoyed it. I'm sure the ladies were fine without us. Speaking of which, where are they?"

"Mother is sick. A feminine complaint. Iselda is with her," William said as he watched them fill their plates.

"Did Alba come?" his father asked.

"She did," he said, no longer certain his clenched teeth were warranted.

"Then she'll be fine. Alba always knows what to do." His father dove into his meal with relish.

"You trust Alba?" he couldn't stop himself from asking.

"Of course, I do. She's been taking care of your mother's needs since before you were born," he said between bites. "Have you eased up on your wife yet?"

"What do you mean, Papa?" He took another bite of venison.

"Son, you've been a bit…how shall I put this…overprotective. If I tried to treat your mother the way you've been treating Iselda, she would bite my head off. Trust me. Women know how to handle childbearing, and the best thing you can do is not interfere."

"But Papa, you don't understand…" he began as he shoved his plate away.

"I understand far better than you do. I went through this with your mother when she was expecting the two of you. One time when she was pregnant with you, she got so angry with me that she wouldn't let me share her bed. She made me sleep in another room for a week. Some sacrifices aren't worth making. After all, a man has needs."

William threw up his hand. "Stop. I don't want to know any of this about you and Mother." Though, in truth, he was interested to hear that his parents had continued marital relations without any health consequences. Perhaps he didn't need to keep his distance from Iselda after all.

"The prospect of being a father can be a bit daunting," his father said. "Try to remember she's the one carrying the baby. Her sympathy will wear thin quickly if you try to interfere."

William let out his breath slowly. "Thank you for the advice, Father. I found it helpful, believe it or not."

His father laughed. "High praise coming from you!"

William excused himself and made his way back to his empty room. Lying awake on his bed, staring at the curtains, he wondered if his parents were right, and he had it all wrong. He couldn't undo nine years of mistrust toward Alba easily, but perhaps he could give her a chance to prove herself.

As for Iselda, he needed to mend things quickly because it was clear now he wasn't treating her as he should. His fears had got the better of him and were turning him into a controlling bully. At a moment like this, alone in a strange place with no family or friends nearby, she deserved his attentive support, not to be ordered around.

He should have been more forthright about his lovers and children, too. As soon as he saw Maribel, he should have warned Iselda about the nature of their relationship. Attempting to hide it was a stupid thing to do, and look at the cost. If he didn't tread carefully, she was going to sail off to Winchelsea without a backward glance. He'd go after her, of course, but even if she accepted him back, they would both know for the rest of their lives that something fundamental was broken between them.

Was she worried about his past lovers? She seemed to accept Maribel easily enough. It appeared they were becoming fast friends, which he found sweet if slightly alarming. But every so often, he saw a look in her eye when they passed a beautiful woman—an unspoken question that filled him with shame.

He needed to find a way to show her that his heart and body were hers alone. The thought brought on a torrent of erotic memories—Iselda on their wedding night, Iselda in nothing but stockings with blue bows, the first time they made love in

Arundel... Before long, he was hard and aching for her. He couldn't wait nine months, ten really, taking into account recovery time. He needed her now, spreading her legs and climbing on top of him, taking him with a vengeance, so warm and eager, her nipples hard as she invited his touch. Maybe she'd even recite some Hildegard.

At that thought, he laughed aloud. What a state he was in if even the thought of Hildegard was arousing! He'd let her recite the entire book if only she'd stay with him and agree to some physical affection. His father was right. There was no way he could last nine months like this.

Some force stronger than him propelled him out of bed and down the hall to his mother's bedchamber. He knocked tentatively. Iselda opened the door. She looked tired but also happier than she'd been since their arrival in Arundel.

"How is she?" he whispered.

"Still in pain, but she's sleeping. She'll be fine this time tomorrow, God willing."

"Can I sit with you?"

She nodded and invited him in. There was only one chair, so he sat on the floor beside her, resting his head against her knees. After several minutes of sitting in silence, she ran a gentle hand through his hair. The tender gesture made his heart ache. He closed his eyes and let himself drift off, sure and more than content that he'd been forgiven.

CHAPTER TWENTY-SEVEN

ISELDA WOKE WITH a start as dawn's light began to creep into Lady Maud's window. Something heavy and warm rested against her leg, and she looked down to see William asleep on the floor, propped up against her. She gave him a little shake. When he opened his eyes and looked up at her, she gestured with her head toward the door. Silently, they tiptoed out of Lady Maud's room.

In the hall, she said, "We should get some proper sleep. Your mother should be fine, since she's made it through the night with no signs of kidney infection."

He nodded. They slipped back into their room after Iselda let a servant know to ask Maribel not to disturb them for several hours.

She pulled off her silk gown and matching silk slippers and started pulling the pins out of her hair.

"Let me help," William said, coming up behind her. He began to pull out the pins, and her hair cascaded down, free at last. He pulled her against him as he worked, holding her gently as he finished the delicate work. When he was finished, he swept her hair aside and kissed her neck.

She gasped, instantly aflame. "William, I've missed you," she said, hoping he would continue.

"*Mmmm,*" he murmured into her hair, cradling one of her

breasts in his hands. "I've missed you too, sweeting. I'm sorry for the way I've acted. It isn't easy to undo nine years of guilt and fear, but I should never have taken it out on you. I won't try to stop you from going where you please ever again, and I won't interfere with your choice of midwife either. I love you too much to let such things come between us."

Oh, my poor, sweet husband.

"I love you too. More than I can say in words."

She turned around and kissed him. This beautiful, talented, imperfect man made her feel so much her heart might burst. It hurt so much when he was keeping his distance. And now she was back in his arms where she belonged.

Their kiss of tender longing turned into something more, and his hands grasped her buttocks, pressing her closer against the undeniable evidence of his arousal.

"Sweeting, I want to make love to you. Would you permit me? I've been told it won't hurt the baby."

She laughed. "Is that what you were afraid of? I could have told you no harm would come of it. And here I was worried... Well, it doesn't matter, since it's not true."

He took a shaky breath, pulling her close. "I'm sorry if I ever gave you cause to worry. No other woman could hold a candle to you in my eyes. There are plenty of pretty faces in the world, but they don't sparkle with intelligence like yours. No one else stands up to my nonsense and puts me in my place like you do. I can't tell you how much I adore that you aren't intimidated by me, that you don't put me on some pedestal as the heir. You see me as I am with all my flaws, and you love me anyway. And I love you, sweeting, with all that I am."

She wasn't entirely sure how she hadn't melted into a puddle from that speech. "I love you too, William." She gave him a slow, languorous kiss. "Now if you really want to show how contrite you are, come to bed with me and give me so much pleasure I lose my mind."

He didn't need a second invitation. Walking her swiftly over to the bed, he pulled off her shift and laid her down. He quickly dispensed with his cotte and shirt and breeches as she watched appreciatively. That chiseled chest was so lovely, his strong arms so capable. And then there were his beautiful long legs and the highly gratifying sight of his arousal.

Heat and moisture pooled between her legs as she watched. After a week without, she was starving for him. He lay down beside her, heat radiating from him. She could smell his delicious herbal scent, something she hadn't noticed until now yet something she knew she'd never not notice again. Laying back, she opened herself to him, looking in his eyes and seeing deep love and passion reflected there.

His skillful hand parted her folds and touched her, tracing lazily around her bud, tantalizing and teasing. "You're driving me mad. Give me what I need, William," she pleaded in a breathy voice. He touched her directly but ever so lightly, stroking her so gently she thought she might die of it. "More, please," she begged.

"You mean like this?" He plunged a finger into her and began to tease her expertly with his thumb. As she bucked and moaned, he added a second finger. She could feel the now familiar waves of her approaching orgasm, and she surrendered herself to pure sensation as he brought her to her peak.

When she was at the pinnacle of sensation, he took his hand away and thrust into her, taking her even higher. It was torture. It was ecstasy. It was everything. All she could do was tremble and writhe as he took her with a primal ferocity that drove her wild. This is what she hungered for. She wanted him to be as mad for her as she was for him.

A loud crack interrupted them, and something gave beneath them. William looked for a moment, shrugged and continued to render her senseless and oblivious to everything but the movement of their bodies. Nothing else existed in this moment. The world could end around them, and they would still be here enveloped in each other.

She came and then came again. At last, he joined her with a cry and collapsed by her side, utterly spent.

As she blinked and tried to make sense of the room around her, something was off. She looked down and…they had broken the bedframe.

She started to laugh. At first, she tried to hold it back, seeing how tired William was, but a loud guffaw escaped her.

"Whatizzit?" asked William, raising his head with what looked like superhuman effort.

She threw her head back and laughed some more. "We broke the bed," she said, gasping for air.

His head flopped back down, and he snuggled closer to her. "We broke the bed," he said in bleary amusement. "Lie down with me."

She curled against him on the oddly angled bed and drifted off to sleep almost immediately.

SHE WOKE TO loud knocking on the door. "Iselda, it's Maribel. The earl wants to know if you'll be joining for lunch."

"It's lunch time already?" she murmured to herself as she got up and found her robe. Going to the door, she opened it carefully so as not to provide a view of naked William, stretched across the lopsided bed. "Maribel, I think we'll need a bit more time. Could you have lunch brought up to us? Please convey our apologies to the earl. We were up all night tending to the countess. She'll be fine, by the way. You can let him know that too."

Maribel couldn't quite hide her smirk as she turned to carry out her orders.

Iselda closed the door quickly and started pulling on clothes.

"No, stay here naked with me," William complained, startling her.

"You're awake."

"Barely."

He was peeking at her out of one heavily lidded eye, as if he could stay half asleep.

"They're bringing us lunch. I have to be decent to open the door and take it."

He sighed heavily. "I suppose you do. And I should hide my nakedness as well, probably."

"I like you indecent, but I don't think the servants would."

She watched him get up and pull on his clothes with some regret. Goodbye chest. Goodbye legs. Goodbye cock.

"What are we going to do about the bed?" he asked.

"I imagine we'll have to tell someone and then they'll fix it." Silly man asking silly questions.

"But what are we going to tell them?"

She smiled. "That our lovemaking was too passionate and could not be contained?" She sauntered over to him and ran her hands down his chest. "No, I suppose that wouldn't do. I think...we'll say...nothing." She whispered the last word in his ear and was delighted to feel him jump to attention against her leg.

"Nothing," he said, pulling her close against him.

"No need to paint a picture. Let them come to their own conclusions." She moved her leg against his prominent bulge and was rewarded with a moan.

"Watch out, sweeting, or we might have to break some more furniture."

"That's what I was hoping."

At that moment, there was a knock on the door, and Iselda went to get the tray of food. Putting it down on the dressing table, she asked, "What piece of furniture should we break next?"

THAT EVENING AT dinner, Lady Maud felt well enough to join them. "I hope you two are well rested after spending half the day in bed?"

Blood rushed to Iselda's cheeks.

"Yes, Mother," William said, as if they hadn't broken the bed and done some perfectly wicked things on a chair. "We are well rested. And how are you feeling?"

They took their seats.

"Much improved, thank you. Alba checked in on me this afternoon and agreed with Iselda that I am improving. I hear you two spoke to her as well?"

"Yes, I encouraged William to speak with her, since she is going to be my midwife. I thought a conversation might help to reassure him that Alba was the right choice." She gave William's knee a little squeeze beneath the table.

"The woman knows her herbs and remedies," William said. "And I have it on the best authority," he said, turning to Iselda, "that the thing I blamed her for was not her fault."

"Thank heavens your wife has an active mind and good sense," his mother said. "Someone needs to save you from your own foolishness, and you never listen to me."

They all said grace, and the first course was served. It was a hearty soup with balls of spiced meat and bits of sausage. Iselda's stomach rebelled, and she could hardly eat a bite. It was all she could do not to run from the table with all of its rich meaty smells.

"I heard there were some difficulties with the furniture in your room," Lady Maud said, and Iselda nearly spat out her watered wine. "The servants are moving your things to the room next door until everything is repaired."

William bit his lips together to keep from laughing, and she said quickly, "That's very thoughtful. Thank you."

Taking bites of bread to quiet her stomach, Iselda managed to survive the first course without incident. To her infinite relief, the second course was vegetable stew cooked with raisins and pine nuts. This was a dish she could enjoy, though the lingering scent of meat still left her a bit queasy. As the bowls were taken away, Lord Arundel cleared his throat.

"William," he said, his expression stern. "We have given serious thought to your request to build a hospital. Though I am concerned about the expense, I can't deny the advantages to our town of having one. With your connections and expertise, I am hopeful we can make it the finest there is. You have my blessing to reach out to the Hospitallers about establishing a presence here."

"Alba helped me talk him into it," his mother added. "She thinks it would benefit the town greatly. Her word carries a great deal of weight in these matters."

William swallowed and stared at his parents, unable to believe what they were saying. After all their protests, they were finally agreeing to his wishes?

It was at this point that the servants came in with an enormous platter of roast venison and began serving everyone. "Thank you," he said at last. "I can't tell you how much this means to me. To us," he said, taking Iselda's hand. "We won't let you down, Father. We'll make it the finest hospital anyone has ever seen."

Iselda wanted to stand up and cheer. At last, William would have an outlet for all his excess energy. There would be something to distract him from hovering around her constantly. It would be a distraction for her too. Establishing a hospital would be a welcome project that would let her engage with the townspeople in a whole new way. Hopefully, she could convince William to let Alba play a role as well, especially if he still planned to establish a maternal health wing.

She beamed at everyone as they tucked into their venison, despite the smell. All was right with the world. Her husband loved her. He had a distracting project. And she had a trencher filled with a second helping of vegetable stew. What more could she want?

"We'll still expect you both to fulfill your duties as lord and lady," Lady Maud said, giving them pointed looks.

Well, there might be one or two things she could wish for, but they were no longer the carefree young people who could pursue their vocations with single-minded determination. Their responsibilities were broader now. They would have to accept that their lives had changed.

Mmm. The carrots were delicious. She filled her belly with stew and still had room for custard for dessert.

They said goodnight to William's parents and made their way to the guest room where they were staying until their bed was fixed.

"Did you ever imagine this is what our lives would be like?" she asked William as they walked.

"I did, actually. The night we were locked in the cellar, I couldn't stop thinking about what it would be like if they forced us to marry. I imagined us together in Arundel. I imagined having children with you. I even imagined losing my mind with anxiety when I found out you were expecting."

"You did?" she asked, laughing.

"I did. And I knew then that I would be deliriously happy with you. My only concern was you. I didn't want to make you miserable or worse yet be the reason you came to harm."

She shook her head. "I know you would never cause me harm."

"I got you pregnant, didn't I? In my mind that wasn't much different than putting a knife to your throat. And I still haven't completely overcome my fear. I'm trying to keep it inside while I'm with you, so I don't drive you mad." He sighed. "I know it's not rational, but then fears rarely are."

Pulling him into the guest room where they were staying, she kissed him on his cheek. "You are a sweet man, and I love you. The future is going to be fine."

"Yes it is, because I'm with you, sweeting."

EPILOGUE

T HE BELLS HAD just rung for Nones, and William was already arguing with his very pregnant wife in the hallway of the new Arundel hospital.

"How many patients have you bled to death today?"

"All of them, of course. Very efficient."

She stuffed a ginger cake in his mouth. He couldn't say he was sorry to have provoked her.

"One of these days, I am going to prove to you that bloodletting is counterproductive. I've been keeping records of your patients' outcomes."

William grumbled. "I agreed to let you keep my patient records because you're better at it than I am, not because I wanted you to build evidence against me."

Brother Joseph's head popped into the hallway. "Do you have any ginger cakes? I just finished convincing a woman that her son's goiter wasn't caused by a finch giving him the evil eye and that he simply needed to eat more fish. I need a treat."

"Of course, here you are," Iselda said, handing him two. "I'm so glad you agreed to move here from Winchelsea. I know William is delighted to work with you again."

"Thank you, my lady. It was my pleasure. Working with Lord William is infinitely preferable to working with Brother Xavier. I had better get back to my patients." He slipped back into the examination room, and the door closed behind him.

"How else are you going to undermine me today, sweeting?" he couldn't help asking with a smile.

"I was hoping you would let me test another of Hildegard's remedies. This one is for a sore throat. My records from Winchelsea were mixed, but I haven't done a specific comparison against Galen's remedy. I was in my apothecary workshop preparing both before I came down."

He exhaled slowly, trying to keep his equilibrium. He loved her with his whole heart, but sometimes she drove him mad. "Why do you continue to question Galen? When are you going to give up and admit that he's a far better authority than Hildegard?"

"Why should I admit to something you've already proven wrong?" she said handing him another ginger cake. "You yourself gave up on anything but ginger cakes when I was troubled with morning sickness."

"That's not fair. They're delicious."

She gave him a triumphant smile. "That's exactly why they work. Who wants to drink something disgusting when their stomach is already upset?"

Rather than admit defeat, he decided to change tack. "How is it going with teaching Alba to read?"

"Quite well, thank you. She's doing well with reading Hildegard. She rarely has to ask me for help anymore."

He groaned. "You should have had her read Galen."

"Asking her to learn Greek might be a bridge too far, my love."

It was a fair point, but he didn't like it. "If she's going to run the maternal health wing of this hospital, I need to know that she is well versed in all the remedies that—"

"She already knows more about maternal health than you ever will. And you've grilled her enough on remedies to know how knowledgeable she is. Give it up and admit defeat, William."

Thankfully, at that moment, they were interrupted by a certain nine-year-old girl, skipping down the hallway.

"Posy," Iselda warned. "I've spoken to you about walking in the hallways."

Looking abashed, Posy murmured, "Yes, my lady." Brightening, she looked up at him, and his heart melted. "My lord, I finished learning the Greek alphabet. Soon, I'll be able to read Galen just like you."

She was her father's daughter, even if he could never say so out loud. He was so glad that Maribel had relented and allowed him to assist Posy with her studies. She was such a bright girl. He and Iselda could hardly keep pace with her voracious appetite for learning.

Even Maribel had a role at the hospital now. She oversaw the servants that did all of the cooking and cleaning, making sure it was always a welcoming place for travelers and the sick.

"Can you run along—I mean walk—to your mama? William and I need to meet with Alba."

Posy dutifully walked until she thought she was out of sight, but he caught her skipping again as soon as she turned a corner. He couldn't help but smile.

"We should go find Alba," Iselda said, taking his hand.

They walked down the hall and turned into the new maternity ward. They could hear the cries of two women in labor as they rounded the corner. Alba came out of the room and greeted them.

"Julieta is tending to them," Alba said, gesturing toward the room with the mothers. "She's gotten much more confident since she's been studying with me." They walked down the hall to an examination room, and Alba shooed William away. "Wait here. This is women only. I'll let you join when we're done."

He watched as his wife disappeared into the room with Alba. The noises from down the hall were quieter but still clearly audible. They set every nerve on edge. It took every ounce of his restraint to hold back from going in and trying to assist with alleviating their pain, even though he knew very well there was nothing he could do. When this happened to Iselda, he was going to have to be kept far away, or he wasn't going to be able to stop himself from barging in.

At least Iselda was healthy. The morning sickness had passed after the third month, and soon, he was able to feel the baby moving within her when she put his hand on her belly. The baby seemed to like the sound of his voice. He hoped no one ever found out how much time he spent conversing with Iselda's belly, feeling the strange rippling of kicks and squirms at the sound of his voice.

The cries of one of the women down the hall grew louder and then, suddenly, they stopped altogether, replaced moments later by the unmistakable cry of a baby. Listening to this miraculous moment, tears prickled his eyes. Soon, he would hold his own babe in his arms, listening to cries and coos, feeling the grasp of his or her tiny fist around his finger. Soon, the hell of Iselda's pregnancy would be over, and he could regain his sanity.

Despite his efforts to keep from torturing Iselda with his fears, he couldn't actually make them go away. They ate at him night and day, and only the end of this terrible waiting would convince him that all was truly well. In the meantime, he did the best he could to keep his sanity by making furious love to Iselda in their new, sturdier bed, and getting regular exercise. He wouldn't be sorry for this long wait to be at an end, though. The thought of being a father, and doing things properly this time, filled him with hope and joy.

"William, you can come in," Iselda called from the door of the examination room.

He wrapped his arms around her from behind, resting his hands on top of her belly.

"You'll be happy to hear that she and the baby are healthy as can be. It won't be much longer now. Have you noticed how she's carrying the baby lower now? That means the baby will be here soon. Are you ready to be a father?"

He knew Alba knew he already was a father, but they all

knew this time was different. "Very ready. Thank you for all your help."

Two weeks later, he was pacing the hall of the hospital while Brother Joseph kept an eye on him from the examination room. Iselda was up at the castle giving birth, and for everyone's sake, he needed to be far away. His father and Michael tried to talk him into going on a hunt, but he had no patience for that. The hospital was where he needed to be. He was useless for any work, but being there was soothing.

He was about to tell Brother Joseph that he was going to the castle whether he was wanted or not when a messenger boy arrived, telling him the baby had arrived. William went running, as he heard cheerful felicitations from Brother Joseph behind him.

When he got to the castle, he took the steps two at a time and bounded to the door of their bedroom. Taking a deep breath to compose himself, he opened the door with a shaking hand. There was Iselda looking tired, but radiant, with their newborn child curled on her chest.

"Are you all right? Is the baby all right?"

Iselda beamed. "Everyone's doing beautifully," Alba answered. "The birth was smooth as could be. Congratulations, my lord."

"It's a little girl," said Iselda. "Your parents will be disappointed, but I'm not."

Tears prickled in the corner of his eyes. "I'm not either. We have a daughter, sweeting. I can hardly believe it. Can I hold her?"

"Of course," Iselda said, picking up the tiny bundle with a fuzzy black cap of hair.

Holding his little girl in his arms, he was overwhelmed with an emotion unlike any he had felt before. It was as if he had been living in a dim twilight without realizing it, and suddenly the sun came up. A tear trickled down his face. "I think we should call her Lucinda. She lights up my world."

Iselda beamed at him. "I love it. Lucinda. It's perfect."

He sat down beside her on the bed, and she rested her head against his shoulder. "Welcome to Arundel, Lucinda," he said. "Your mama and papa love you very much."

About the Author

Leslie Vollard has a longstanding passion for the Middle Ages. Her obsession with all things medieval dates back to college when she dug through archives at the Bibliothèque Nationale in Paris to study the 12th century troubadour, Arnaut Daniel. In her work, she brings courtly love, chivalry, and the troubadour tradition to life. Romance reigns supreme in her steamy novels about how love conquers all.

Leslie lives in Long Island with her delightfully nerdy husband and two cats. She loves gardening, baking, and reading love poems in dead languages.